Acclaim for Krista McGee

"Good things come to those who wait—and pray."

—*Kirkus Reviews* of *Starring Me*

"Ripe with glitz and glamour of celebrity, the drive of ambition, and the angst of peer pressure, *Starring Me* is the perfect book for teenage girls. Krista McGee crafted strong characters who believably zoom in on their faith and decisions through the different lenses of their experiences."

–Nicole O'Dell, author of the Diamond Estates series and founder of Choose NOW Ministries

"Spunky chick meets dreamy boy and auditions for a teen version of *Saturday Night Live*. What's not to love?"

—Shannon Dittemore, author of *Angel Eyes*, regarding *Starring Me*

"[A] touching, fun, edifying, campy, quick and downright delicious teen read."

—USAToday.com, regarding *First Date*

"McGee's debut novel is an absolute gem. Anyone who enjoys reality television and a well-told story shouldn't hesitate to read this great book."

—*Romantic Times* TOP PICK! review of *First Date*

"How would you like to live out the dramas of your teen life on national television? Krista McGee has crafted a cute tale of dating, faith, and being the girl God has called you to be."

—Jenny B. Jones, award-winning author of *There You'll Find Me* and A Charmed Life series, regarding *First Date*

Right Where I Belong

Also by Krista McGee

First Date
Starring Me

Right Where I Belong

Krista McGee

THOMAS NELSON
Since 1798

NASHVILLE DALLAS MEXICO CITY RIO DE JANEIRO

Published in Nashville, Tennessee, by Thomas Nelson. Thomas Nelson is a registered trademark of Thomas Nelson, Inc.

Thomas Nelson, Inc., titles may be purchased in bulk for educational, business, fund-raising, or sales promotional use. For information, please e-mail SpecialMarkets@ThomasNelson.com.

Publisher's Note: This novel is a work of fiction. Names, characters, places, and incidents are either products of the author's imagination or used fictitiously. All characters are fictional, and any similarity to people living or dead is purely coincidental.

Library of Congress Cataloging-in-Publication Data

McGee, Krista, 1975–
Right where I belong / Krista McGee.
p. cm.
Summary: After her father's third divorce, seventeen-year-old Natalia decides to move with her stepmother, Maureen, from Spain to Florida to learn more of Maureen's faith and to discover who she is away from her father's expectations. Includes reading group guide.
ISBN 978-1-4016-8490-7 (pbk.)
[1. Fathers and daughters—Fiction. 2. Stepmothers—Fiction. 3. Christian life—Fiction. 4. Self-actualization (Psychology)—Fiction. 5. Spaniards—United States—Fiction. 6. Moving, Household—Fiction. 7. Tampa (Fla.)—Fiction.] I. Title.
PZ7.M4784628Rig 2012
[Fic]—dc23 2012023813

Printed in the United States of America

HB 04.19.2018

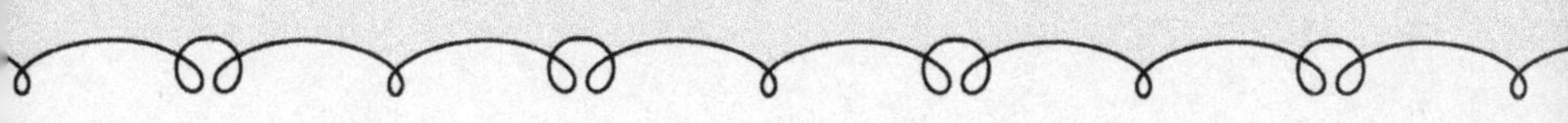

To Eliana—"God
answered" when he gave
you to Daddy and me

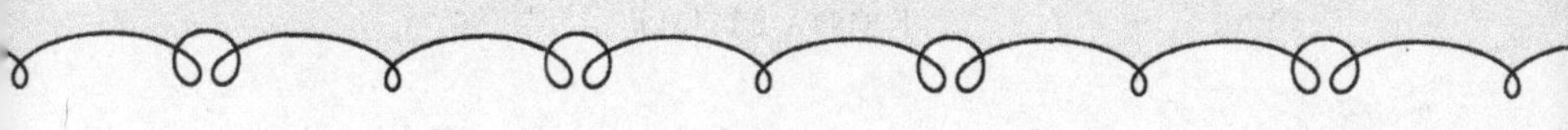

Chapter 1

"I am leaving your stepmother."

"Let me guess." Seventeen-year-old Natalia did not fall for the woe-is-me, martyred expression on her father's face. Not again, anyway. "She is not making you happy. You've found someone else. Life is too short to be tied down to one woman."

"Natalia Ruth Montoya Lopez! You do not speak to your papa in that tone of voice."

Shame clawed at Natalia's stomach. *He's right. Help me, Jesus. What do I say to him?*

Natalia inhaled deeply. "I'm sorry. But you keep leaving all the women in your life. How do I know you will not leave me too?"

Papa turned Natalia toward him, his face softening. "*Hija*. I will never leave you. You are my daughter. My flesh and blood. But women are different. You are young and you don't understand. You fall in love and you fall out of love. Nothing can be done about that. It is part of life."

"So this is what I have to look forward to? Falling in love with a man and then having him tell me a few years later that he doesn't love me anymore? What about 'till death do us part'? Doesn't that mean *anything*?" Natalia hated the anger that kept bubbling up, but she didn't know how to stop it.

"For some it does, *mi corazón*. Your grandparents were married for forty-seven years. And they were truly happy. I have often wondered if something is wrong with me. I just cannot seem to keep that feeling. I try . . ."

"Oh, Papa, please. You do not try. I have seen this, now, three times."

"Natalia!"

She held up one finger. "Mamá—I was four. I can still remember the yelling. I would hide under my bed with the door shut and *still* hear the two of you."

"That woman had a temper." He looked out the window. "You didn't know the half of it."

"Yes, I do! I'm not saying she was perfect, but neither were you. And if either one of you had just accepted that fact, you might still be together."

Papa turned around, opening his mouth to speak, but Natalia held up two fingers and continued. "Isabelle never did anything to you. She was like a slave: cooking, cleaning, cowering in fear. I remember she'd take little Ari outside in the middle of the night just so her crying wouldn't wake you. And you kept her around for how long? Three years?"

He sighed. "Isabelle. No man can handle such a timid woman. It was nice for a while. A nice change from your mother's yelling. But then . . . there was no passion. A man cannot live without passion, hija. It was her own fault. I cannot help being a man and having a man's needs."

The image of her father and his "needs" rushed in full color into her brain, and Natalia tried not to gag. "And now we come to number three. Maureen." Natalia stood inches from him. "I think she was the best one yet. She left her home and her family. Moving from the United States to Spain was not easy. Yet she did it. She learned the language, she adapted to our culture, and still you reject her."

Natalia shook her head. "*I* have seen it coming, but I know the signs. I do not think she has any idea. You are going to break her heart, Papa. And for what? So you can do this all over again with a fourth and a fifth and a sixth?"

Natalia's throat felt like it was closing in on itself. She couldn't speak. She willed herself not to cry. *Why can't I just stay angry? It's so much easier to be angry.*

Her father had hurt her so many times that she had learned to put up a wall around her heart, hardening herself to his outbursts, his ridiculous logic. But her heart broke for Maureen. She had seen good in Papa. She had loved him unconditionally, and Natalia had foolishly hoped he would live up to Maureen's vision of who he was.

How childish that hope was.

"Natalia," Papa said, like he was explaining to a toddler why she couldn't have a cookie before dinner. "Someday you will understand. For now, help your stepmother. She depends on you."

Natalia turned and walked away, refusing to listen to any more. *God, help me stay quiet. Better not to say anything at all than to say something I will regret.*

"Natalia!"

She kept walking, out of the living room, down the hallway of the spacious apartment, into her room. She shut the door and considered locking it, but her father wouldn't come. He would yell and get angry, but he would not try to sit down and work things out. He would let her stew and then, when Natalia emerged, he would act like everything was fine, as if they did not just have an argument. She had seen this dozens of times before. Just one of many reasons why the man couldn't keep a wife.

Five years ago Maureen had come to Madrid with her company, which was in partnership with her father's. Several companies from around the world had merged. Because Maureen's position was supervised directly by Papa, they worked together often. After a few months he was bringing Maureen home to work after dinner. A few months after that he was bringing her home for good. From the beginning she had felt more like a friend to Natalia than a stepmother.

Natalia walked to her window. She took a deep breath, trying to will oxygen into lungs that felt dry and thick. Ragged breaths escaped. She pulled back the curtain to see the plaza below. Mopeds and smart cars lined up at a stoplight eight floors below. Children were playing soccer, parents were pushing toddlers in swings, fathers were pushing their babies around in their carriages. So many happy families. Natalia let the curtain fall back into place and sat on her bed, finally giving in to the wracking sobs she had held on to for so long.

I will never, ever allow myself to fall in love. I won't do to anyone what my father does to these women. And to me. Never. Do you hear me, God? Make me single. Have me travel the world or work with orphans or whatever. But don't make me fall in love. I won't do it. I can't.

Natalia sat in her favorite spot at Retiro Park—a bench overlooking the small lake where couples drifted in boats and children skated along the sidewalks. She gazed at the statues of lions that guarded an ancient gazebo, the pillars reflected in waves in the waters below.

"Churros for you." Natalia's best friend, Carmen, handed her the warm pastry covered in cinnamon sugar. "And ice cream for me."

Natalia bit into the churro. Heaven. *"Gracias."*

Carmen splayed her hands in a Spanish "of course" sign and bit into her frozen treat. "Feeling better?"

"About my father's divorce? Or about his dating a woman six years older than me? Or about watching my stepmother go from a strong woman to a blubbering child?" Natalia moved her feet back as a rollerblader sped past.

"It has only been a week."

"Exactly." Natalia closed her eyes. "And Maureen just told me last night that she is leaving. Moving back to Florida."

"But you and Maureen . . . ?"

"She's like the mother I never had."

Carmen smiled sideways. "You have a mother."

Natalia raised her eyebrows. Carmen knew that Mamá was far too busy with her career to give much time to her only child.

"Poor Maureen." Natalia took another bite of the churro. "She is terrified to go back home. But she feels like staying here will keep her from being able to get over Papa. He is her boss, after all."

Carmen tossed the paper from her dessert into a trash can. "But what will she do?"

Natalia shrugged. "I don't know. Neither does she."

"She'll find something. Maureen is amazing. Beautiful, smart, funny."

Natalia nodded. Maureen had been her rescuer in more ways than she could count. She made Natalia feel important, loved, during her preteen years when she felt awkward and ugly. She spent time with Natalia.

"Who will teach me about God when Maureen is gone?" She hadn't even considered that her spiritual mentor would be leaving.

"You don't need this crutch of faith to help you." Carmen turned away and ran a hand through her long, silky black hair. "You are too smart to keep going on with this. People are talking. You used to be so well respected, but all this talk of 'salvation' and 'eternal life' is making you look foolish."

Natalia sighed. Over and over again, she had tried to explain her faith to her friend. But Carmen, like so many Spaniards, saw faith as a weakness, an embarrassing part of their history. When Natalia tried to tell her that what she had was a relationship with a God who loved her, Carmen only recalled the Spanish Inquisition and other atrocities carried out in the name of "religion."

"Natalia, think logically. There is no evidence that God exists. None. No evidence of an afterlife or a creator.

Science has disproven all that superstition. Why would you go backward? You don't believe the earth is flat. Belief in the existence of God is just as ridiculous."

"Science can't disprove the existence of God any more than religion can prove it. Faith is involved on either side of that debate. But I know God exists. I have seen him at work in my life. I have seen him change me. I'm sorry you don't like the changes, but . . ."

Carmen shook her head. "It isn't that. Well, it is, I guess. I *don't* like it. But I guess if that is what you need, then I should just keep quiet and let you believe it."

"Could you be any more condescending?" Natalia laughed. "You're talking to me like I'm Ari, waiting in line to see Saint Nicholas! God is not Santa."

Carmen put her hand up in protest. "Can't you hear how silly that all sounds? An invisible Savior who speaks to you through a two-thousand-year-old book and little voices in your head?"

"I know it sounds silly to you. And it pains me more than I can say that it does. But that is all the more reason why I need Maureen. She understands." Realization hit Natalia, an almost-audible voice from God speaking to her soul. Natalia jumped up.

"What is it?" Carmen pulled Natalia back to the bench.

Peace settled over her. She knew this was from him. Of course.

"Natalia, *por favor.*" Carmen clapped her hands, startling Natalia from her thoughts.

"I need to go with Maureen." Natalia stared across the pond to a family eating a picnic lunch on the grass.

"To America?"

Natalia nodded. *"Sí."*

Carmen pulled the remaining churro from Natalia's hand. "They must have put something other than sugar on this."

"No. I mean it." Certainty settled over Natalia as soon as the words came out of her mouth. "She needs me. It's my turn to help her. I can't abandon her the way Papa has."

"What about me?" Carmen planted her hands on her hips. "If you really believe this, then should you not stay here and keep trying to get me to believe it?"

Natalia laughed. Her friend was using any tactic possible to get Natalia to stay in Madrid. "If my staying here could make you believe, I would stay. I'd sit right down here in the middle of the ground and not move an inch until you believed." She sat cross-legged on the dirty sidewalk, caring little that those passing by looked at her as if she were losing her mind. "But I can't make you believe. Only God can. So I will keep asking him to help you."

"Get up, Natalia!" Carmen whispered. "What will people think?"

"What do I care what people think? I'm leaving!"

Carmen pulled Natalia up by her wrist, shaking her head in mock disgust. "How can you be so flippant about this? Do not let your zeal over your newfound faith take you away from everyone who loves you. Please! At least finish high school."

"I know you're saying this because you care about me." Natalia straightened her jacket and dusted off her skirt. "This is my home, my people, my country. I will miss you so much. But I need to go with my stepmother. I just cannot believe I didn't think of it sooner."

"Sooner?" Carmen stood. "It has been a week."

"I need to speak with Maureen. And my father."

"Hopefully they will talk you out of it." Carmen grabbed her backpack and threw it over her shoulder. "Do not do this, *amigita*. You will regret it." Carmen stared at Natalia, shook her head, then walked off.

Natalia felt her heart breaking with each step. Maybe she *was* out of her mind. Maybe Carmen was right. Did she really want to leave everything she knew just for—?

She stopped herself. She was leaving for a God who loved her, who had sacrificed everything for her. A God who knew just what it was like to leave the familiarity of home out of obedience to his Father.

Peace washed over her in a way Natalia could never explain, an experience so intimate and amazing that all her momentary doubts vanished. God was with her in this park. He would be with her as she left. More difficulties would come, but Jesus would be there as she faced each of them.

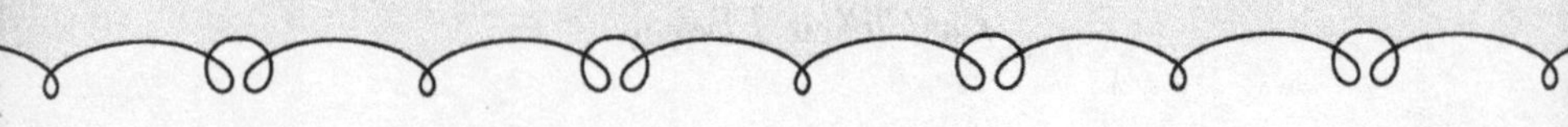

Chapter 2

"Good-bye, fragments." Brian Younger dumped his grammar workbook into the trash can beside his locker. "Good-bye run-on sentences that should have a comma somewhere in there but I never remember where so I get ten points off my essays. Good-bye—"

"Really, man?" Spencer Adams picked up Brian's discarded workbook. "You might need to look over this during the summer. If you want to graduate next year, that is."

Brian put a hand through his red hair and looked down at Spencer. At six foot six, Brian was half a foot taller than the big-mouthed most-popular boy in school, but that didn't deter Spencer one bit.

"Maybe I don't want to graduate." Brian refused to take the book from Spencer's hands.

"Don't want to graduate?" Lexi Summers, friend and fellow "freakishly tall" student at Tampa Christian School, shoved herself between the feuding boys. "What are you talking about? I've already got the countdown going." Lexi looked at her watch. "Three hundred fifty-five days, five hours, and ten minutes."

Spencer dumped the workbook back in the trash. "I'm with you, Lex. Get me outta this place. I'm ready for some freedom."

Because Brian's dad was the pastor of the church attached to the Christian school, Brian got his share of "I hate this school" speeches. Spencer topped the list of complainers.

"Why can't you be excited about graduating and not hate the school at the same time?" Lexi put an arm around Brian. "I love this place."

"Hey, no PC." Spencer shook a finger in Lexi's face. Physical contact was against the rules at TCS. "See what I mean? When we're at college, no one's gonna yell at us for giving our friends a hug."

"Or give us demerits for making out with a sophomore in the hallway." Lexi snapped a finger in Spencer's face.

Brian tried not to laugh.

"At least someone wants to make out with me," Spencer bit out, slamming his locker door, then walking away.

"Don't worry about him, Lex. Spencer's a jerk."

"I was going to say the same thing to you." Lexi smiled. "Don't worry about me. It takes a whole lot more than Spencer Adams to ruin my day."

Brian wished he could say the same. Spencer Adams had been making his life miserable for years. Just because the guy's dad was loaded, because he had good looks passed down from his Cuban model mother, because he could play every sport well and all the girls at school drooled all over him, was that reason for Spencer to treat Brian like gum stuck on his shoe?

Brian walked over to his dad's office, trying to get Spencer out of his head. *At least I get a two-month break from the guy. Count your blessings, right?*

"My boy's a senior." Dad stood from his desk and pulled Brian into a hug. "Ready for this summer?"

"I guess."

"What's wrong?"

Brian sighed. "I just wish I was smart and athletic instead of just so incredibly good looking."

With the complexion only boys with bright red hair were afforded, Brian's pale skin, blue eyes, and freckles had been the cause of ridicule most of his life. He had been called "Brian the Friendly Ghost," "Vampire Boy," and a host of other names, none of which were synonymous with "good looking."

"It's a curse we Youngers have." Dad smiled. His formerly red hair had been muted with gray, and faint wrinkles replaced his freckles. "I've got some good news for you."

Brian slumped into the leather chair across from his dad's desk. "Lay it on me."

"I got you a job."

Brian sat up. "Where?"

"Working with Mr. King."

Dad forgot that Brian didn't know the names and occupations of every member of the church. "Who?"

"George King." His dad leaned forward. "He owns a demolition company."

"Demolition?"

"Yes, he goes into old buildings and guts them."

"I get to spend the summer tearing stuff down?" Brian asked. "Awesome."

"Yep, you'll be working all summer on an old mansion right on the bay."

"A mansion?"

"Apparently it's in pretty bad shape." Dad's phone rang. He held up a hand to Brian. "Hi, Joan . . . Manny's back in the hospital? I'm so sorry." He grabbed a sticky note. "Room 524. Got it. I'll try to get up this afternoon . . . I'll be praying for you."

"Something serious?"

"Manny Johnson." Dad placed the sticky note on his computer monitor. "He's got cancer and hasn't been doing well lately."

"Do I know him?"

"Neither of the Johnsons come to church much." Dad shrugged. "But they call when times are tough."

His dad loved his congregation, but it bothered Brian that people just called when they needed something. Or wanted to complain. He promised himself that he would never go into the ministry. Not after seeing how hard it was on his dad and their family.

"So, an old mansion?"

"Old." Dad nodded. "George said it was built in 1913. It has been sitting vacant for about a decade."

"What?"

"The owner was in a nursing home, but she refused to sell it. So it's just been sitting there. She died last month, and her family sold it right away. George said it was pretty nasty inside."

"And we're just tearing it down?"

"You'll be gutting the inside so the new owners can remodel. George said it'll take a good two months to get it all done."

"Two months? How big is this place?"

"About six thousand square feet," Dad said. "Oh, and guess who the new owners are?"

Brian leaned over the desk toward his father. "Us?"

"You wish." Dad laughed. "The Adamses."

"As in Spencer Adams?" Brian slouched back into his chair, praying it was some other Adams family. Any other.

Dad nodded. "Yep. I'm sure you'll be seeing him around the site."

Great. Why couldn't the house be owned by a supermodel? Or a movie star? Come on, God, you're killing me. Is this some kind of a test? Because if it is, I think I'd rather just fail.

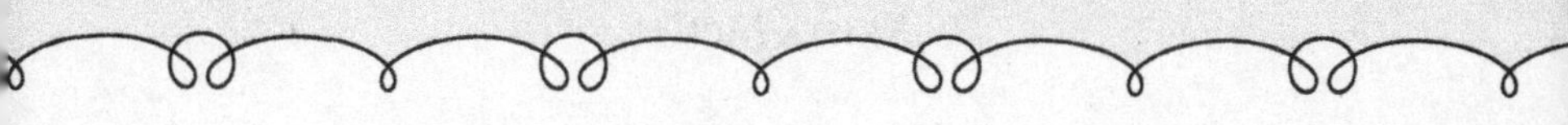

Chapter 3

"Why would you want to come to Florida with me?" Maureen stood in her bedroom, throwing clothes into suitcases, tears coursing a well-worn path down her cheeks.

It was best to remain silent. Natalia reached in a suitcase and folded one of Maureen's blouses. Upset or not, Maureen hated for her clothes to be mistreated.

"I'm going back to family and friends who warned me not to marry your father. I can just imagine the 'I told you so's' I'm going to get." Maureen tossed a pair of fuzzy slippers across the room. Natalia retrieved them.

"And they were right. Why didn't I listen to them? He didn't share my faith. We barely knew each other. But I was so sure he meant it when he said I was the love of his life." Maureen could barely speak between sobs. She took a ragged breath. "But I was just one of a long line of women. Nothing special. And now I have to go back and acknowledge just how wrong I was."

Natalia took Maureen's hands and shook her head. "I know you're hurting. Believe me, I know. But I, for one, am incredibly thankful you married my father. If it weren't for you, I wouldn't know about Jesus. You may not be my biological mother, but you are my spiritual mother. I'm sticking beside you whether you like it or not. So if you want to go back to Florida, I'll go. If you want to go to Timbuktu, I'll go there too. My father may not see how special you are, but our heavenly Father does. So stop telling me to stay here and help me pack."

A few minutes later Natalia left the apartment and took the Metro to meet her father at his office. Papa wanted to meet at his new girlfriend's *piso,* but Natalia refused to set foot in that woman's apartment. She could not force Papa to end that relationship, but she certainly did not have to enter into one of her own.

"Mija." Papa bent to give Natalia a kiss on both cheeks. "You have something important to tell me?"

Natalia sat in a soft leather chair that faced her father's large but meticulously clean desk. If only he would be as careful with the women in his life as he was with his business. "Maureen is hurting, Papa."

He raised a hand. "I know. It will be hard for her at first. But she is a strong, capable woman. And she is beautiful. She'll find love again. With someone far better than me."

Natalia wanted to roll her eyes, but she resisted. God would not be pleased with her disrespecting her father. No matter how much he deserved her disrespect. "This move back to Florida, it will be very difficult." Natalia touched her forefinger to her thumb. *"Muy dificul."*

Papa sighed, leaning back in his chair. "I have tried to help. I will pay alimony. I will pay for her moving expenses. I have plenty of connections all over the United States. I could get her a job. She refuses all of it."

Natalia's stomach clenched. Did he really think Maureen's pain could be softened with his money? "She is too proud to take anything from you. She needs what you will not give her."

Papa leaned forward. "I wish you would meet Victoria. She is a wonderful woman. Exactly what I need."

Natalia bit back a dozen angry responses. None of them would be beneficial. Or appropriate. "We are talking about Maureen. Papa, I would like to move to Florida with her."

Natalia held her breath. She had imagined this conversation in her mind all the way over on the Metro. She still wasn't sure how her father would respond.

"I think that's a great opportunity," he said after a moment of uncomfortable silence. "I went to college in America, you know. Finishing high school there will help you get into the school of your choice."

She had hoped her father would be angry at her wanting to leave, not see this as yet another opportunity to make her choose her career path.

"I knew I wanted to go into business when I was twelve years old."

Natalia couldn't count how many times she had heard her father mention this. Usually in the context of her being seventeen and still not knowing what she wanted to do.

"You are seventeen, corazón. And still, you have no idea what you want to do. Correct?"

"Correct." Natalia sank down in the chair.

"If you want to be a success"—he glanced around his spacious office—"you must have a plan for that success. Know what you want and go after it with everything you have."

Natalia stared at the carpet.

"So, yes, go to Florida." Papa stood and walked to Natalia. He pulled her up from the chair and escorted her to the door. "Do well in school there. That, combined with recommendations from your teachers here, and you will be able to get into a good college, get a good degree, and become a success. Like your papa."

Natalia stood stiffly as her father embraced her. This was it? She was leaving her home, leaving him, and all he could say was "do well in school there"?

"I do wish you would meet Victoria before you leave. You would like her. She is making a new man out of me."

Natalia exited the building as fast as she could, trying not to picture her father and Victoria. The "new man" he was becoming was devastating Maureen, and he couldn't even see it.

Papa was looking for love and fulfillment in the arms of a woman. Even seventeen-year-old Natalia could see he would never find what he was looking for there.

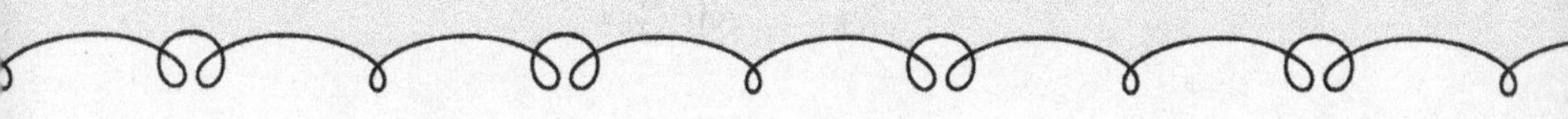

Chapter 4

"So you'll be living where?" Natalia's mother, Anita, asked. For the third time.

"Right outside Tampa, Florida, Mamá." How much of their conversation was her mother actually hearing? Between checking her phone and looking around the plaza to see if she knew any of the passersby, she had a difficult time focusing on her daughter. "It's in the southeast portion of the United States."

She glared at Natalia and laid her cell phone next to her glass of red wine. "I know where Tampa is."

"Sorry. Anyway, it's in northwest Tampa. Maureen says it's just a few minutes from the beach."

Mamá responded to yet another text message, then looked at Natalia with eyebrows raised. "And you're sure you want to move there with this woman? You haven't known her very long. You know you're welcome to move in with me."

Her concern lasted only as long as it took for her to

spot someone she knew across the Plaza Mayor—Madrid's town center—a huge square filled with restaurants, souvenir shops, and other small businesses housed in the bottom floors of what used to be the fortress to protect the town from invaders centuries ago.

Mamá waved her phone in the air and motioned for her friend to call her. After blowing the woman an air kiss, she once again turned to face Natalia. "What was I saying?"

"I can always stay with you." Natalia rolled her eyes.

"What?" Her mother stiffened.

"Mamá, you don't have time for me. How often are you at home?"

"When I was seventeen, I just needed a place to sleep and store my clothes. I have raised you well, and you are ready to venture out on your own. But you don't need to go all the way to America if you don't want to."

Natalia bit back her desire to argue with her mother's comment. She had not raised Natalia. That woman was even more work-obsessed than her father. But Natalia didn't want to argue. This was her good-bye lunch and she wanted it to go well.

"Thank you, Mamá, but Maureen could use help and I would like to go with her."

"*Vale.* All right. I did speak to your father about it, and he seems to think a few years in the United States will be good for you. We both went to college in the States, you know."

Natalia was surprised to hear her parents had spoken. They usually used her as a mediator.

"We are hoping this will help you choose a career, get a little more motivated."

And there it is. The one thing in the world they can agree on—Natalia needs to buckle down and choose her career. God, I need your help here.

"Mamá, I am going because I believe that is what God wants me to do."

"It's already three o'clock!" Her mother jumped, picked up her phone, and scrolled down the screen with her finger. "I'm supposed to meet a friend at four over in Las Rosas. I'm sorry, sweetheart." She stood, Natalia taking her cue. After a quick kiss on both cheeks, her mother wished Natalia luck on her trip and left with what they both knew was an empty promise to visit.

Natalia stayed at the table after her mother left, waving away the waiter, and put on her oversized sunglasses to hide her tears. Her mother always changed the subject when Natalia tried to speak with her about her faith.

She looked over the plaza as people passed by. How many of those were mothers and daughters who talked, who shared secrets and stories? Did any of them sit at a table like this, phones off, and discuss their lives and their feelings?

Natalia left the plaza, soaking in the sights and sounds and smells of her native city. She would miss the smell of the *Jamón Serrano*, the leg of ham hanging from the butcher's windows, being cured before sliced paper thin for people to enjoy with bread and cheese, drizzled with olive oil. The smell of churros. She'd miss the narrow cobblestone streets that wove in and out of the city, the old-world charm that seamlessly mixed with modern luxuries—a Metro system, taking people on underground trains anywhere they wanted to go, with stops outside of palaces and cathedrals; luxury hotels built inside what used to be convents in the sixteenth century. She could get on the Metro from anywhere in Madrid and exit at a bullfighting arena, a world-class museum, an ultrachic mall.

A group of young people about Natalia's age crossed the street in front of her, arms linked, laughing. She thought of all the friends she was leaving. Although they disagreed with her faith, they were still good friends. Natalia had grown up with her classmates, sharing years of memories and moments that would all be left behind.

Would the Americans at her new school welcome her? Would she have friends or be an outcast? The little she knew of Americans—other than Maureen, of course—was what she saw on television: beautiful, gossipy, and boy crazy. But Spanish television shows didn't accurately reflect Spaniards, so hopefully American shows didn't reflect the average American either.

Natalia made her way past the crowds of people down the escalator to the Metro.

At least one, God. Help me make at least one friend in Tampa.

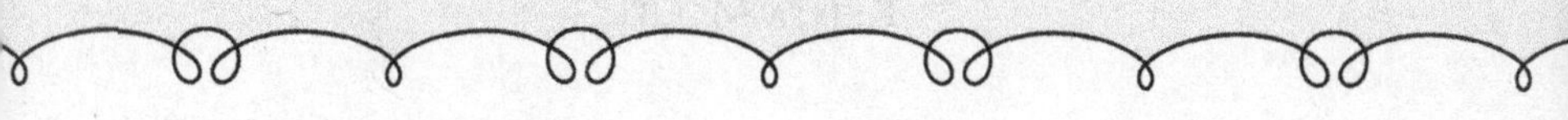

Chapter 5

"What did he say?" Natalia had asked that question dozens of times since she and Maureen first landed in the United States.

Although Natalia's education had been in English, her ears could not adjust to the various accents and slang terms being thrown around by the stewards, immigration officers, and airport workers. All of her English teachers had been from England, and none of the people she encountered sounded like them.

She and Maureen had first landed in LaGuardia Airport in New York. After an overnight flight from Madrid, a tired and heartsick Natalia followed the massive crowd from the plane to the Customs line and had been separated from Maureen because hers was not an American passport. Natalia had to ask three times before she understood that the Customs officer wanted to know if she had brought any hazardous materials with her. All she heard were a series of mumbles and grunts followed by raised eyebrows.

When she didn't understand, the man simply mumbled and grunted louder. Thankfully, the gentleman behind her—also a Spaniard—was able to translate.

"I have been taking English since I was seven," Natalia said. "So why am I having such a hard time understanding it?"

"The New York accent is difficult to get used to," the man said, forefinger touching his thumb in a familiar Spanish gesture.

Their next layover was in Atlanta. Standing at the lunch counter, Natalia tried to adjust to what she was hearing—very different from what she heard in New York.

She turned to Maureen. "Why did she ask that woman what kind of Coke she wanted? Don't they sell other drinks here?"

Maureen explained that many southerners referred to all soft drinks as "Coke," so when he asked Natalia what kind of Coke she wanted, she could answer "Sprite."

"But not Coca-Cola Light," Maureen continued. "It's called *Diet* Coke here."

Natalia rubbed her temples, trying to ward off the Georgia-sized headache pounding in her brain. Meanwhile she and Maureen were passing through yet another gate to board yet another plane. And, again, Natalia had no idea what she was being asked.

"He wants to see your boarding pass," Maureen said. "Just show it to him, with your passport."

"Spain, huh?" The older man looked through Natalia's passport and whistled. "My wife has always wanted to visit there. Heard it's real purty, all that good food and them flamenco dancers." The man did a little twirl, his arms raised above his head, clapping to an imaginary beat.

Natalia looked at Maureen, who shook her head and smiled. "Southern people are very friendly." She answered Natalia's unspoken question as the two made their way through the terminal and into the airplane.

Natalia grunted. "I think I like New Yorkers better. I may not understand what they're saying, but at least they move a little quicker. These people act like they have all day!"

Maureen laughed. "Language isn't the only difference between Spain and the US. Our cultures are pretty different too. Not as different as other places, though. I had some major adjustments when I moved to Madrid."

"Like what?" Natalia squeezed into the middle seat, a heavyset woman on one side, Maureen on the other.

"Kissing."

"What?"

"We don't greet with a kiss in the States. It's a handshake, a hug if you're really close. But never a kiss."

"Really?"

"I was stunned at my first business meeting with your dad's company. All these people coming and kissing both my cheeks. It was awful. Until your dad came along. One look at him, and I couldn't wait for the daily greeting." Maureen's smile faded and her eyes began to fill with tears. Again.

Her stepmother was grieving, but Natalia didn't know anyone could cry as much as that woman had in the weeks since the divorce. She had hoped stepping back onto US soil would help. Apparently it did not.

Natalia looked out the window as the plane made its way from Atlanta to Tampa. *What am I doing? I don't understand the way anyone talks. I don't understand the way they act. God, did you really mean for me to come here, or was this just my own stubborn idea?* She thought this would be good for her, good for Maureen. But maybe she should have listened more to Carmen. *Maybe I should have stayed.*

Natalia's mind continued to wander as the plane descended into the Tampa International Airport. She took a few deep breaths and tried to convince herself that this was a good decision.

Forty-five minutes later she was ready to get on the next plane back to Madrid.

"It'll show up." The airline employee assured Natalia as she filled out the paperwork for her missing luggage. "This just happens sometimes when there are several legs to a flight."

"Legs?" Confused, Natalia looked up at Maureen. Would she *ever* learn American slang?

"It means stopovers. Because we were on so many different planes, the luggage got mixed up."

"How long until it arrives?" Natalia stared at the man behind the counter. He shrugged and slid a form across the counter.

Maureen pulled a pen from her purse and filled out the information required, Natalia standing beside her. Was this a sign? Her luggage didn't even want to be here.

Maybe I should just go home. This certainly isn't starting out well.

Maureen handed the completed form back to the man and dragged herself to a chair a few feet away. Gazing into her stepmother's face, Natalia knew she could never leave.

Suddenly, Maureen burst out laughing. People around her looked at her as if she were crazy. Natalia looked at her as if she were crazy. The woman hadn't laughed in weeks. "Maureen?"

Maureen wiped tears from her eyes—tears that, for once, weren't from weeping. "This is all so ridiculous. It's like a really bad comedy. 'Everything that can go wrong, does go wrong.' No job, no husband, no money. And no luggage."

Natalia didn't really see the humor in their situation, but she was so happy to see a smile on her stepmother's face, she didn't care. Maureen's blue eyes swam. "Oh, Natalia. I can't believe you're here. But I'm so glad. Thank you."

The switch from laughter to sentimentality was abrupt, but Natalia squeezed the hand that Maureen placed in hers.

Maureen sighed. "I am dreading this first meeting with my sister. We've talked on the phone. I've Skyped with the girls. She keeps telling me how excited they are that we are coming. But what is it really going to be like? I am divorced. Broken. Embarrassed."

"Maureen." Natalia appreciated her honesty. That was one of the traits that endeared her to Natalia from the beginning. "You are a strong woman and your family will see that. Besides, you've been away from them for years. How many times have you told me how much you've missed your sister and how you hated being away from your nieces? You're back! This is exciting. You are home, where you understand everyone and you don't need to kiss anyone. And what about those public subs? You've been talking about having a foot-long roast beef sub since we left Madrid."

Maureen let out a halfhearted laugh. "Publix, Natalia, not public. I want a Publix sub. And I do want to see my sister and hug my nieces and smell the Gulf of Mexico from my backyard." She dabbed her eyes with a tissue. "I'm sorry, sweetie. This is just so much more difficult than I anticipated."

The shrill ring of Maureen's phone screamed from her purse. Both women jumped, then laughed. Maureen dug around for her phone, barely finding it in time to answer.

It was Maureen's sister, Carol. She was waiting outside. Maureen took a deep breath and stood, Natalia following behind her. She looked longingly at the Departures screen, seeing a flight to Madrid leaving in forty-five minutes.

I could take it. Natalia walked through the baggage-claim area and took her first steps into the infamous Florida humidity. Her papa would pay the fare. Staying here with a grieving stepmother, a sea of strangers, surrounded by people whose accents she didn't understand and whose customs she didn't like was certainly not appealing. *Maybe my lost luggage is a sign from God that I should go back.*

Natalia took one look at Maureen's vulnerable, tear-stained face and knew she could never be so selfish. *She needs me,* Natalia reminded herself. *And I need her.* Trying her best to forget about the lost luggage, forget about the home and the friends she left behind, Natalia smiled as she greeted Maureen's sister—and her future.

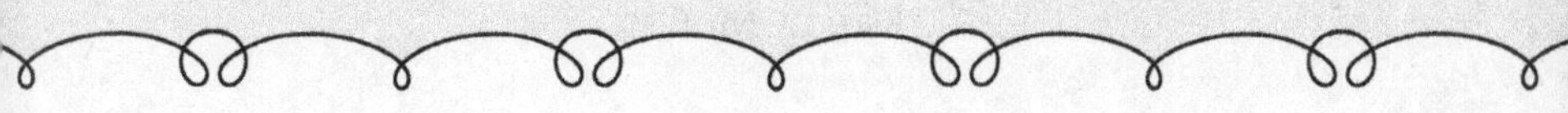

Chapter 6

"First thing we gotta do is tear down the paneling," Mr. King said.

Brian had gotten to the work site at six o'clock. Mr. King insisted on an early start, and Brian decided now would be the perfect time to learn the fine art of coffee drinking, so he gagged down another sip of the gas station house brew.

"It doesn't have to look pretty." Mr. King pulled away at the ancient wood paneling. "But you do need to make sure you don't cut through any wires."

"And how do I know where those are?"

"No telling in a house this old. It's probably been rewired several times."

Brian glanced at the crowbar in his hand. "So be careful not to cut through wires that may or may not be all through the walls we are tearing down."

Mr. King slapped Brian on the back. "Exactly."

Brian looked at James, his coworker. "You done this before?"

"Started when I was your age." James smiled. "I finish up college next year, so this'll be my last summer. I'm going to miss it."

"Ever been electrocuted?"

"I wouldn't call it electrocuted."

Brian didn't have the time—or the desire—to hear that explanation.

"I'll be working with you boys most of the time," Mr. King said. "But I need to run over to the kitchen to give that crew the rundown. You okay without me?"

"Sure." Brian gripped the crowbar.

"Don't worry." James laughed. "You'll be fine. Plus, this is great for the physique." He flexed a large bicep at Brian. "The girls will be falling all over themselves to go out with you by the time this summer is over."

"All right, then." Brian threw his tool at the wall. "Let's get started."

Five hours later his entire body hurt. And they'd only gotten to half the walls in the large room. The paneling was so old it refused to come down in one piece. Jagged edges were all over the floor. Brian wore gloves, but splinters made their way into his wrists and ankles.

"Look who we have here."

Brian turned to see Spencer, sipping a giant soda and smirking in his polo shirt and plaid shorts, not a hair out of place.

"Spencer." Brian tried to smile, but he was sure it seemed more like a grimace. Acting really wasn't his strong suit. "I heard your dad bought this."

"This mansion will be the perfect place to host the homecoming dinner, don't you think?" Spencer smiled.

With you as homecoming king, I'm sure. "Yes, perfect."

"Hello, Brian." Mr. Adams walked in behind his son. His girth filled the doorway. Mr. Adams was a successful defense attorney. His billboards dotted I-275. Brian rarely saw him at school, though, so he had only met the man a few times.

"Nice to see you, Mr. Adams." Brian shook the man's hand. "This is going to be a great place."

"It better be, for the price I paid." He glanced around. "Bay-front property doesn't come cheap. Neither does a complete remodel. But my wife insists."

Mr. Adams had recently remarried. His new wife was also a model, just like the first Mrs. Adams. *How does a guy who looks like he swallowed a VW Bug get women who look like that?* Brian thought of the billboards again. *Right. That's how.*

"You look tired, Brian. If you'd joined the football team, you'd be used to working out."

Brian was about as interested in football as Spencer was tactful. "No time for sports, man. Some of us have to work."

"Spencer is working." Mr. Adams squeezed his son's shoulder. "At my law firm."

"In the air-conditioning." Spencer took another sip of his soda.

"Don't mock the help, son." Mr. Adams turned to walk out of the room. "They keep things running so we important people can do our work."

Brian rolled his eyes.

"Think you're smart enough to find your way out of

here?" James said, once he was sure the Adams men were out of earshot. "I'm ready for lunch."

"I don't know." Brian scratched his head. "I'm just the help. Here to serve the important people."

"Don't let those guys get to you." James walked ahead of Brian. "A little hard work is good for everyone. That's what my dad says." James looked back at Brian. "And he's a senator."

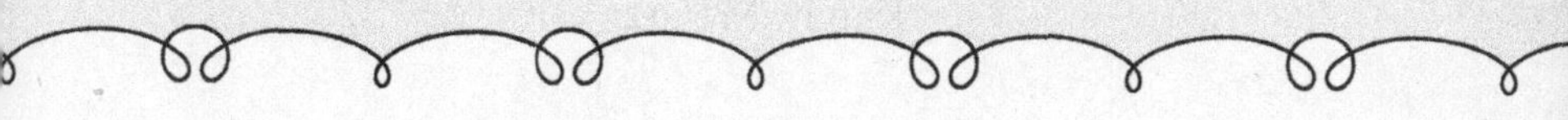

Chapter 7

"Wouldn't this be just perfect?" Joanne, Natalia and Maureen's Realtor, gushed. "This place was built in 1984, but the entire kitchen has been remodeled. The bathrooms too. And this is upgraded vinyl in the entryway. Doesn't it look just like tile? You'd never know if you didn't look close. Go ahead, touch it. Amazing, isn't it?"

Natalia wished that woman would stop talking. Just for a minute. She hadn't kept quiet for more than thirty seconds the entire torturous day. As soon as Maureen and Natalia entered a house, Joanne would spout off the dimensions, the architectural details, the upgrades. Natalia couldn't stand it. She wanted to be left alone so she and Maureen could have a private walk and talk about the possibilities without having Joanne jump in singing, "And don't forget, you're just a mile away from the mall!" or "Look at these fixtures! Top of the line. Try it. Come on, you know you want to!"

"I appreciate all you've done for us, Joanne, really."

Natalia tried her best to sound polite, to show grace, as Maureen had taught her. "But do you think Maureen and I could talk privately for just a few minutes?"

"Why sure, honey!" Joanne drawled. "I've got a great little place about five miles from here I'd like you to see. Let me call my partner and see if it's available this afternoon."

When the door shut behind Joanne, Natalia sighed. "Do all Americans talk that much? Because if they do, I don't know if I can stand it."

"Don't stereotype, Natalia. There is no such thing as 'all Americans.' There are thirty million individuals." Maureen raised her eyebrows.

Natalia let out a slow breath. "Guilty. Again." She shook her head. "But you have to admit. This place is . . . what is that word . . . a dump?"

Maureen laughed. "Well, I don't know if I'd go that far. But I am on a tight budget. I don't want to live off your father's alimony. I want to make my own living and be independent."

"What about child support?"

"That's for you. I don't want to use it for a house or anything at all related to me."

"Maureen . . ."

"No, Natalia. I've got to do this. You don't understand. If I'm ever going to be able to move on, I have to make a clean break from your father."

She could see the tears forming in Maureen's eyes, so she quickly changed the subject. "But all this dust! And the furniture. It's so . . . big."

"American design tends to be a little less streamlined

than Spanish design. When I first moved to Madrid, I remember thinking that Spanish apartments appeared sterile and uninviting. And the furniture seemed like it belonged in a dollhouse. Now that I've lived there for five years, this does look a little big and a tad messy."

"A tad?"

"Okay, maybe a little more than a tad. Americans just tend to have more things, and things get dusty. But we can shop at Ikea and you can be in charge of dusting every day."

"No maid?"

Maureen shook her head. "Here I am just a middle-class woman living paycheck to paycheck. I don't even know what that paycheck is going to be at this point. I've got enough savings to last about three months, then I'm done. No maid. No new clothes or eating out. I tried to tell you this before we left, Natalia. This is a much different way of life than what you're used to."

"It's all right." Natalia prayed God would help her adjust to this new lifestyle. "Where you go, I go, remember? Just promise me I won't have to share a room with cockroaches!"

~

Two hours and three houses later an exhausted Natalia and Maureen returned to Carol's house. There the pair was greeted by Maureen's two nieces and her frazzled sister.

"Aunt Maureen! Guess what?" Little Calla asked, her four-year-old face beaming. "I made you something! But you have to close your eyes. You too, Natalia. Close your eyes!"

Eight-year-old Nora grabbed Natalia's hand. "Close your eyes! We don't want you to see it!"

The girls had attached themselves to Natalia, caring little that she was a "stepcousin." The little blond-haired, blue-eyed girls were adorable, and Natalia hoped their presence would cheer Maureen, whom they loved even more than they loved Natalia.

Eyes closed, Natalia felt her way past the large dining room table to the kitchen, which held the overwhelming smell of burnt caramel.

"Ta da!" the girls sang out in unison.

"We made a flan!" Calla clapped her hands together. "We wanted to make something Spanish and Mom said this was a Spanish dessert. Do you like it?"

"Wow." Maureen looked at the dark brown lump of congealed custard. "Flan! I do love flan." Her eyes widened as she peered at Natalia, warning her without speaking that they had to eat this, no matter how bad it tasted.

"Georgie came in while we were cooking"—Calla pointed at the beagle eagerly panting beside her small leg—"and I had to take care of him because Mama says he is my job because I wanted him. So I gave him a treat, and it just took a minute. But Nora was in the bathroom at the same time and she didn't know I was helping Georgie and the sugar got a little burned at the bottom of the pan and Mama—"

Carol placed her hand over Calla's mouth. "What she's trying to say is that it might not taste like what you're used to."

"But it's still good." Nora's curls bounced as she nodded. "Just a little crunchy."

"Crunchy flan." Maureen cautiously dipped her fork into the now-fossilized dessert. She took a large drink from her glass of water, then placed the flan in her mouth. "Mmmm . . ." Maureen tried to say more, but she probably could not open her mouth.

Natalia gulped as the two girls turned their big blue eyes to her. She couldn't refuse their gift. But one look at Maureen's face, and she knew she'd be tasting this flan for a week.

Just then the front door opened and Jack, Carol's husband, walked in. The girls ran to greet him, giving Maureen and Natalia just enough time to dump their desserts into the trash and return the empty plates to the table.

"Wow! You ate the whole thing?" Nora gasped as she ran back into the kitchen. "You loved it! I knew it! I've got more." As she made her way to the island in the center of the kitchen, Carol cut her off.

"That is sweet, Nora, but don't you think we need to save some for Daddy?"

Jack shot Carol a look that said, "I'll get you for this" but smiled as he was served a heaping pile of the girls' Spanish concoction.

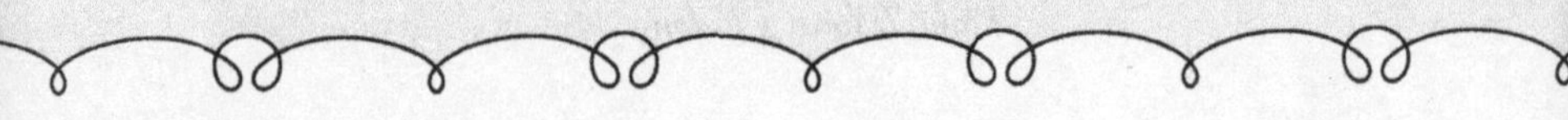

Chapter 8

"I think that's the last of it." Jack grunted as he dropped yet another oversized Ikea box on Natalia and Maureen's new living room floor.

Carol had stayed home with the girls so Jack could help the pair set up their new town house. After several days of searching, their Realtor found a new three-bedroom/two-bathroom town house just minutes from the beach right in Maureen's price range. Surprisingly there were no delays with the contract or closing, allowing them to move just two weeks after their arrival in Tampa.

Natalia could see God's hand in the entire process—finding a house they both liked, that Maureen could afford, in a community with a pool, gym, and yard maintenance. Maureen was even able to take out a loan for a few thousand more than the mortgage so they could decorate the place. It was perfect.

Unfortunately, Maureen's discouragement had only grown in the weeks since the two returned from Spain.

"If God worked so hard to provide for us here, why didn't he work in Spain? Why didn't he make your father want to stay with me? It's hard to be thankful for a house when my life has fallen apart."

Natalia had learned to stay quiet. Her attempts at helping Maureen either resulted in tirades or tears—neither of which was pretty. Or beneficial.

"All right, ladies, I'm going out to get some lunch. I need a Big Mac and some fries to get me through the rest of this day." Jack laughed, stretching his back muscles and grimacing with the effort. "You guys want something while I'm out?"

"I would love a salad."

"No," Maureen snapped. "We'll take care of our own lunch. Jack, you've done enough. Go ahead home and we'll put these things together."

Jack and Natalia both looked at Maureen as if she were crazy. "Maureen, don't be silly. It would take you guys forever to put all of this together. Besides, your sister would skin me alive if I came home now. Natalia wants a salad. What about you?"

Defeated but still angry, Maureen gave Jack her order and watched as he walked out the door. As soon as his car pulled out of their driveway, Maureen began to cry.

"Why does my sister get a guy like him? They've been married ten years, and he still does whatever she asks. He treats her like a queen . . . He's a great dad. It's not fair!" Maureen slid down the wall to the hardwood floor.

Natalia vacillated between anger at Maureen for wallowing in self-pity and anger at her father for causing Maureen so much pain. She finally decided the best thing she could do would be to pray—pray for Maureen to get over her dad and pray for herself not to strangle Maureen in the meantime.

Natalia grabbed her suitcases, which had arrived five days after she did, and took them up to her room. A bare mattress on a metal frame sat underneath the lone window and boxes were piled along three walls. Inside those boxes were her nightstands, dresser, and headboard. Jack was right: this would take forever.

I may not be able to put my things together, but I can at least make my bed.

She walked over to the pile of bags and found the one with her sheets—bright red jersey cotton to go with her red-and-white floral bedspread. Natalia relaxed as she placed them on her bed. She wasn't used to beds being so high, and she would need to return to the department store and get a bed skirt to cover the ugly black rollers at the base of the bed frame. She folded down the bedspread and placed her pillows against the wall, then surveyed her work.

It's a start. She smiled.

"Lucy, I'm ho-ome!" Jack bellowed.

Who was Lucy and why was Jack calling for her? Natalia still hadn't deciphered what he had meant when he said Carol would "skin him alive" when he came home. Natalia doubted she'd ever fully understand Americans.

". . . and I brought backup!"

Natalia came down the stairs and smiled when she realized she knew what he meant by "backup"—thanks to the American cop shows so popular in Europe.

"You're smiling like the cat that ate the canary." Jack laughed at Natalia.

"What?"

"The cat that ate the canary," Jack repeated.

When will people realize that saying something twice doesn't make it more intelligible? Natalia looked behind her stepuncle and froze midthought.

She had never seen hair quite so red. It had golden streaks and was wavy, the locks cut short but spiked. Below the hair was a giant. Her father, a little under six feet, was considered quite tall in Spain. But this young man stood almost half a foot taller. Natalia had to crane her neck to see his face. He had a warm smile—very white—with a strong nose and full, rosy lips. He was paler than most of the boys she knew in Spain, making his hair look even brighter and his big blue eyes, framed by blond lashes, brighter still.

Not traditionally handsome, but certainly attractive. Very attractive. Carmen would go crazy over those blue eyes. Not me, of course. I am not even thinking about boys, not getting involved. Ever. But I can admire some nice eyes every once in a while. For Carmen's sake.

"Natalia, this is Brian Younger the younger." Jack laughed and Brian rolled his eyes.

"That joke never gets old, does it, Jack?"

"Never!" Jack smiled and slapped Brian on the back.

"Little Brian Younger?" Maureen gasped, eyes wide. "But you were always such a tiny thing. When did you get so tall? *How* did you get so tall?"

Natalia was so happy to see Maureen distracted she almost missed the young man's answer.

"Good to see you too, Miss Maureen." He laughed, wrapping Natalia's stepmother in a hug, the older woman's head buried in Brian's chest. "I hit a growth spurt between my sophomore and junior years in high school. Eight inches in one summer."

Maureen stepped back to survey him. "Eight inches! I don't even think I would have recognized you. And how are your parents?"

"Doing great." An older gentleman walked in and squeezed Brian's shoulder.

"Brian Younger the older!" Jack bellowed.

"Pastor Brian, I have missed you."

Pastor Brian walked toward Maureen and hugged her, whispering into her ear. When he pulled away, Maureen excused herself, dabbing at the tears in her eyes. The pastor looked apologetically at Jack.

"It takes time." Jack sighed. "This hasn't been easy." He gazed over at Natalia. "But this beautiful young woman has certainly made it easier. This is my stepniece, Natalia. Natalia, these are the Brian Youngers. The old guy is our pastor and the young guy is trouble."

She wasn't sure what to make of that comment, and, thankfully, she didn't have time to respond. The younger of the Youngers came and hugged Natalia in the same warm embrace he had given Maureen, bending down to be closer to eye level. Instinctively, Natalia kissed his right cheek and moved to kiss the other.

"Oh, I forgot! Americans don't greet like we do. I'm sorry."

"You can kiss me anytime you want to." The younger man laughed, his face turning an adorable shade of pink. Natalia felt her stomach jump. *No, Natalia. Do not even think about him like that. No boys, remember?*

"Excuse my son. Obviously, he's starved for attention.

Growing up in a pastor's home can do that to you. It's nice to meet you, though. Jack and Carol have told us what a blessing you've been to our Maureen. To leave your family and your home to come be with your stepmother . . ." The pastor's voice cracked and he cleared his throat. "Well, you're already an example to us. We can't wait to get to know you better."

Maureen walked in, her eyes red. She smiled at the men and walked over to Natalia. "She is special."

The room was silent for a moment, then Brian Younger the younger spoke up, breaking the ice. "Since you asked, I am eighteen and about to begin my senior year. My birthday is in May, and my parents decided to wait until I was six to start kindergarten because I was so little."

Pastor Brian shook his head. "Always have to bring that up, don't you, son?"

Brian smiled at his father. "I am currently working demolition, running the ESL program at church, and planning to go on a mission trip to Costa Rica in September. In general, I have turned out fantastically well—despite my upbringing." He winked at his father. "And I'm sure I owe most of it to my elementary Sunday school teacher."

Shaking her head, Maureen laughed softly. "I'm glad you didn't lose any of that humility I so admired, Brian."

"Enough chitchat." Jack rubbed his hands together. "I brought these men along to work. Pastor Brian only works one day a week, you know, so I figured he was overdue."

Apparently sarcasm is a national pastime. I think I'll make it here just fine.

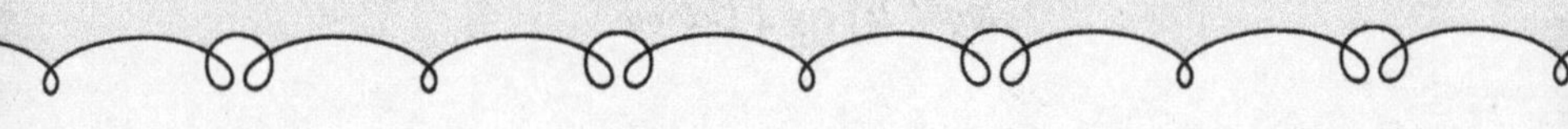

Chapter 9

"Over a decade working in upper-level management in international corporations, and I can't even get an interview with a small firm here!" Maureen slammed her laptop shut and stood from the table, her chair scraping loudly against the tile floor. "Divorced, unemployed, unattractive—"

"Maureen, you are beautiful and intelligent."

"And unemployed."

"Because of the recession. You know that. But something will work out. God has the perfect job out there for you. You just haven't found it yet."

"Just like God had the perfect marriage for me?" Maureen spat. "I'm sorry, Natalia. But God and I aren't on very good terms right now."

Natalia walked over to Maureen and took her hand. "Someone very wise once told me that the trials we face in our lives help shape us into the person Christ wants us to be."

Maureen shook her hand from Natalia's, walked into the living room, and fell into an overstuffed chair. "Oh, Natalia. It's easy to say that to someone else. It's much harder to believe it when it's happening to you."

"So you don't believe anymore?" That couldn't be true. Not after all the conversations she and Maureen had had, all the times Maureen had shown her verses that spoke to both their hearts. Maureen wouldn't forsake the God she loved.

"No, it's not that." Maureen sighed, raking her hand through her short, blond hair. "I don't know. I don't know anything anymore. I wake up every morning thinking today is going to be different, but it never is. Every night I go to bed angry, hurt. Alone. I don't know how much longer I can take this."

"Maybe you should talk to someone," Natalia suggested. Not for the first time.

"No," Maureen shouted, crossing her arms and closing her eyes. "This is humiliating enough without crying to Pastor Brian or Carol about my problems."

"If your arm was broken, would you feel the same way?"

"What?"

"If you fell from the stairs and broke your arm"—Natalia sat on the couch across from Maureen—"would you go to the doctor and get it taken care of? Or would you sit at home and try to fix it yourself?"

"That's not the same."

"Maureen, your heart is broken. Your spirit is broken. There's no shame in getting help so you can heal. That's what the body of Christ is for, right? Pastor Eduardo back home always said that. We help each other—mourn with those who mourn and weep with those who weep."

"I don't know. Right now, I just want a job. I need a job. Once I have that then maybe I can think about seeing a counselor. Maybe." Maureen stood and walked back to the table, then opened her laptop.

The conversation was over. For now, anyway. *All I can do is pray for her. God, help her. Make her see how much she needs you right now. Help her to forgive Papa and to forgive herself so she can move on.*

Natalia walked up the stairs and smiled when she entered her room. The Youngers and Jack had put everything together. No boxes in sight. Her dresser—tall, light-colored with six drawers—stood to her left, the bed sat under the window, the red curtains functioning as a backdrop to her headboard. On the right, she had a small desk with a rolling chair.

Pulling the chair out, Natalia turned on her laptop. As she waited, Natalia looked at the picture on her desk—her last day of school. All her friends were smiling, Natalia in the center. They had thrown her a huge party. She laughed when they brought out hot dogs, fries, and apple pies.

"We want to get a taste of what you'll be eating from now on," Carmen had joked.

Natalia clicked on to the Internet and pulled up her e-mail. A note from Carmen, the title *Please Come Back!* screaming at her.

Natalia read the message and laughed, amazed that Carmen could sound just as dramatic in an e-mail as she could in person.

After the morning she had, Natalia debated whether or not to consent to Carmen's plea. Going back home was so tempting. Maureen was falling apart, and Natalia didn't seem to be helping. At all.

Natalia's eyes drifted to her Bible. She opened the front cover and saw the verse Pastor Eduardo had written on the first page the day he baptized her. "'For I know the plans I have for you,' declares the LORD, 'plans to prosper you and not to harm you, plans to give you hope and a future.' Jer. 29:11"

He had handed her the Bible and shown her that verse. "Remember this, Natalia. There will be times when your faith is shaken, when you don't understand what is happening. Remember that God has plans for you. And those plans are good. Trust him. He will never, ever let you down. He will never leave you."

Okay, God. You have me here. There is a plan. A good plan. I will trust you.

Natalia thought back to Carmen's e-mail, then jumped up. "School!"

After running down the stairs, Natalia almost ran into the back of Maureen's chair. "I have to register for school! You said it starts at the end of August. That is just two weeks away! I need to get the book list and buy uniforms and—"

"Calm down, Natalia." Maureen looked up and sighed. "There's a Christian school right at the church. I called the principal while we were still in Spain. Your father has paid your tuition already. We do need to get you registered, but it's not a big deal. The school is much smaller than your school in Madrid—just a few hundred students . . ."

Maureen stopped speaking when she realized Natalia had stopped listening.

"You mean everyone there is a Christian?"

"Well, I don't know about that. But the teachers are all Christians, and Bible is one of the subjects taught."

"Someone is going to teach me Bible every day?" Natalia was so excited she could barely contain herself. "I have so many questions. I was just praying the other day that God would help me understand what I am reading. And look at the answer. A Christian school!" Natalia hugged Maureen. "Can we go now? I want to see it. I can't believe you didn't tell me this. That is the best news I've heard since we came here."

Maureen shook her head and mumbled something about hoping Natalia wouldn't be disappointed, but she was barely listening. Natalia grabbed her bag and threw on shoes, then was up the stairs and back down in less than thirty seconds.

Maureen wasn't quite so fast. Natalia waited impatiently, imagining what the school would look like and what it would be like to have teachers who were Christians and classmates who shared her faith instead of ridiculing her for it.

Ten minutes later the pair pulled up to the church.

"I know you said the school was associated with the church, but I didn't realize it was part of it." Natalia tried to imagine where the classes were held.

"Yes, my Sunday school class was in the high school building. That building over there"—Maureen pointed to her right—"is the elementary building. The portables behind that are where the middle school classes and art classes meet. The choir and band rooms are in the same building as the sanctuary. The school offices are here, right next to the high school building." Maureen pointed straight ahead, toward what looked like a house. "This used to be the church's parsonage."

"The what?"

"The house where the pastor and his family lived," Maureen said. "Years ago, many churches provided housing for pastors. When the school started twenty years ago, the parsonage was turned into the administration building."

"But where do the Youngers live?"

"They own a house about ten minutes from here, right on a lake. It's beautiful."

"But I thought he worked here full time?" Natalia asked.

"He does." Maureen shrugged. "The church pays him well. He's not wealthy, but he makes enough so he can provide for his family."

Natalia was shocked. At her small church in Spain, the pastor had to work another job because the church could barely afford to pay for its building. She couldn't imagine a church having enough money to pay a pastor to live on.

"The pastors' offices are over there, in the same building as the sanctuary."

"Pastors? There is more than one?"

"Sure. Pastor Brian is the senior pastor, then there's Pastor Mike, the associate pastor. And, there's the youth pastor and the music minister."

"And the church pays them all?" Natalia asked, bewildered.

"Of course." Maureen opened the door to the administration building.

Natalia had more questions, but she'd have to wait until

later. The secretary, a kind-looking woman in her fifties, stood behind a tall counter filled with brochures, letters, and assorted potted plants.

"Good morning. Welcome to Tampa Christian School! How can I help you?"

"My name is Maureen Lopez." She winced at the last name. "I don't have an appointment, but I was wondering if we could see Mr. Lawrence. My stepdaughter will be going to school here this year, and we wanted to plan her schedule and maybe get a tour of the school grounds."

"Of course! But the guidance counselor, Mrs. Williams, will need to help you with the schedule. She's out of town this week—gone to camp with the little ones."

"Oh." Maureen sighed, giving Natalia an "I'm sorry, maybe later" look.

"But," the secretary continued, "Mr. Lawrence is in. I'm sure he'd be happy to talk with you and show you around."

Before Maureen could respond, the secretary picked up her phone and pressed three buttons. In less than a minute, the door behind Natalia opened.

"Maureen!" boomed the principal—a tall, wiry man who looked to be about the same age as Natalia's father. He hugged Maureen, then moved to hug Natalia. Unsure of what to make of this man, Natalia hugged him back, tentatively, then stepped away.

"Come in, come in!" he said, walking toward his office. He suddenly turned. Natalia almost ran into him, so abrupt was his movement. "Oh! I'm sorry, Natalia. I already feel like I know you, so I didn't even think to introduce myself.

I'm Mr. Lawrence, principal here at TCS." He stuck his hand out and Natalia shook it, smiling. This was one of the most energetic men she'd ever met.

"Pastor Brian was over here just this morning, bragging on you and saying what a help you've been to Maureen. Little Brian was pretty impressed too." Mr. Lawrence winked.

"Little!" Maureen laughed. "I barely recognized him when he came over this weekend."

"You're telling me." He motioned for the women to enter his office. "I said good-bye at the end of the school year, looking down at his little red head, and came back in the fall looking up! Have a seat, ladies."

Natalia sat in the plush leather chair, Maureen beside her in a matching chair. Mr. Lawrence walked behind a large mahogany desk and pushed aside a stack of papers.

"Résumés," he explained. "We need a PE coach, a band director, and a Spanish teacher. All by the end of the month. Lots of applications for band and PE, but none for Spanish. That's always hard to fill."

Natalia looked at Maureen, eyebrows lifted.

Maureen shook her head emphatically.

Mr. Lawrence caught the exchange and clapped his hands. "Señora Lopez!" He laughed. "Of course. You would make a great Spanish teacher. You were always the kids' favorite Sunday school teacher."

"Teaching Sunday school and teaching Spanish are *very* different, Jim." Maureen frowned.

"But a teacher is a teacher," Mr. Lawrence countered. "And you are a teacher."

"No." Maureen sat up straighter, her chin up. "I am an international corporate businesswoman."

"Maureen." He leaned forward. "I have no doubt you are a very gifted businesswoman. But teaching, while paying less, is not a career to shun. Here, it is a calling. We get the privilege of investing in the lives of young men and women. And those young people go out into the world and take what we've taught them, being lights in a dark world. This is one of the most fulfilling jobs you could ever have."

Maureen laughed. "I'd forgotten what a salesman you are, Jim. And I agree, teaching is a calling. But it's not *my* calling."

"How do you know?" Natalia asked. "You have been looking for a job for three weeks. Nothing is opening up. And here there just 'happens' to be an opening for a Spanish teacher. Don't you think God could be in this?"

"I like this girl." Mr. Lawrence beamed.

"I do too," Maureen responded, frowning. "But I don't agree. I have no desire to be a Spanish teacher."

Her tone made it clear that the conversation was over. Mr. Lawrence recognized it too, but a wink from him when Maureen's head was turned let Natalia know that he would pray Maureen changed her mind.

"Got the last of the desks moved out of Mrs. Kennedy's room." Brian Younger Jr. poked his head in Mr. Lawrence's office. His crystal blue eyes widened when he saw Natalia.

"Brian." Mr. Lawrence stood. "I was just about to give Miss Natalia here a tour. But I'm sure she'd rather see the school with you than with me."

Natalia glanced from Mr. Lawrence to Brian. "No, I don't want to take up your time. I can see you are busy."

Brian's dirt-stained T-shirt revealed a more muscular body than Natalia had expected from such a thin boy.

God, I know I prayed for a friend. But this can't be it. I've sworn off boys. Friendship could lead to something else. Something I won't allow.

"It would be my pleasure, Natalia." Brian beamed. "I dropped in to pick up my supplies list, and Mr. Lawrence put me to work. On my day off, no less. I could use a break. Please?"

Natalia looked into Brian's blue eyes and her heart sank. "All right, then. But just a quick tour. I'm sure there is more work that Mr. Lawrence needs done."

"Yes, there is." Mr. Lawrence turned to his credenza and pulled out a stack of papers. "But Maureen here has to fill out all this paperwork, so you can take your time."

"Yes, sir." Brian's white teeth seemed to sparkle.

Natalia forced herself to look away from his adorable smile. And his beautiful eyes. And his muscular arms. *This is going to be the longest tour ever.*

Chapter 10

"Chemistry."

Natalia looked at Brian. *Oh yes, definite chemistry.*

"No. Not for me." She shook her head, trying to rid herself of those errant thoughts.

"You already took chemistry?" Brian flipped through the key ring Mr. Lawrence had given him.

She closed her eyes. *Idiot.* "I did. Yes. So no chemistry at all for me this year."

Brian's light eyebrows came together. "All right."

Natalia stared at the floor as Brian slipped the key into the door.

"This is Mrs. Stevenson's room." Brian opened the door and Natalia entered.

The classroom looked just like all the others in that hallway—blue walls, brown carpet, two bulletin boards, a whiteboard, and twenty desks. But Brian managed to make each room interesting, with his background information on the teacher or funny stories about things that happened in the room.

"She teaches algebra, which is not the most exciting subject. But"—he turned out the lights before continuing—"one dark and stormy afternoon, we walked into the classroom to find Mrs. Stevenson had disappeared."

Natalia laughed. "Disappeared?"

"Hey, this is a horror story, not a comedy. Wipe that grin off your face."

She did as she was told. Or she tried to, anyway. She couldn't help a small grin from lifting the corners of her lips.

"As I was saying." Brian cleared his throat. "On a dark and stormy afternoon, when even the sun was too frightened to come out, we were visited by . . . Mr. Monotone."

"Mr. Monotone?"

"He talked just like this." Brian imitated the teacher, his voice remaining exactly the same with each word. "'Class, I am your substitute. Take out your books and we'll discuss the FOIL method. That's right. It is so exciting.'"

"He didn't really talk like that." Natalia shook her head.

"You accuse a *pastor's son* of lying? How dare you." Brian clutched his heart. "And I haven't even gotten to the worst part yet."

"Sorry." Natalia laughed, enjoying herself far more than she had intended. "Go on."

"The combination of Mr. Monotone's boring voice combined with the boring subject caused the star of the class, best-looking guy in the school, and all-around amazing, almost-super hero—"

"I assume we are talking about you?"

Brian's grin was wide. "Aw, you flatter me, Natalia."

She normally hated the English pronunciation of her

name, with the long *l* and the flat *a*, but when it came from Brian's mouth, it was endearing.

"But you guessed it." Brian spread his arms. "Star pupil, Brian Younger Jr., every girl's fantasy and every boy's nightmare, fell asleep right in the middle of class."

"How terrible." Natalia laughed.

"Oh, that's not all." Brian folded his arms. "If I had just fallen asleep, it would have been nothing. Oh no. I fell asleep and started having a nightmare. I was stuck inside the algebra book, being chased by square-root signs and little *x*'s."

"Oh dear." Natalia smiled as Brian bent toward her. Her eyes widened as his face was just a few inches from hers.

"You have no idea." The smirk on Brian's face faded, just for a moment, and Natalia stepped back, refusing to allow herself to enjoy his nearness.

"So the *x*'s were chasing you?" Natalia prompted after an awkward moment of silence.

"The *x*'s." Brian got back into character, mock horror filling his eyes. "They were terrible. Chasing me around the odd problems, knocking me into numbers. I was running for my life."

"And then what?"

"Then the fire alarm went off."

"That's not good."

"No, and it was right when I was about to be pushed down into a quadratic equation."

"So what did you do?"

"What any normal person being chased by an algebra problem would do." Brian shrugged. "I jumped out of my chair and screamed. Except that you can't jump out of these chairs. So I ended up falling out, screaming at the little *x*'s to leave me alone."

"You're joking with me." Natalia couldn't imagine that actually happening in a room full of students.

"Do you think I could make something like that up?"

Natalia looked at Brian for a moment. "Yes, I think you could."

"Well, thank you." He stood a little straighter. "But, unfortunately, that is totally true."

The door to the classroom opened and a young man walked in. Dark hair and eyes, muscular, quite good-looking, but with a smile that indicated he knew just how good-looking he was. He reminded Natalia of her father. Not a good first impression.

"I'm Spencer Adams." He held his hand out to Natalia. "Mr. Lawrence told me Brian was showing the new girl around. I couldn't allow that. I'm the class president, so it's really my responsibility." He looked over his shoulder at Brian. "You understand, right, Younger?"

Brian's face turned pink, but he didn't say anything. His shoulders slumped, though.

"Actually"—Natalia removed her hand from Spencer's—"Brian is doing a fabulous job."

His face lit up and Spencer scowled. "Of course he is. But he's got work to do. Right? He's on the crew fixing up my family's new mansion. You'll have to come see it when it's done."

"It sounds lovely," Natalia said. "But I think this is the end of the tour, right, Brian?"

He nodded.

"Fine." Spencer grabbed Natalia's arm and pulled her to the front of the room. "But let me offer you a word of advice. Younger, here, may be the pastor's son, but he's a loser. Doesn't play sports, doesn't do well in school, spends all his free time here." Spencer spat out the last word like it was a virus. "Not the kind of guy a girl like you would want to be seen with."

Natalia bristled. She knew this boy's type. And she did not like it. "And what makes you think that after a two-minute conversation you could have any idea what kind of a girl I am?"

Spencer's face went from shock to pleasure. "I like your spunk. We're going to get along well."

She turned to Brian. "Can we go please?"

A huge grin splitting his face, Brian looked from Natalia to Spencer. "We sure can."

Once the pair was sure Spencer was gone, Brian gazed down at Natalia. "I'm sorry. Spencer's the big man on campus."

"What?"

"Oh, sorry." Brian rubbed the back of his neck. "It's so hard not to use clichés."

"No, use them. But then explain them so I know what they mean. It's like a whole new language inside a language."

"Okay." Brian sat in a desk and motioned for Natalia to sit beside him. "'Big man on campus' is like the guy all the girls like and all the guys want to be."

"You want to be like him?"

"No, that's kind of a saying too." Brian stretched his legs out, his foot brushing Natalia's.

Her toes curled at the touch, and tingles rose all the way up her leg. She yanked her foot away.

"Sorry." He blushed.

Natalia looked away. *I will not let myself be attracted to him.*

"So Spencer is popular, then?" She needed to get the conversation back on neutral ground.

"He's the captain of the football team, star basketball player, gets straight As in school, and his parents are filthy rich. They paid for the new science lab I showed you. So, yeah, I guess you could say he is popular."

"Wow." Natalia liked Spencer even less than before. There were plenty of his type at her school in Madrid.

"I know." Brian hung his head. "He's impressive."

"No, that wasn't an impressed 'wow.' He sounds like a—what is the word?—jerk?"

"No." Brian sighed. "I'm sorry. I didn't mean to make him sound bad. I wish I could be all those things. Well, except for the parents. Mine may not be rich, but they're awesome and they love each other. Spencer's folks got divorced a few years ago. His dad remarried as soon as the divorce was final. It was pretty tough on him."

Brian is actually defending this boy.

"But I'd sure like some of his skills. I don't play any of the school sports. And he's right; I'm not the smartest guy here."

Natalia wished Brian could see that he was far more attractive than the arrogant Spencer. But she couldn't tell him that. *He might think I'm interested. And I'm not. Definitely not.*

"Speaking of school . . . tell me about Bible class."

Brian's face lit up. "My favorite class. This year we'll get my dad. He teaches the seniors. We get a semester of apologetics and then a semester of life management."

"Apolo . . . what?"

"Apologetics—how to defend your faith. My dad wrote his thesis in seminary on that. It's his favorite subject."

"I have been praying for someone to teach me that." Natalia stood and walked around the room, barely able to contain her excitement. "My friends in Spain think I'm crazy for becoming a Christian. I've tried to tell them why I believe what I do, but there's so much I don't know."

Brian leaned back. "Wow, no one ever gets excited about taking apologetics."

"What?" Natalia stopped pacing. "How could they not? To know how to answer people with questions and criticisms. Isn't that what we're commanded to do? To have an answer to any who ask?"

"Oh man, my dad will want to adopt you." Brian stood and smiled. "You'll have to come over for dinner sometime and pick his brain. He'd love that."

"Pick his brain?" The image that popped into Natalia mind was disgusting, and she shuddered.

"Sorry, another cliché." Brian headed toward the door and held it open. "It means to ask questions and find out what another person knows."

"I'd love to do that, then." Natalia walked out in front of Brian. "To pick his brain." It still sounded strange coming from her lips, but she was determined to learn "American."

He showed her the rest of the school, but all Natalia could think of was apologetics. She wanted to invite herself to Brian's house right then.

But that would mean spending time with him. And I can't. I already feel some of my resolve weakening after just a couple of hours. I am not made to be anyone's girlfriend. Although if I were, I would want someone like Brian. He is kind and funny and he loves God. Really loves God. And isn't afraid to talk about him. But I can't like him. I won't.

"I have to go." Natalia interrupted Brian's story about the former band teacher and her antics.

He stopped midsentence, his brow wrinkling. "Oh, all right. I'll walk you back to the office."

"No, please." Natalia began walking away. Quickly. "I can find it. I've taken enough of your time."

Brian called after her, but she ignored him and kept walking. *Too much temptation. A godly guy who can laugh at himself and has a great family? Oh, Lord, why couldn't Spencer Adams have given me the tour? He's not tempting at all.*

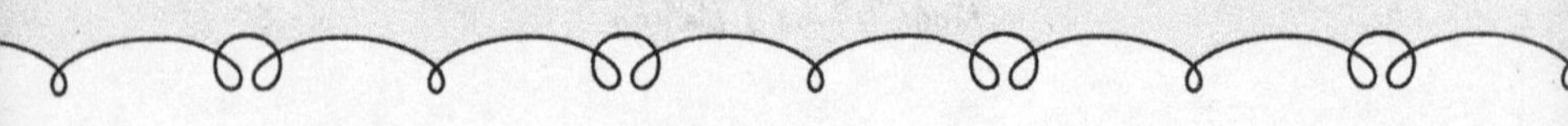

Chapter 11

"I am a complete idiot." Brian walked into his dad's office and threw himself into the chair.

Gazing up from his computer, Dad took his glasses off. "No Younger is a complete idiot. Partial, maybe. But not complete."

"Mr. Lawrence made me give Natalia Lopez a tour of the school."

Dad leaned back in his seat. "That should be a good thing. I saw how you were looking at her the other day."

"She's beautiful, Dad. Of course I was looking at her."

"So what's the problem?"

"I actually let myself believe, for a minute, that she might be interested in me."

"And why wouldn't she?"

Brian looked at his dad. "I'm not exactly the class Casanova."

"Nor would I want you to be."

"I know, Dad." Brian slumped farther into the seat. "But she's out of my league. I forgot that until Spencer Adams came up and reminded me."

"So you're letting Spencer tell you how to think?"

"No." Brian sighed. "Forget it. Why can't I be attracted to a girl who'd actually like me back? Like Lexi Summers. She'd probably go out with me."

"She is a wonderful girl." Dad smiled. "Your mother and I would approve of her."

"But she's like my sister." Brian shrugged. "We've known each other forever."

"So what happened with Spencer and Natalia?"

"She saw him. And she talked to him. Now she knows I'm the class joke."

"Did she treat you differently after Spencer came in?"

Brian thought back to Natalia's response. "No. Actually, she kind of put Spencer in his place."

"So why are you upset?"

"Because, Dad, I'm basically a geek. But a geek that isn't even all that smart. What do I have to offer a girl like that?"

"She moved all the way out here to help her stepmother, son." His dad leaned forward. "She's probably struggling with a lot of things. You can offer her your friendship."

Brian sighed. "Yep, that's me. Everybody's best friend."

"Nothing wrong with that."

"Oh, I almost forgot." Brian clapped his hands. "She can't wait to take apologetics."

"Really?" Dad's face broke into a huge smile.

"Yeah, she said she's been praying for someone to teach her how to defend her faith."

"I like this girl." Dad nodded.

Me too, Brian thought.

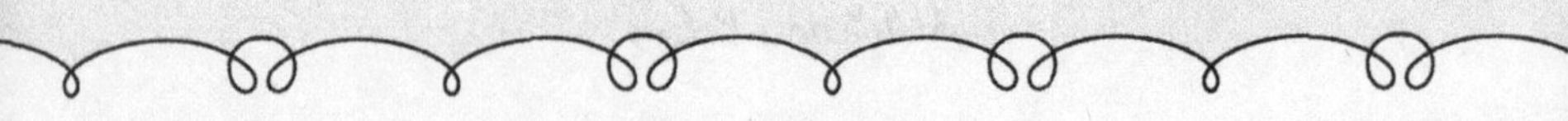

Chapter 12

Looking out the window—for the fifth time in as many minutes—Natalia let the blinds click back into place.

Earlier that morning Natalia had received a phone call from one of the seniors at Tampa Christian School. A female student. Her name was Addy. Natalia had been trying to get Brian out of her head since her tour the day before. The attempts had been largely unsuccessful. She hoped a female friend could help her forget about the blue-eyed giant.

"Addy Davidson?" Maureen had asked. "I used to teach her in Sunday school. She's a sweet girl. Her parents were missionaries in Colombia. They were killed when Addy was just a little girl. Her uncle Mike flew down there, picked her up, and raised her all by himself."

"Wow," Natalia said. "You know a lot of the kids here, don't you?"

"I spent several years teaching the third- and fourth-grade Sunday school classes." Maureen smiled. "Life was pretty great back then. I was constantly getting promotions, was involved with the singles group at church, taught Sunday school. But I didn't think it was great. I wanted more. I was bored, living where I'd always lived. I wanted to see more of the world, to be more successful. Look where that got me. Right back here, unemployed and divorced and bitter."

Natalia, trying to avoid yet another meltdown, asked, "What else can you tell me about Addy?"

"Oh, Addy? Actually"—Maureen laughed—"she's a bit of a celebrity right now."

"A celebrity?" Because of her mother's and father's occupations, Natalia had been forced to meet more celebrities than she cared to remember. Most were self-centered and demanding. She was suddenly less excited about her lunch plans.

"Carol kept me posted about it when we talked. The show was on right when your father left, so I didn't watch it. Apparently, though, Addy was on a reality TV show competition to win a date with the president's son."

"Oh!" Natalia gasped. "Did she win?"

"No, but she was a contender right up until the end, and I remember Carol saying that Addy had presented the gospel to one of the show's producers—right on the air. I think that's why she didn't win. But everyone here was so proud of her. She's fairly shy so that couldn't have been easy for her."

Natalia was excited again. A girl her age who cared more about talking about Jesus than winning something as huge as a date with the president's son. Would Addy even want to be her friend? Natalia had only been a Christian for a couple of years, and she certainly didn't have missionary parents.

The doorbell rang, interrupting her thoughts.

Natalia rushed to the door, then made herself pause a moment before opening the door.

"Hi, Natalia, I'm Addy." The young woman held her hand out in greeting.

Still unused to the American greetings, Natalia put her hand in Addy's and squeezed. Addy was certainly reserved. Not at all like Brian and Spencer, or even Jack and the girls.

Addy was taller than Natalia by about two inches, her brown hair a shade lighter than Natalia's, and her eyes a warm brown. She was very pretty, but she didn't try to flaunt it.

"Addy," Maureen said, walking past Natalia to hug the young American. "It's so good to see you! I didn't get to see all the episodes of your show, but I heard you made quite an impression on America. And on the First Son."

Natalia was thrilled to see Maureen so happy. She stepped aside as Maureen led Addy into the living room.

"This is a great place, Miss Maureen." Addy took a seat on the tan couch and avoided answering Maureen's question.

"You don't have to call me Miss Maureen, Addy. I'm not your Sunday school teacher anymore."

"It's a habit." Addy laughed. "But Mr. Lawrence did tell me he's asked you to be our Spanish teacher. So maybe I can call you Señora Maureen. He wanted me to try and convince you to take the position. I'm planning on taking Spanish 3 this year, and I'd love to have you as my teacher."

Maureen's smile melted, replaced by a scowl. She stood.

"I've already told Jim I'm not interested. I wish he would let it go. I didn't leave a good-paying job in the corporate world to . . ." Maureen paused, closing her eyes. "I know you were just doing what you were asked to do, Addy. Why don't you and Natalia go ahead and go, enjoy your lunch. I have some phone calls to make." She headed to the kitchen.

Addy looked apologetically at Natalia. "I didn't mean to upset her. I didn't know . . ."

"It's all right." Natalia grabbed her purse as she led Addy back to the door. "Maureen is having a hard time adjusting. I think her teaching Spanish would be a terrific idea. She is a gifted teacher. I've benefited from that gift—she's taught me about the Bible, answered my questions, helped me to know how to study and pray. I think she just has to get past the idea that being a teacher is below her."

Natalia opened the door to Addy's red compact sedan, sat down, and buckled in as Addy did the same.

"Maureen would fit in well at TCS. There are several teachers right about her age, some married, some divorced, some single. All are great. And I'm not just saying that because Mr. Lawrence told me to."

Natalia laughed. "She just feels so embarrassed. I don't understand. This isn't her. The Maureen I know is the kindest, happiest woman I've ever known. But this divorce—my father," Natalia added angrily, "has changed her. I had hoped that my being here would help. But I don't know."

Natalia stopped. She was surprised at herself for being so honest with a girl she barely knew. But Addy didn't seem put out by it.

"I think what you did is amazing," Addy said. "I left

home for the TV show I was on, and I went kicking and screaming. God had to really shake me up to make me look past myself and see the reasons he had me there. But you came willingly, and not just for a month. I can't even imagine how hard it is to leave your parents and your friends and your country."

Addy pulled into the parking lot of Dixie's Diner, a place unlike any Natalia had ever seen before. It was small and filled with what looked like broken-down tables and chairs, potted plants hanging from the ceiling, and plastic menus caked with samples from the various "southern-style" dishes it boasted.

"What does 'southern style' mean?"

"Basically, it means extra butter and gravy, with everything fried—the meat, the vegetables, even the desserts. It's great!"

Natalia wished for a nice paella—a Spanish rice dish made with chicken or shrimp, no butter, gravy, or fried foods. But she was determined to at least give the new food a try. Addy was thin, so Natalia hoped that meant the food wouldn't cause her to have to trade her form-fitting jeans for the elastic-waisted pants that seemed so popular to the other patrons of the restaurant.

Natalia reluctantly ordered the "Dixie De-Lux"—chicken-fried chicken, mashed potatoes, corn, and a roll. She was sure that she would be in a carbohydrate coma for weeks afterward, but Addy had insisted.

"Dixie has owned this diner since the days when Orange Station was just a little town, far outside the Tampa city limits. Tampa has grown, and we're basically just a suburb of it now. But Dixie is still here. She's about seventy-five years old and still works a few days a week. These recipes were her grandmother's—about a hundred years old. They are amazing. I promise!"

Natalia waited, nervously, for her lunch and listened as Addy filled her in on what to expect from Tampa Christian School.

"TCS is the only school I've ever attended." Addy took a sip from her iced tea—another item Natalia "just had" to try. "There are about forty in our graduating class. We're one of the larger ones. A couple years ago, there were just twenty-one graduates."

Natalia was shocked. Although she had attended a private school, it was much larger, with the graduating classes averaging two hundred.

"There are advantages to the size." Addy had obviously noted Natalia's surprise. "Our classes are small, so we get to know each other well. With only one hundred fifty or so in the entire high school, you have a much better chance of making the sports teams or being in school plays. What are your extracurricular interests, by the way?"

"What clubs was I part of?"

"No, not exactly. I mean like sports or drama or choir."

"Those are clubs."

"What?"

"Clubs that you join. Some private, some public. But what does that have to do with school?" Natalia was confused. Apparently, so was Addy.

"No, I mean *school* sports and arts."

Was her English failing her? Natalia had no idea what this girl was talking about.

"Our school has girls' volleyball, basketball, soccer, and softball teams," Addy said. "We also have cheerleading. If you're in one of those, you have practices after school during that sport's season and you play teams from other Christian schools in the area. Band and choir are both offered as electives. If you take one of those, you'll have some after-school practices and performances as well. Don't you have that in Spain?"

"Okay, slow down a little. *School* sports and music?"

"Yes." Addy nodded.

"Wow, we definitely don't have that at my old school. Students who wanted to be involved in those types of activities joined a club."

"Well, we have Little Leagues here, those are like clubs, where kids from around the community can play sports."

"Little Leagues?" Natalia replied. "I suppose that's similar. But your schools also offer sports?"

"Yes. Do you play?"

"I played football—what you Americans call soccer—for fun. But mostly I spend my time studying. I have to get into a good college, after all."

"You don't sound excited about that."

Natalia thought of her parents. "It is not exciting. But it's what is expected of me." Not wanting to discuss that any further, Natalia began eating her southern fare.

The pair ate in silence for several minutes. Natalia listened to the conversations going on around them, pleased that her understanding of "American" English was improving.

Addy pushed her plate away, having only eaten half of

what she ordered. "Oh, we also have a girls' Bible study that meets once a week, if you're interested."

"Oh yes." Natalia pushed her plate away as well. Dixie was not as delightful as Addy claimed. "You have Bible class *and* do a Bible study?"

"And there's youth group and Sunday school." Addy smiled. "Not too many girls come. We average ten or twelve."

"What do you study?"

"Different things." Addy took the check from the waitress and pulled out her purse. "By the way, lunch is on Mr. Lawrence. He insisted. Anyway, sometimes we study a book of the Bible. Other times we read a book together and discuss that."

"I'd love to be part of that. I've been so isolated in my Christian life. I still can't believe I actually get to take Bible as a class!"

"Seniors get Pastor Brian." Addy raised her eyebrows.

"He seems very nice. Isn't he?"

"He's great." Addy leaned in. "But I've heard he's really tough. Last year's seniors said it's more like a college class than a high school one."

"How wonderful." Natalia couldn't wait. College Bible!

Addy shook her head and grinned. "I'm glad you're here, Natalia. I think you're going to be a great addition to our senior class."

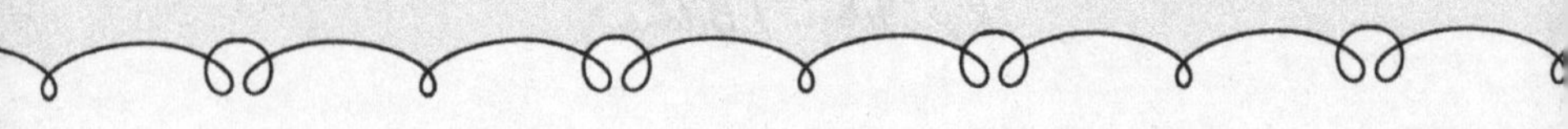

Chapter 13

"You'll be happy to know I've accepted the job at Tampa Christian School," Maureen announced as she walked into the town house, slamming the door behind her.

Natalia *was* happy, but Maureen didn't want to hear that. A week had gone by since she had been offered the job by Mr. Lawrence, and despite her constant scouring of the Internet and newspapers, Maureen had not found any other job possibilities. Natalia knew Maureen would eventually have to take the job available to her. And Natalia felt that job was from God, and the more Addy told her about TCS, the more confident Natalia felt that it would be a great place for Maureen.

"I just signed my contract," Maureen spat out as she sat on the couch and placed a pillow on her lap. "I am getting paid about a third of what I made starting out in your father's company. But there won't be any raises here. No promotions. Nothing. All my education, all my experience, everything goes out the window."

"Maureen." Natalia sat next to her, wanting to scream at her for not seeing the opportunity she was being given but knowing that wouldn't help the situation. "You are trading one set of gifts for another. And you've always told me how much you love the Spanish language and how terrible your high school Spanish teacher was. What was her name? Señora Manzeloswi?"

"Midzowanski." Maureen smiled in spite of herself. "She *was* pretty bad. She couldn't even pronounce half the words in our Spanish 2 textbook. 'HO-la, chih-cahs,' she'd say. She wouldn't even try to speak with a Spanish accent. It was awful!"

"But you have been exposed to true Spanish." Natalia grinned. "From the Mother country. You can teach these poor American kids correct pronunciation, proper grammar. You're like a missionary to the monolingual!"

Maureen reached over and hugged her. "Oh, Natalia, I don't know what I'd do without you here. I'm sorry I haven't helped you very much. I feel like our roles have reversed. You're the mother and I'm the child. I'll get better. I promise. This is just so much harder than I thought it would be. All of it is so much harder."

"We'll get through this, Maureen. And I, for one, am quite relieved that you'll be at school with me. You can protect me from awful things like chicken fried chicken."

Both laughed. Natalia had not enjoyed the southern food, but, thankfully, Addy was very understanding. In fact, she had called later that night and offered to take Natalia to a local Spanish restaurant.

"It's supposed to be the real thing," Addy promised. "In

fact, it's called a tapas bar. When I told that to my uncle, he thought I said 'topless bar' and got this shocked look on his face." Even Maureen had chuckled at that.

"Tapas are very Spanish," Natalia assured Addy. "They are similar to what you call appetizers, except you share them with a whole table and that is your meal. If this place is really authentic, we can even get some chorizo. That's my favorite!"

"What's chorizo?" Addy asked.

"Just wait and see."

"Oh, Natalia," Maureen said, snapping Natalia out of her reverie. "I almost forgot. When I was in the meeting with Mr. Lawrence, he asked me about your community-service hours."

"My what?"

"Students are required to have a certain number of community-service hours in order to graduate."

"What am I supposed to do?"

"Anything that benefits the community," Maureen replied.

"Well, that clears it all up." Natalia raised her arms in surrender. "I don't litter and I go shopping. Isn't that beneficial? I can go shopping a little more if that would help."

"Sorry, it doesn't work that way. It has to be a service, like tutoring kids or volunteering at a community center. Oh, I know." Maureen placed a hand on Natalia's knee. "Little Brian said he runs an ESL program here. That's English as a Second Language. He offers classes at the church. Most of them are Spanish speakers. You could help with that."

The thought of working with Brian was not unpleasant. But Natalia feared that working so closely with him every week might be difficult.

"Well?" Maureen asked.

"I don't know. Let's keep looking for other options. If I can't find anything else, I'll do that."

"Hmmm, where have I heard that before?" Maureen laughed.

Natalia was so happy to hear her laughing, she didn't stop to wonder if God was using her stepmother to guide her to this ESL ministry. She was sure God wouldn't want her to be around a guy she was attracted to.

Why purposefully court temptation? I'm sure there will be some other community service I can do. Preferably with a woman. Or an ugly old man.

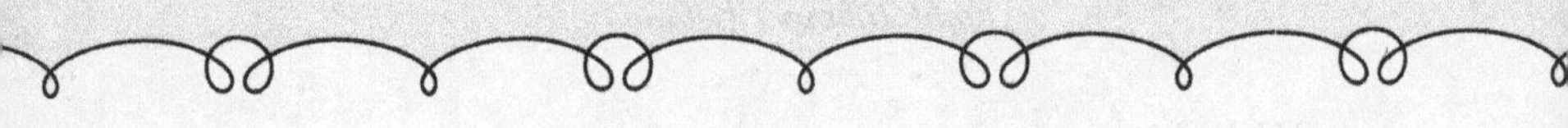

Chapter 14

"Ah yes." Natalia leaned back in her chair. "*This* is good food!"

Addy had picked up Natalia from her house that evening to take her to the Spanish restaurant. Natalia quickly discovered that the food was, in fact, quite authentic. The owners were from Salamanca, as were their chefs. Upon hearing they had an actual Spaniard in the restaurant, two of the chefs came out to personally greet her.

Natalia was thrilled to speak to someone in her native language, talking about places they knew in Spain and things they missed here in the States. Both men had lived in Tampa for over a decade, and their accents sounded more Latin American than Spanish. But it was Spanish. And for that, she was grateful.

Once the men excused themselves, Natalia looked at Addy. She had been sitting quietly during the entire conversation.

"I'm sorry for taking so long. I was just so excited."

"Don't apologize." Addy shrugged. "That was great. I

know a little Spanish, so I could pick up on some of your conversation. But your accent is different. It almost sounds like you lisp when you speak."

"Lisp? What does that mean?"

"Like when you said *gracias*," Addy said. "You pronounced it *gra-th-ias*."

"Of course. It's the Latin Americans who have a different accent. *Ours* is the mother tongue. Just like British is the mother tongue of English."

Addy laughed. "So since you learned English from your British teachers, does that mean you speak better Spanish *and* English than we do?"

"I guess so." Natalia winked. "But since you're in Spanish 3 this year and Maureen will be teaching you, you'll be able to learn from the best."

The conversation continued to be light and fun as the waiters brought out the different appetizers, called tapas. Addy confessed that she wasn't sure she liked the chorizo.

"Properly pronounced *chori-tho*," Natalia had corrected. The sausage-like links were a little spicier than what Addy was used to. Natalia was happy that Addy liked the octopus.

"*Pulpo*, we call it," Natalia had said. "It's one of my favorites too."

Addy put her napkin down and looked at Natalia. "If you don't mind my prying, how are you doing? I understood enough of your conversation with the chefs to know you miss Spain. I know you must miss your family and friends. I've seen how upset Maureen is. You seem fine with all this change, but I don't think I would be. Are you really all right?"

Natalia took a sip of her water and thought about Addy's question. Natalia had plenty of friends in Spain, but she rarely talked with any of them about how she was feeling. In fact, she couldn't remember any of them asking how she was feeling. They'd argue and debate and joke, of course. But Natalia had spent too many years guarding herself from hurts that she wasn't even sure she knew how she really felt about most things.

"I'm okay," Natalia said quietly, cautiously. "I miss it, yes, but I know this is where God wants me. And to get to go to a Christian school . . . I can't even tell you how exciting that is."

"I take so much for granted." Addy tilted her head. "Wasn't there anyone in your school who was a Christian?"

"Not that I knew of. Some of my friends believed in God, but not a personal God. They certainly didn't see any need to study the Bible or pray. My closest friend is an atheist, and she would argue with me all the time about why my faith is silly and I need to give it up."

"Wow. What did you say to her?"

"I defended my faith the best I could and shared the gospel with her every chance I got."

"I admire that." Addy took another bite of the *pulpo*. "I was around people for a whole month this spring who didn't know Christ, and I was scared to death to even let them know I was a Christian. God had to really shake me up to make me share my faith."

"Maureen told me about that. You talked to the producer of your reality TV show on air, right? That's bold."

"It wasn't easy, but God used my weakness. And now

Jonathon, the president's son, is really growing. We talk about our Bible studies and share prayer requests. It's exciting."

"So is there really a romance there? Or is that just rumor?"

Addy's face turned a bright shade of red, and Natalia knew she had touched on a sensitive spot. "I'm sorry. You don't have to answer that." Brian Younger's face suddenly popped into Natalia's mind. *I can't even go to dinner with a friend without thinking of him. What is wrong with me?*

"No, it's all right. Actually, we are still praying about that."

"You're praying about a boy?" Natalia's glass clinked against the tiles on the table. "What do you mean?"

"We are definitely interested in each other, but we want to take things slow and make sure God is honored in our relationship. We've got plenty of time to get serious down the road."

Natalia smiled. This was the kind of friend she had been praying for. She told Addy as much.

"I'm glad God brought you here, Natalia." Addy returned her smile.

"Me too," a familiar voice said. Natalia turned to see Brian Younger the younger standing behind her. She strained her neck to look up at his bright red head and smiling face.

"What, no kiss for an old friend?" He laughed, pulling a chair out to sit beside Natalia.

"Do Americans not ask permission before invading a dinner table?" Natalia peered at Addy.

Addy, obviously unsure whether or not Natalia was serious, looked to Brian.

"I was invited by your stepmother, thank you very

much." Brian grabbed a slice of bread and placed chorizo, cheese, and a tomato on top.

"What?" Natalia asked, still in shock. Her heart raced as he sat down. What excuse could she invent to leave the restaurant as soon as possible?

I am not interested. No boys, no dating, no romance. God! Help me. Surely you don't want me tempted like this.

"As I was saying," Brian mumbled as he swallowed the last of his food, "Maureen called to ask me about the ESL program. She said you needed some community-service hours." Brian paused to take a sip of Natalia's water. She blinked in surprise. "I told her that was amazing because just this morning I was praying that God would bring someone who is bilingual along who could help me. So many folks come in speaking no English at all." Brian helped himself to some *pulpo*. "And all I can say is, *Hola, me llamo Brian, y tu?*"

Natalia wasn't sure which was worse—Brian's manners or his accent.

"So." Brian forced Natalia to look him in the eye. "*¿Que pasa?*"

"What?" His blue eyes momentarily distracted her.

"I don't know. That's all I remember from Spanish class."

"I'm not sure." Natalia stared down at the table—anywhere to avoid his eyes. "Let me think it over a little more. When do you need to know?"

"We meet every Thursday. So how's tomorrow sound? That enough time?"

"No. I'll see you Sunday at church. I might have an answer then."

Brian's eyes registered shock, and then something else.

Natalia thought he seemed intrigued. But that couldn't be the case. She looked away from Brian's eyes to her half-eaten chorizo.

Brian cleared his throat, reached in his pocket, and pulled out a ten-dollar bill. His relaxed demeanor returned. "Thanks for the food, ladies. It was *muy bueno*!" He winked.

Natalia sat, her back straight and eyes forward, refusing to watch the young man leave.

"Interesting," Addy said as the bell above the door signaled Brian had left the restaurant.

"What's interesting?"

Addy smiled and took a sip of her soda. "That was interesting."

"I don't understand."

"I think Brian Younger may have just met his match."

Natalia folded her arms. "I am no one's match."

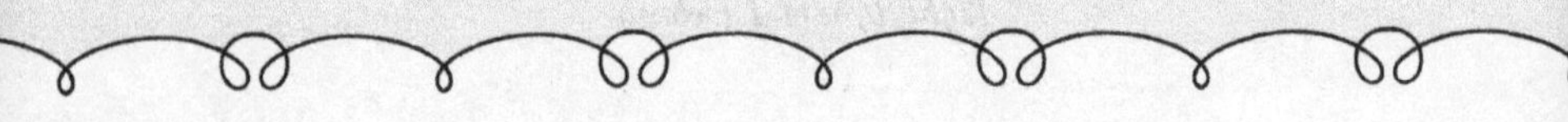

Chapter 15

Is there any problem a good day of shopping can't fix?

Addy picked Natalia up from her town house at ten the next morning. With school starting the next week, Natalia had lots of shopping to do. Maureen was busy with her lesson planning so Addy volunteered to help.

Natalia's father had insisted on sending enough money to cover all her schooling expenses. Maureen wasn't thrilled to have to accept anything from Oscar, but Natalia explained that she was still his daughter. Maureen might be cut off from her soon-to-be ex-husband, but Natalia was not. Maureen reluctantly agreed, but the less Maureen had to see, the better.

"So where do we begin?" Natalia buckled into the passenger seat of Addy's sedan. Shopping had been her favorite pastime in Spain, and she was excited to be heading out to stores, even if it was just for school supplies and uniforms.

"The uniform store. It's better to get that over with."

"What do your uniforms look like?" Natalia gazed out

the window at all the billboards. *How do people focus on driving with these everywhere?*

"Nothing special. Plaid skirts or khaki pants and your choice of navy or green polo shirts."

"Polo shirts? What are those?"

"You know, knit shirts with collars and three or four buttons," Addy said.

"That seems awfully casual. No blazers? No dress shirts?"

Addy laughed. "This is Florida. We'd burn up in blazers and dress shirts. Is that what you wore in Spain?"

Natalia nodded. "Everything was quite formal. We'd get in trouble if our shirts were untucked or our blazers wrinkled."

"Wow. I'd be in trouble every day! No school sports and no wrinkles? It sounds awful."

"It wasn't awful at all." Natalia's face heated. "Rules build character. Dress for success. A proper uniform reflects a proper student."

"Is that what they told you?"

"That is what my parents say." Natalia shrugged. "Too bad uniforms can't tell me what I should be, though. That is what my parents really want."

"They want you to know your major already?"

"They want me to know my *career* already." Natalia didn't want to continue this discussion. The stress of those thoughts was too much to consider. "But polos and khakis. That's nothing, I'm telling you."

"Most of the TCS students hate wearing uniforms. That's one of the biggest complaints you'll hear."

"Well, that's silly." Natalia shook her head. "Complaining

about uniforms. I'll just have to straighten these Americans out." She smiled. "They need to know how good they have it—Bible classes, Christian teachers, no blazers or ties . . ."

Natalia stopped as Addy pulled into a parking space at the uniform store. She was overwhelmed as she walked into what looked like a mini-department store, filled with every kind of uniform imaginable.

"I thought you said the colors were navy and green?" Natalia asked.

"They are, but this store houses uniforms for most of the private schools in Tampa."

Natalia was surprised to learn that each school had its own uniform requirements, some even had their own plaid. Addy navigated through the aisles and found the Tampa Christian School section. Natalia was not impressed with the stiff cotton skirts, but she found several in her size, along with some pants, and went in line to check out.

She spotted a mall across the busy street. Natalia longed to spend a few hours in there, catch up on the latest fashions, and maybe buy a few cute pairs of shoes to liven up the dull uniforms. But she promised to live within Maureen's means. Middle-class living would not be easy. *Good-bye, Jimmy Choo. My feet will miss you dearly.* "Now for books." Natalia laid her purchases in the backseat of Addy's car.

A few minutes later Addy pulled into the parking lot of the largest bookstore Natalia had ever seen.

"If they don't have our summer reading books, there's a bigger bookstore down the street."

"Bigger than this?" Natalia asked, overwhelmed at the selection.

Addy was able to find one of the books, a Jane Austen novel that had been required reading for Natalia when she was in the ninth grade. The second, a book by C. S. Lewis, was not available.

"*Till We Have Faces* isn't very well known," Addy said. "But Mrs. Jenners, our English teacher, says it's his best. We may have to go to a Christian bookstore for that one."

Natalia wanted to know about Christian bookstores, but in less than three minutes, Addy had pulled into a Walmart parking lot. Natalia had heard a lot about this store from Maureen and others. She walked in and was relieved to know that, in Spain, they had a store even bigger—Carrefour. That store was two stories tall, with a moving sidewalk that took customers and their carts from one level to the next. At least, this once, she didn't feel overwhelmed. This Walmart was only one story and didn't have nearly the variety that Carrefour had.

Addy had the school supply list in her purse, and the girls made their way to the far end of the building where the back-to-school displays were set up. Again on familiar territory, Natalia made quick work of finding the items she needed and placed them in the cart.

"All done." Addy crossed the last item off their list.

"Is that all?" Natalia smiled. "That was fun. I love shopping."

"I can tell." Addy laughed. "I've never seen anyone get so excited about cereal."

"You have so many choices. We don't have nearly so many. Of course, you are lacking in the cheese department. And no Jamón Serrano."

The girls walked their cart out to Addy's car and found Spencer Adams making his way into the store.

Spencer stopped and smiled at them. "Addy. And, Natalia, right?"

"Right." Natalia pushed the cart to the side so an oncoming car could pass. "How are you, Spencer?"

"Doing much better now that I've seen you two lovely ladies."

Natalia wanted to groan. *But that would not be polite.*

"Shopping for school supplies?"

"I sure am." Spencer smiled again.

He thinks we should just melt over that smile.

"Listen, I was hoping I'd see you again, Natalia." He leaned in. "I know you were just being nice the other day, but Brian Younger really is a loser. I mean, he's nice and all that. But he's not the kind of guy you want to be seen hanging around with."

"Really?" Natalia raised an eyebrow. She knew guys like this, guys who thought they knew exactly what a girl wanted. *Arrogant boys seem to be an international phenomenon.* "I appreciate your concern, but I do believe I am quite capable of deciding with whom I do and do not want to associate."

Spencer walked away, his bright smiled having faded.

Addy spoke quietly beside Natalia. "That's twice in two days! And you handle it so well."

"What are you talking about?" Natalia reached for the car door.

"First Brian, now Spencer. Boys are throwing themselves at you, and you just put them right in their place!"

"What does that mean, 'put them in their place'?"

"You know, it means . . . how do I explain it?" Addy slanted her head to the side and pursed her lips. "It means that you let them know you were boss."

When Natalia crossed her arms and furrowed her brows, Addy tried again. "Another cliché. I guess I don't realize how many we use. Okay, what I meant to say was that two boys think you are very attractive and you don't even give them the time of day." She caught herself. "You don't flirt back."

"Why should I? I don't want to date. No use making anyone think otherwise." Natalia turned the vents of the air conditioner toward her. Standing outside all that time was brutal. "But what do you mean *two* boys? Spencer was the only one flirting. And I think it is more because I'm new and have a foreign accent than anything else."

"Brian Younger," Addy reminded. "He's friendly and he jokes with everyone, but he hardly ever flirts. I don't even think he's had a girlfriend. But he was flirting with you. Big time."

"Don't be silly. He was just trying to encourage me to help him in his ministry."

"If that's what you want to think, all right." Addy laughed. "But I know what I saw. And he is a great guy. I would definitely approve of that match. And Spencer—he's probably the most popular guy in school. He has all kinds of girls lined up, wanting to go out with him."

"I'm not interested in dating," Natalia said, louder than she intended, from the look on Addy's face. "I'm sorry. I really don't mean to be rude. I just do not intend to date."

"Because you don't want to get involved with an American?"

"No, because I don't want to get involved with anyone. Jesus is the only man I want in my life."

Natalia could tell Addy wanted to know more, but Natalia wasn't ready yet to share the reasons behind how she felt. She was flustered at the thought that Brian might actually be interested in her, and upset that she hoped it would be true.

What was that verse Pastor Eduardo preached on before she left? Natalia tried to recall. Paul said that the things he wanted to do, he didn't, and the things he didn't want to do, he did. *I understand that exactly. I don't want to think about Brian. I don't want to be attracted to him.*

As Addy pulled into Natalia's driveway, she turned to Natalia. "I respect how committed you are to Christ, Natalia. You really challenge me to make sure I keep him first in everything. But he wants good things for you. Don't be afraid to accept the good things along with the difficult."

"You think dating is a good thing?"

"No, it's not that." Addy shook her head. "I just get the feeling you have a wall up around you. You'll let people get just so close, then no more. I'm not talking about boys either. I feel it too. I'd like to be your friend, Natalia. I love having fun and eating and shopping together, but I'd like to know what you're thinking and how you're feeling. I want to help you. I know this move can't be easy. You miss your friends and your family. I know Maureen is struggling. Let me in. Please."

Natalia wasn't sure how to respond. She was shocked that Addy, who had known her for such a short time, could see into her so easily.

"Thank you, Addy." Natalia looked straight ahead. "But I am just a private person."

"I understand." Addy smiled. "I am too. But I've learned that even private people need to make some things public. With people they can trust. I hope I can earn that trust with you. I'm praying for you. I see God working in you and it's exciting. I'm so glad God brought you here."

Natalia thanked Addy, then grabbed her packages and walked into the town house.

Help me, God. Help me to be as strong of a person as Addy believes that I am.

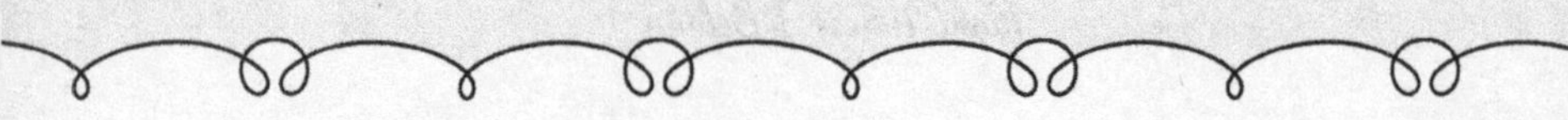

Chapter 16

Natalia opened the door to the town house to find Maureen curled into a ball on the couch, a dozen crumpled tissues on the floor.

"Maureen!" Natalia dropped her purchases and rushed to her stepmother. "What happened? Are you all right?"

Maureen moaned and blew her nose, her face covered in tears, her eyes so red and puffy she didn't even look like herself. She was crying so hard that she couldn't speak. She tried, but the only sounds that came out were sobs. Natalia was distraught, unsure of what to do.

Maureen lifted a sheet of typed paper and thrust it into Natalia's lap. Opening the paper—also soaked in tears—understanding dawned on her.

The divorce was final.

Maureen had still held out a glimmer of hope that it wouldn't actually happen, that Papa might change his mind. Natalia knew that wouldn't happen. In her weekly conversations with her father, he shared that he was blissfully happy with Victoria, his much younger new woman. They had been vacationing in southern France, shopping in Morocco. She was trying to convince him to buy a vacation home in Fiji, but Papa thought someplace closer—the Canary Islands, maybe—would be better.

Her father was always rushed, always happy when Natalia spoke to him. She, of course, relayed none of her conversations with her father to Maureen. She didn't want her stepmother hurt any more than she already was.

Maybe I should have said something. If I had known she still had hope, still thought my father would regret his decision and come back, I would have said something.

Tears Natalia hadn't meant to shed fell from her eyes as she sat rubbing Maureen's hand, silently mourning with her the loss of her marriage, her dreams.

After several minutes, Natalia asked, "Maureen, let me call someone. Carol? Pastor Brian? You need to talk. You can't go on like this."

"No!" Maureen sat up. "This is humiliating, Natalia. You have no idea. I left Tampa proud—I had a great-paying job in Spain. Everyone was so impressed. Then I married a man who was richer and better looking than any of the men here. And Carol and Pastor Brian, they warned me not to marry him. I came back for my wedding shower, and they cornered me. Was I sure I knew what I was doing? Was he a Christian? Had we dated long enough for me to really know him?

"I laughed at them, Natalia. I laughed in their faces. I told them Oscar was my soul mate, and I didn't need time to make sure of that. I told them God wouldn't have brought me to him if he didn't intend for us to be together—I was sure God planned the whole thing. And since God planned it, then Oscar would eventually become a Christian. Of course he would. He just needed time."

Maureen sobbed, gulping air and throwing aside the now-empty box of tissues. "How can I go back to them now and tell them they were right? That I made the biggest mistake of my life and I'm going to have to suffer the consequences of that decision forever?"

God, help me. Natalia needed the right words to help her stepmother, and at the moment, none were coming to mind. "Do you really think they would condemn you? Your sister loves you. I can see that. So does Pastor Brian. Neither of them seems like people who enjoy watching others suffer. I think they'd be happy to help you if you'd just let them."

Maureen's eyes softened for a moment, then hardened. "No, Natalia. I can't. I won't. I have to deal with this myself. It's my fault I got here. My own stupid choices. I didn't listen to them before, so how can I go crying to them now?"

Natalia wanted to argue, but Maureen wouldn't listen. She had made up her mind. God would have to change Maureen's heart. Natalia vowed to pray even more for her. She couldn't stand to see Maureen suffering so much.

She held Maureen's hand until her stepmother fell asleep, then Natalia made her way up to her room. How could she judge Maureen for not asking for help when Natalia did the same thing? Addy had just offered to help her, and Natalia refused. Natalia thought of her stepmother downstairs, lying on the couch and drowning in grief. With a deep breath, Natalia picked up the phone.

"Addy?" she asked tentatively. "I need to talk."

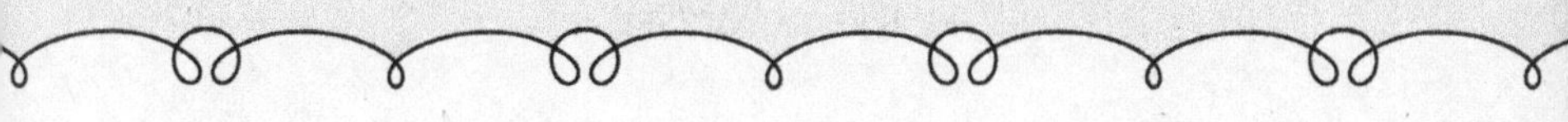

Chapter 17

"What's wrong, Natalia?"

Addy's kind voice made her cry even harder. She hated this. *I shouldn't have called her.*

"Natalia?"

"I'm sorry." She took another deep breath.

"Did something happen with Maureen?"

Suddenly Natalia found herself spilling out the whole story—the divorce papers, her father's new fiancée, Maureen's depression.

"The worst part is that I hear more from my friend Carmen than I do from my own parents." Natalia looked at her computer, where yet another e-mail from her best friend sat unopened in her in-box. Anger bubbled up inside, anger she hadn't even known was there.

"I'm sorry, Natalia. Have you talked to them about how you feel?"

"Right." Natalia laughed. "We do not talk about feelings in my family. We talk about to-do lists."

"Maybe that's why it's so hard for you to talk about how you feel. You're not used to it."

"Maureen and I used to talk about that kind of thing." Natalia remembered nights when her father worked late. Maureen would come home and they'd talk about everything from God to school to their favorite movies. "That hasn't happened in a while, though. I miss that Maureen. I'm beginning to wonder if she'll ever get over this."

"Do you talk to God about how you're feeling?"

"What?"

"Jesus promises to make our burdens light. He wants to help you, Natalia. Just like he wants to help Maureen. You might not be able to help her see that yet, but you can turn to him. Maybe she'll see him in you and realize she doesn't need to be struggling through this on her own either."

"I hadn't really thought of that." Natalia closed her eyes. "I feel like I'm drowning, and all I can do is just keep my head above water."

"All the more reason to let God help you. Let him be your life raft. I'll help too." Addy's laugh was soft. "I'll sit and help you row back to shore."

"Thanks, Addy." Natalia would never have had a conversation like this with Carmen.

"Can I make one more suggestion?"

"Sure." Natalia dried her eyes with a tissue.

"I've found the best way to deal with difficulties is to try to focus on helping others. It's so easy just to think about myself, you know?"

"I barely know anyone here, though. And I think Maureen and I are both tired of me trying to help her."

"What about the ESL ministry? Brian has a classroom full every Thursday, and his main helper, Anthony, just left to go back to college in Tallahassee. Anthony is Cuban, so he was able to work as an interpreter. Brian doesn't have anyone to do that now."

Natalia was torn. Addy was right about needing to think about others. But couldn't she be involved in a ministry that didn't require her to work so closely with Brian? His face came to her mind more often than she wanted to admit, even to herself. When she saw him in church on Sundays, her heart raced and she couldn't keep her eyes from the back of his red head during the service.

She admired that he was often bent over his Bible, taking notes and nodding at his dad as he preached. Most of the other teens were nodding off or texting with their phones hidden in their palms. Brian was certainly different.

"He doesn't have anyone to interpret?"

Addy shook her head. "And you've heard his Spanish. If you don't come in and give him a hand, he might lose the whole class."

Natalia laughed. "That is certainly true. I'm just not sure I can handle hearing him murder my beautiful language every week."

"I'm sure he'd be very grateful for some private tutoring."

Natalia didn't like how enticing that thought was. "No, this relationship will be strictly business."

"Sure, Natalia." Addy laughed. "You keep telling yourself that."

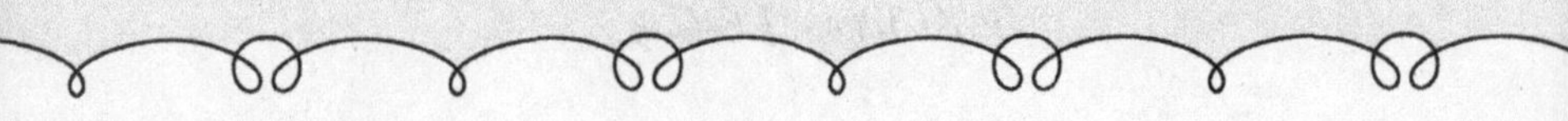

Chapter 18

I am here for community-service hours. Natalia walked into the church's main entrance, looking for the ESL classroom. *I am not here to spend time with Brian. I am not attracted to him. I am not going to keep thinking about him. But what am I doing now? Thinking about him.*

Spotting the classroom, she glanced in but found no one there. She checked her phone. She was a few minutes early. Natalia walked back toward the entrance and found a plush wing-backed chair to sit in as she waited for the class to begin.

"*¡Hola, mi ayudante!*" Brian's huge frame filled the doorway.

Natalia winced at his horrible pronunciation, hoping to mask her delight in seeing him.

"That means, 'hello, my helper.' At least, that's what this says." Brian held up an electronic translator.

"The words were correct." Natalia refused to look Brian in the face. "But I think you'd better leave the Spanish to me. What do we need to do?"

He grabbed Natalia's arm and lifted her to her feet. She

was sure the heat from his touch raised her temperature at least five degrees. She pulled away and crossed her arms.

Brian looked at her for a moment, then smiled. "All right. Business it is. First, we need to set up the classroom. I like to put the chairs in a semicircle so we can all see each other. There are about fifteen who come on any given Thursday. Ten of those are here every week, the other five vary. I've got cookies and drinks out in my truck. We'll set those up in the back.

"We begin with a short devotion. That's where I'll need your help. Some of our students speak very little English, so I'll need you to translate. After that, we get to work and it's all English. This week they'll all be telling a little about themselves. I told them you were coming, so they have been working on a one- to two-minute introduction."

"You told them I was coming? When? I only called you this morning."

"I told them last week." Brian winked. "*You* may not have known then, but I did."

"How did you know I would come?"

"God told me." Brian grinned broadly. "He and I are very close." Brian winked again, and Natalia hoped her face didn't reveal how unnerved she was by this young man.

She had no idea how to respond to him. Thankfully, she didn't have to because Brian abruptly left the room to get the cookies and drinks.

Natalia set up the chairs and looked around the room. Posters with the parts of speech filled the back wall. To the side was a poster board full of photographs of what Natalia assumed was the group. Brian stood in the middle—a huge redheaded column, arms wrapped around shorter, smiling Hispanics.

"Those are last year's graduates," Brian said as he returned to the room and began laying out the snacks. "We had a great group. Most have moved on—some are taking classes at the community college. These two"—Brian pointed to a couple at the end—"became Christians. I was able to connect them with a Spanish-speaking church a few miles away. They are plugged in and loving it. They've invited all of the others too. It's been exciting to see them grow."

Natalia couldn't help but look at Brian's face as he spoke. Pure joy. He loved those people. *He certainly has his father's pastor's heart.*

She wanted to ask if Brian planned on going into the ministry, but she didn't have time. A man in a plaid shirt and jeans walked in and planted a kiss on Brian's cheek.

"Brian," the man said, his accent changing the name to "Bree-ahn." Natalia liked the change. *"¿Cómo estás, amigo?"*

"Victor! I am doing very well." Brian slapped the man's back. "And your English is way too good to make me try to use my rotten Spanish."

"This is true." Victor put his hands out expressively.

"Victor." Brian pointed toward her. "This is Natalia. She'll be helping us this year."

This year? I just signed on to get my community-service hours. Of course, at three hours a week, it'll take me all year.

"*Señorita* Natalia." Victor took her hand and kissed it. "*Muy bonita*. For once, Brian was not exaggerating."

Natalia looked over to see Brian's cheeks turning pink. "*Gracias, Señor* Victor. I am happy to be here."

The door opened again and this time a group of five entered. Natalia tried to remember all the names. Just when she thought she had them, another group entered.

"Just in time." Brian walked over to hug each of the members.

He's so comfortable. With everyone. I can't even imagine that.

"Grab a snack and a drink and then sit," Brian directed.

Pastor Mike, the associate pastor, stuck his head in the doorway. "All good, Bri?"

"Yes, sir." Brian stuffed a cookie in his mouth. "Wanna sit in?"

"Not unless you need me. But I'll be in my office if anything comes up."

Natalia looked from the door to Brian. "Is this supposed to be Pastor Mike's job?"

"Not exactly." Brian gulped down some juice. "He's in charge of outreach, and this counts as outreach. But he's got a ton of other ministries he's involved in. I worked with him in here from the time I was a freshman. He let me take it over last year. It works great. He gets to catch up on paperwork on Thursday nights, and I get to be in charge. Win-win."

Brian introduced Natalia to the group, and she noticed several of the members look from their leader to his new helper with winks. *Don't even go there.*

When Brian asked Natalia up to the front to translate, her mouth went completely dry.

What if I mess up? What if I can't do it fast enough and these people don't get the message? She closed her eyes, willing herself to pray. As she did, Brian began his own prayer quietly.

"God, we thank you for this time together. Help me have wisdom as I talk about your Word and help Natalia as she translates my words. Use us to glorify you. Amen."

Natalia felt herself calm, peace washing over her. Until Brian looked over and smiled.

Don't look at me, Natalia wanted to scream. *I can't focus when you're looking at me.* So she stood a step behind him, her eyes on the faces smiling at her. Faces of people wanting to hear God's Word in their own language. *Help me do this, God.*

Brian took out a worn Bible and opened it to the center. "I'm going to talk about Job."

Brian paused, and Natalia realized that was her cue to begin translating. Switching from English to Spanish so quickly was more difficult than she had expected, but once Brian got into his message, they found a rhythm. Natalia was able to listen to Brian and translate at the same time.

"Did Job have a right to complain?" Brian asked, waiting for a response.

"Sí," Maria, an older woman, responded. "His children were taken from him, his money, his land, his health. If anyone had a right to complain, it was him."

"That makes sense." Brian nodded. "How many of you have experienced some of these things?"

Hands all around the room went up, and there were stories behind each one.

"This story is in here for you," Brian said. "For all of us, whenever we think God is being unfair or we have a right to complain. Do you know what God finally told Job at the end of this book?"

Natalia waited with the rest of the room for his answer.

"He didn't say anything." Brian shut his Bible. "He didn't have to. He reminded Job that he is God. He is sovereign. He knows what we can never know and he works in ways we don't see. We can trust him, even when terrible things are happening. He is holy."

Natalia finished translating and bit back a tear. She needed to hear this message. She wished Maureen could hear this message as well.

"I don't want to minimize your pain." Brian looked at the people in the room, compassion filling his eyes. "I know what some of you have gone through, and I can't even imagine it. But God is bigger than your pain. He will meet you in it, help you through it, and he will bring you out of it."

One of the members shouted "Amen," and Natalia echoed that in her heart.

"So you can choose to be like Job, trusting God no matter what. Or you can be like his wife who said, 'Curse God and die.' It's your choice. I pray you will trust him."

Brian closed in prayer and paused. "If you want to talk afterward, you know I'll be here. So will Pastor Mike. But for now, I'm done. It's your turn. Natalia wants to know all about you. In two minutes or less. And in English. So who will go first?"

Natalia was a little surprised at how quickly Brian went from serious to humorous, but the transition seemed very natural. Everything about Brian Younger seemed natural.

"I will go first, since I was the first one to meet the pretty lady." Victor stood and walked to the front of the room. "I am Victor. I am fifty-seven years old, and I am from Cuba. I moved here twenty years ago with my family. I work as an auto mechanic until this year, when I get fired for not talking good English. So I am here. Señor Brian teaches me English and he teaches me Bible, and I go back to work soon because of his good job."

The group members clapped, and Victor pointed to the man sitting beside him to go next. One after the other, the members spoke of moving from their home countries. Natalia understood their tears.

But they have sacrificed so much more than I have. Their families, their reputations. Everything. She was humbled at the joy the people had in spite of their difficulties. And her respect for Brian grew, hearing his praises from so many of the members.

Natalia was sad to see the evening end. She kissed each of the people as they left, feeling a connection with them she never could have imagined.

"They're great, aren't they?" Brian threw an empty carton of cookies in the trash. "I knew you'd get hooked."

"Hooked?"

"Reeled in?"

Natalia had no idea what he meant.

"You like them."

"I do." Natalia snapped the cap on a container of orange juice. "I feel very at home with them."

"So what's your story?" Brian sat down, his blue eyes exploring hers.

The gaze was more than Natalia could handle. She took out her phone. "Oh dear. It's already nine thirty. Maureen is probably sitting out in the parking lot. I'd better go."

"I can give you a ride next week, if you want." Brian stood, and Natalia could tell he was confused by her actions.

"No, that's fine." Natalia nearly stumbled out the door. "I will see you—later."

Natalia rushed out to the parking lot and threw herself into Maureen's car. *How can an evening be so amazing and so frustrating at the same time? And how in the world will I be able to do this every week this year?*

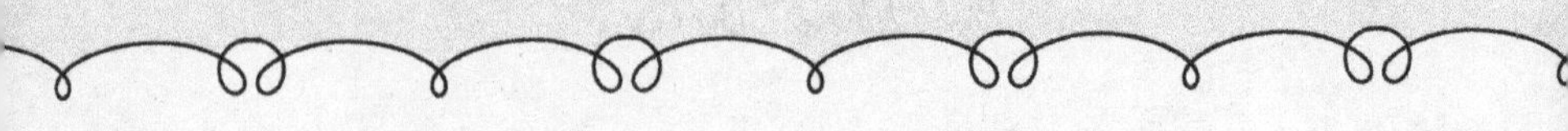

Chapter 19

"Your dad is a senator, you're majoring in premed, and you're working here?" Brian looked at James.

He grabbed Brian's crowbar. "Watch out for the wire."

Brian sucked in a breath. "Good thing you're studying to be a doctor. You may need to use those skills on me before the summer's out."

James slowly peeled a layer of drywall off. "Let's hope not."

"Seriously, man. Why work demo?"

"My parents want me to appreciate manual labor." James shrugged. "I was just going to work here one summer, but I got hooked."

"It is kind of fun." Brian pulled the rest of the drywall down and threw it to the middle of the room. "Helps me get out my aggressions."

"Like Spencer Adams?"

"How'd you guess?" Brian began working on another section of the wall.

"I knew guys like that when I was in high school." James grunted. "I know guys like that in college."

"You don't know Spencer." Brian looked at James. Brown hair, a tan, and muscles. Wasn't that what all the girls wanted?

"My dad knows his dad."

Brian mimicked Mr. Adams's commercial. "'Car accident? Hurt on the job? Call the law firm of Adams and Finley. We're here to help.'"

"Adams supported my dad in the last election."

"You don't sound happy about that."

James grimaced. "His support came with a whole lot of strings attached."

"Really?"

"He and my dad ended up having a huge fight."

"Why?"

"Dad wouldn't give him what he wanted."

"Mr. Adams didn't like that, huh?"

"Not at all." James grunted again.

"Explains why Spencer always expects to get his way."

"He learns from the best."

Brian took a sip of water. "Thing is, Spencer pretty much does always get his way." Brian thought of Natalia. Spencer also had his eye on the beautiful new student.

James looked at Brian. "With a dad like that, though, his life can't be easy."

"Mine should be so tough." Brian strained to pull out an eighty-year-old nail.

"Come on, man, you've told me how great your dad is. Would you really want to trade him for Mr. Adams?"

"No way."

"I've heard the way he yells at his employees, and at my dad. Imagine how Spencer gets treated."

"Don't go making me feel sorry for him, James." Brian finally got the nail out.

He laughed. "I'm just saying, sometimes perfect lives aren't as perfect as they seem."

Footsteps approached the dining room where he and James were working.

"Finally coming in to help us, Mr. King?" Brian called out.

"Mr. King isn't helping?" Mr. Adams walked in, his expensive business suit a stark contrast to the piles of rubble he stepped over.

James's eyes widened. "He just stepped out, Mr. Adams. He'll be right back."

"My multimillion dollar home is left to the two of you?" Mr. Adams glared at them. "I figured out who you are, by the way." He leveled his gaze at James. "You're lucky I didn't have you fired."

"For what?" James laid his crowbar down.

"For being related to Senator Perkins," he spat. "Do you know how much money I donated to that campaign?"

"No, but I bet you do," James muttered under his breath.

Brian bit back a laugh.

"Excuse me?" Mr. Adams's face was inches from Brian's. "I've given plenty to your dad too."

Brian knew he was referring to his donations to the school. *Amazing how people think the pastor personally benefits from gifts given to the church or school.* But it would not be wise to contradict him.

"I was just telling my son this morning how much of a

responsibility it is to be an Adams, how lucky he is, how grateful he should be."

James met Mr. Adams's gaze. "How fortunate for him he has a father who won't let him forget that."

The businessman's face turned red. "There are other demolition companies out there. I can ruin this one. Believe me. So you better watch yourself and treat your betters with respect."

Brian waited until the man was out of earshot before saying, "As soon as we see one of our betters, we will."

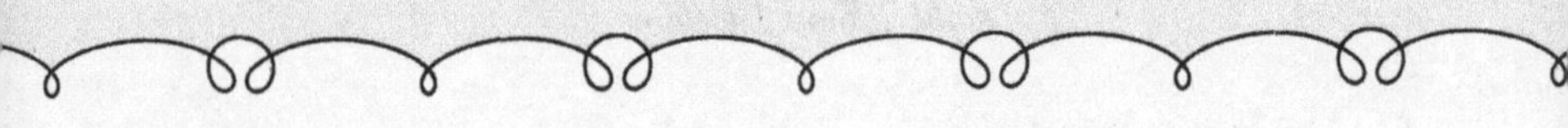

Chapter 20

"Another great night." Brian cleaned up the trash left on the tables after the last of the ESL group members left.

Natalia tried to convince herself that she was not attracted to him. *So why does my heart act like it's going to jump out of my chest every time he looks at me?*

"So I heard you telling Victor that your mom is a broadcast journalist in Madrid."

Natalia nodded. Brian had been trying to get her to open up more about her personal life, but she was afraid. She needed to keep their relationship as distant as possible.

"So have you gotten to meet any celebrities?"

Natalia grabbed another chair and spoke while walking to the corner. "A few."

"Antonio Banderas?" Brian stood beside her. "I loved him in *Puss in Boots*."

Natalia rolled her eyes as Brian tried to dance the tango by himself. "No. I've never met him. Most of the celebrities I've met are only famous in Spain. It's no big deal, really."

"Sure it is." Brian kept stacking chairs. "So what does your dad do?"

"It's complicated."

"A secret agent? Like Antonio Banderas in *Spy Kids*?" Brian's eyes widened, as did his smirk. "You can't say or he might get kidnapped, and then you'd have to go to a private island and fight crazy bad guys to free him—I'll take your silence as confirmation."

"What is it with you and Antonio Banderas?"

"I just love Spanish people." He shrugged. Then his face turned that adorable shade of pink. "I mean . . . it seems like a cool country . . . bullfighting and all that manly stuff."

Natalia found his awkwardness endearing. Too endearing. "I'd really better go."

"Wait." Brian grabbed her arm. She turned to face him. His nearness, combined with the close contact, was almost more than she could handle. Almost.

"No, really." Natalia pulled away, practically sprinting toward the door.

"But I'm taking you home," Brian called out as she pushed the door open. "I called Maureen earlier. There's something I wanted to talk to you about, and I knew we wouldn't have time in here."

Natalia prayed he wasn't about to ask her out. *And if he is, how could Maureen, of all people, even agree to it? She hates men.*

She remained silent as Brian poked his head in Pastor Mike's office to say he was leaving.

Brian started his old pickup truck and put it in gear. Pulling out of the church parking lot, he finally broke the silence. "So you're probably wondering what I wanted to talk to you about."

"Look, I don't—"

"Let me say it, then you can argue with me, okay?" Brian smiled, but Natalia wondered if that's what she was like—always arguing with him whenever he spoke. She hoped not. "I want you to go on the mission trip to Costa Rica with the youth group."

Natalia released a loud exhale. "A mission trip?"

"Yes." Brian spoke quickly, obviously excited about this endeavor. "We went last year, and it was amazing. We spend our mornings working on a church. The churches there need lots of work, and most of the people can't pay for it. So we paint and make repairs for them. Then, at night, we run a Vacation Bible School for missionary kids at a language school."

"Language school?"

"It's called the Spanish Language Institute, right in San José." Brian almost missed the turn into Natalia's neighborhood. "Missionaries go there to learn Spanish. Some stay a whole year, some just stay a few months. But when they're done, they go off to serve in a Spanish-speaking country."

"I never thought about what missionaries had to do before going overseas."

"Me neither. That's one of the great things about this trip. You get to talk with missionaries and hear their stories. They're just regular people."

"As opposed to . . . ?"

"I don't know." Brian pulled in front of Natalia's town house and put the car into Park. "Growing up in church, we had dozens of missionaries come through, and they all seemed kind of weird."

"Weird?"

"You know, all those stories about living in the jungle and eating fried bugs or running from armed warriors."

Natalia couldn't tell Brian she hadn't ever even seen a missionary. Her church supported some, but she'd never actually met any.

"Anyway, lots of the missionaries that go there have kids. There's a Christian school for them, and they also learn Spanish."

"It must be hard for them to leave home."

"And grandparents and Twizzlers and PlayStations." Brian nodded. "Tell me about it. And all for their parents' call."

"Call?"

"You know, people in ministry say God calls them there."

"Oh, right. Call. Go ahead—the children."

"Right." Brian unbuckled so he could face Natalia. "We run a Vacation Bible School for them. And they love it. We want them to know how special they are, and how they are honoring God with their lives, just like their parents are. We bring candy and treats from the States. They get very excited about that. And we just love on them."

Brian's eyes lit up when he talked about the children. *He's going to be a great father someday.* Natalia pushed the thought away as soon as it entered her mind.

"And you want me to come on this trip? Why? I haven't been a Christian very long, and I don't know anything about repairing churches or teaching children."

"You can learn all that." Brian dismissed Natalia's concern with a wave of his hand. "Plus, it's an amazing experience. And we could really use another translator." Brian grinned. "My buddy Anthony came last year, but he's at college now and can't get away."

"When is the trip?"

"September."

"When would I need to decide?"

"Pretty soon," Brian said.

"You don't give a girl much time to make decisions, do you?"

Brian laughed, and Natalia found she loved the sound of it. "Sorry. But it'll be worth it. I promise. I think Addy is going this year too. She chickened out last year, but a lot has changed for her since then."

"So I hear."

Natalia's front door opened and her stepmother's face appeared through the crack in the door. *If you don't want me sitting in a parked car with a boy, Maureen, you shouldn't give him permission to take me home.*

"I'll pray about it, okay?"

"So will I," Brian said. "But I already know the answer."

Natalia opened the truck door. "And what if you're wrong?"

"Then I'll owe you a trip to Dixie's Diner. How about that?"

A vision of the carbohydrate-filled lunch popped into Natalia's mind and she grimaced.

Brian threw his hands up. "Sorry. I was just kidding."

He thought she was disgusted at the idea of going out

with him. Natalia considered correcting that assumption. *No, better to let him think that. The less I encourage him, the better.* She didn't know why he would be interested in her, but she knew why he shouldn't—her family was far too messed up to drag anyone else anywhere near it.

"Thanks for the ride, Brian." Natalia shut the truck door. "I'm sure Maureen will be able to take me home from now on."

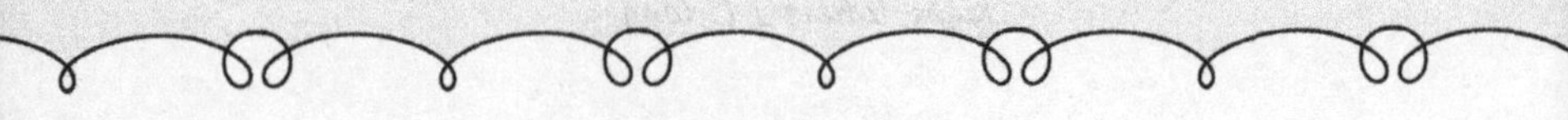

Chapter 21

Brian watched until Natalia was inside her house. Then he hit his steering wheel as hard as he could.

"Ouch." Not the best idea.

He pulled out his phone and punched in Addy's number. The two of them had gone to school together since kindergarten. He wouldn't classify them as best friends, but until her stint on the TV show, both were among the class "outcasts."

"Hey, Addy. Is this a bad time?"

"Brian?" She sounded tired.

He looked at the clock. It was after nine o'clock. "Were you asleep? I'm sorry."

"No." Addy cleared her throat. "I was just reading. Is everything okay?"

He sighed. "I need some help."

"With what?" She sounded alarmed.

"Natalia." Brian pulled out of Natalia's neighborhood and drove home.

Addy laughed. "Oh, that kind of help."

"No, not that. I mean, not that I wouldn't mind it being that. I want to be friends with her, but I keep getting mixed signals. She's amazing with the ESL group. She has connected with them so quickly. And when we're in class, she's happy and talkative. But when it's just the two of us, she clams up."

"She is an amazing person."

"I know," Brian said louder than he intended.

"And she needs friends. Things are tough at home right now."

"I know that too. And I want to be her friend." *I'd like to be more than that, but no use pushing it.* "But it's like she won't let me."

"I think it's really hard for her to open up."

"But I just want to help." Brian turned onto his street.

"Then keep doing what you're doing. Just be yourself. She needs to laugh."

"And I'm the class clown."

"You say that like it's a bad thing."

"Sometimes I'd like to be the class hunk. Or the class brain. Or the class jock. Being the class clown gets a little old."

"Oh, Brian, you're growing up." Addy had a smile in her voice.

"All right, Grandma." Brian laughed. "Now that you've got a boyfriend, you think you're all mature?"

"We are talking about Natalia, not me."

Brian threw his car into Park. "Does Natalia have a boyfriend? Back in Spain?"

"Oh no. She doesn't seem to think she'll ever date."

"Ever?"

"Her family's so messed up, I think she's afraid she'd be messed up too."

"I'll let you go." Brian locked his truck and walked up the sidewalk to his house. "Thanks. I feel a little better."

Brian ended the call and thought of Natalia. Something he had been doing a lot lately. *She needs to spend some time with a healthy family.* He opened the door to his house. *I think I know just the one.*

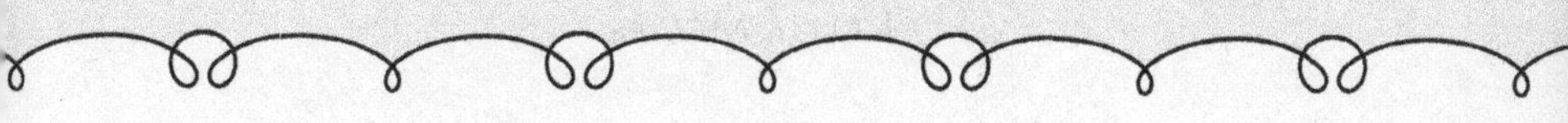

Chapter 22

"Are you ready?" Addy stood at Natalia's doorstep in her school uniform.

"I just feel so underdressed." Natalia smoothed her skirt. Again. "You're sure none of the others will be wearing a blazer?"

"It's going to be ninety-four today." Addy grabbed Natalia's backpack as they walked to her car.

Natalia buckled up and took a deep breath. She didn't even remember going to a new school ever. She was so used to knowing everyone and everyone knowing her. *What was I thinking, switching schools—and continents—my final year of high school?*

"Relax." Addy looked over at Natalia. "It'll be fine. We're in almost all the same classes."

"That's nice."

"And the school is small, so you definitely won't get lost."

Natalia nodded. "Right."

Addy stopped at the end of Natalia's street and glanced in her rearview mirror. "You know what? Let's pray."

"What?"

"We're fine, no cars are coming. Come on." Addy closed her eyes and Natalia, with a glance at the side mirror, did the same. "Jesus, help Natalia. I can't imagine being at a brand-new school for my senior year. Help her feel comfortable and make friends. Give her a great year this year, God. Bless her for her obedience. Amen."

Natalia sighed. "I should have done that three hours ago." She felt like a weight had been lifted. "Thanks."

"You were up at four thirty in the morning?"

"I couldn't sleep." Natalia picked a piece of lint off her navy polo shirt. "I get a little nervous sometimes."

"I understand that. But you're going to be exhausted by the end of the day."

"I know."

"But you still have to come to the Dream Cone with us."

"Oh, I forgot about that." Addy had told Natalia that she and her best friend, Lexi, always went to an ice-cream parlor after their first day of school. "What was the dessert you said you always get?"

"A Chocolate Avalanche. It's amazing. Chocolate ice cream on a chocolate brownie with chocolate syrup on top."

"I don't know how you can eat like that and stay thin." Natalia laughed.

"My friend Kara swears I'm going to weigh five hundred pounds someday." Addy pulled into the school parking lot. Natalia found it difficult to take a deep breath. "We have homeroom together. All the seniors are together for homeroom."

Natalia didn't have time to respond because a very tall, muscular young woman ran up to Addy and lifted her off the ground. "My best friend."

"Can't breathe," Addy panted.

"Oh, sorry." The girl dropped Addy and struck a pose. "Notice anything different?"

"Are you kidding?" Addy walked around the girl. "You look amazing. You must have lost, what, twenty pounds?"

"Twenty-two." The girl grinned. "Forget Weight Watchers. I got the Gram and Gramps Summer Vacation Program. They put me to work on their farm, fed me salads and grilled chicken. I lost fat, gained more muscle, and look out. I am going to kill on the volleyball team this year. And basketball . . . oh boy. Calvary Christian better just get ready. They are going down this year."

Addy stopped her friend with a hand on her shoulder. "Hang on, Lexi. I want to introduce you to Natalia. She's the one I told you about who moved here from Spain."

"Natalia!" Lexi hugged Natalia, and Natalia quickly understood how Addy felt a few minutes before. *"Estoy muy alegre que estés aquí, amiga."*

"Muy bien español." Natalia smiled.

"The Gram and Gramps Summer Spanish Program?" Addy asked.

"Sí." Lexi laughed and turned to Natalia. "They're originally from Puerto Rico. Mom and Dad both grew up speaking Spanish, but neither have passed it down to us kids. So my grandparents believe it's their responsibility to keep us from being too *Americano*."

"Where do they live now?"

"They own a cattle ranch in Texas." Lexi motioned toward the school, and the girls began walking across the parking lot to the senior high building.

"And you go there every summer?" Natalia wanted to think about anything but walking into a classroom of strangers.

"No, my sisters and brothers and I take turns."

"How many siblings do you have?"

"Seven." Lexi shrugged. "I'm number six."

"What a large family." Natalia had a half sister, but she barely saw eight-year-old Ari. Ari's mother, Isabelle, only let Papa see her on holidays.

"You'll have to come out to the house sometime." Lexi linked her arm through Natalia's as they walked out of the parking lot. "We live on a lake. Ever been waterskiing?"

"No, I've never waterskied. I've gone snow skiing, though. Is it similar?"

"Not really." Lexi held open the door, and Natalia saw teens scrambling into classrooms and throwing their backpacks into lockers against the wall. "When you snow ski, you have to lean forward. In waterskiing, you lean back. But don't worry. I'm a great teacher. Aren't I, Addy?"

There was a story behind the looks the girls gave each other, but Natalia didn't have time to hear about it. As soon as they walked into Mrs. Stevenson's classroom, Natalia remembered the story Brian had told her, when he had fallen asleep and dreamed about algebraic equations.

You are not going to start thinking about him first thing, Natalia Lopez.

"Over here," Addy said as she found a top locker and

began unpacking the contents of her backpack. "There are three top lockers in a row. What are the chances of that?"

"Jesus loves me." Lexi opened the locker next to Addy. "Good thing you're my best friend. Come on now, Natalia. You better claim this one fast."

Natalia opened the locker and looked inside. *At least this is the same as back home.* She dug through her backpack to find the magnetic whiteboard she had purchased. She stuck it to the inside door, and Lexi grabbed the marker from her hand before she could snap it into place. Lexi pushed Natalia aside and wrote in huge letters: WELCOME TO TCS!!!

"There." Lexi returned the marker to its place. "Now you are officially welcomed."

The locker next to Natalia's opened, and she turned around.

"Hi, Natalia."

Spencer Adams. Natalia tried to turn back, but he stopped her with a hand to her shoulder. "We're neighbors. Isn't that a coincidence?"

"Yes, I suppose it is." Natalia stepped back as Spencer stepped closer to her. But she miscalculated and bumped into Lexi, who lost her balance and bumped into Addy.

Natalia turned around to apologize and found both girls falling to the ground. She tried to stop Lexi by giving her a hand. But Lexi, weighing about forty pounds more than Natalia, just pulled the lighter girl down with her. Before she knew it, Natalia was on the floor beside Lexi and Addy, the former laughing hysterically.

"Now *that's* how you begin a senior year, ladies." Lexi

stood and Natalia tried to do the same, hoping that, in her fall, she hadn't flashed anyone.

Spencer turned his broad smile on the girls. "Here, let me help you."

Lexi sat back down and held a hand out to him. "Why, certainly."

Spencer grunted as he heaved Lexi up, then put a hand out for Natalia. She scrambled to her feet in an attempt to avoid having to hold the boy's hand.

"Don't be shy." Spencer grabbed Natalia's arm and pulled her up.

"Senior year, Spencer." Lexi smiled at the dark-haired boy. "You ready for it?"

"Of course I'm ready." He waved Lexi aside and looked at Natalia. "You have any questions, just come to me."

He walked to his seat and Natalia watched as Lexi's eyes followed him. "Could I be you? Just for a day?"

"What?"

"To have Spencer Adams drooling over me. Just for a day. I could die happy."

Addy nudged her friend. "You can do so much better than Spencer."

Lexi raised her eyebrows. "Okay, Miss First Girlfriend. Whatever. I lose weight, get in shape. And does he notice? Do any of the boys notice? No. I'm still just plain old Lexi."

Lexi's skin was a beautiful caramel color, her hair was dark brown and curly, pulled into a tight ponytail. Her uniform hung loose on her, but Natalia could tell beneath that was a strong physique.

"I love fashion," Natalia said to Lexi. "And I've always

wanted to give someone a makeover. Head to toe—new clothes, new hair, new makeup."

"I'm listening." Lexi smiled.

"Would you let me make you over? We'll make you so stunning that Spencer will be dying to ask you out."

Lexi's grin widened. "You know what? You've got a deal."

Natalia shook Lexi's outstretched hand as the bell rang. Natalia followed Addy to a desk near the front when Brian rushed in the door.

"You're late." Mrs. Stevenson pointed to the clock above the lockers.

"Sorry." Brian ran to the back of the room, looking for a locker. "Truck wouldn't start. I had to get a ride from my mom."

"I'll let it slide today, but this better be the last time."

"Right." Spencer laughed. "How many demerits did you get last year for being tardy?"

Crouched down in the corner, Brian opened the only available locker. "I think it's time to start class, Spencer. Don't want to take up Mrs. Stevenson's time."

Natalia couldn't understand why Spencer would dislike Brian so much. *He's one of the nicest boys I've ever met.*

Mrs. Stevenson opened the class in prayer and then began discussing the student handbook. Natalia opened hers when she felt a tug on her hair.

"Hey," Brian whispered. His breath on her neck made the hair on her arms stand on end. "What's your schedule?"

Mrs. Stevenson glared at Brian, and Natalia no longer felt his presence behind her. She wanted him to lean forward again. *No, what am I thinking? Stop it.*

"Here's mine." Brian slipped a sheet of paper onto Natalia's desk.

Natalia looked down. They would have Bible, speech, and choir together. Natalia held up three fingers.

"Awesome."

Mrs. Stevenson stopped reading the handbook and looked at Brian. "Do you have something to share with the class, Mr. Younger?"

"Just that it's awesome to be a senior, ma'am."

Some of the kids in the class laughed, but Spencer and the guys around him simply rolled their eyes.

The day went by quickly. Natalia was excited about Bible class, and she seemed to be the only one not upset that Pastor Younger jumped right in with his first lecture that day. Her AP classes were going to be hard. Especially AP United States History. The class was filled with juniors, so none of her new friends were with her. *And what do I know about US history? Columbus, Washington, Lincoln. That's about it.* Her electives seemed easy enough. They were at the end of the day, and Brian was in both of them. Lexi and Addy were both in speech.

The final bell rang and Brian jumped from his seat in the back of the choir room to walk beside Natalia. "So how was the first day?"

"It was fine."

"Fine? That's it? Could you be more specific?"

Natalia smiled, trying to avoid brushing against Brian with her arm. The temptation was overwhelming. She remembered the school's No Physical Contact rule and justified her distance. *It's not because whenever I touch him my skin catches on fire. It's because I want to respect the rules of the school.*

"More specific? Like what?"

"Like how was this different from your school in Spain?" He held the door open for her as they walked toward the high school building.

"Students would never come late in Madrid." Natalia smiled at Brian. "And they wouldn't talk during class. And we'd have quite a bit of homework the first day."

"So we're lazy, obnoxious Americans, huh?"

She watched as Spencer walked toward her. "Some of you."

"Natalia." Spencer stood between her and Brian. "A bunch of us are headed to my place after school. And you are invited."

Natalia hated his tone, as if she should be honored to be among the chosen to come to his house. "Thanks, Spencer, but I'm going with Addy and Lexi to the Dream Cone."

"We've got ice cream at my house. The best. And tons of toppings. Come on."

Spencer obviously had little experience taking no for an answer.

"I hope you have a wonderful time, Spencer." Natalia turned her back on him and opened her locker. "I'll see you tomorrow."

Natalia looked down and noticed Brian's smile covered his face.

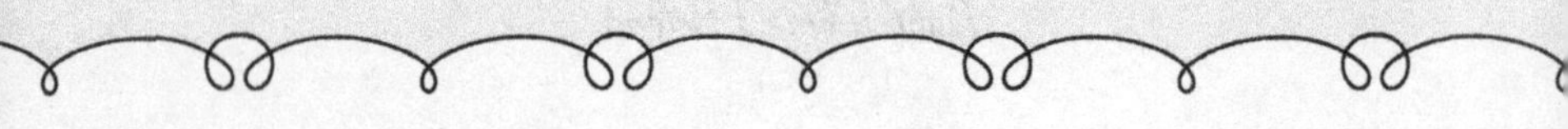

Chapter 23

"Your mother owns a boutique?" Natalia sat in the car and looked at Lexi. They were parked in front of an upscale clothing store, the window dressing sporting clothes straight out of Natalia's favorite fashion magazines.

"Yes." Lexi unbuckled and groaned. "But I've always been a tomboy. My older sister, Sheri, is the fashionista. She's always been the pretty one. My little sister, Mandi, is into art."

"So you can't be into fashion because your sister is into fashion?" Natalia opened the car door and followed Lexi to the shop.

"I've never really wanted to." Lexi shrugged. "You can't play basketball in high heels."

"Oh, Lexi." Natalia smiled. "You've been missing out on so much."

"Smile." Addy held up a camera and snapped a shot of Lexi and Natalia. "I'm making a photo documentary of your day. It'll be perfect for the yearbook."

"As long as you make sure there are as many pictures of me playing sports as there are of me getting a makeover," Lexi said.

"I'll do my best." Addy opened the door to the boutique, and Natalia breathed in the smell of new clothes.

"This place is great." Natalia looked around.

"Thank you." A beautiful Hispanic woman stepped out from behind the counter. Her name tag read "Sheri," and Lexi hadn't been exaggerating about her older sister.

"Hey, Sheri. Natalia is going to give me a makeover. She promises that the boys at school will fall all over themselves once they see the new me."

Natalia laughed. "I promised that?"

Addy snapped a picture.

Sheri put a hand on Lexi's shoulder. "I've been trying to get her out of these shorts and T-shirts for years. I can't wait to see the final product."

Natalia walked over to a rack and searched through the clothes.

"She needs everything, Natalia." Sheri joined her. "Dresses, pants, blouses. Buy as much as you want. It's on the house. Mom's going to be thrilled."

"Don't you have to go back to college soon?" Lexi stuck her tongue out at her sister.

"Not for another few weeks, sister dear. Maybe I should help."

"Not a chance." Lexi eyed her sister's neon shirt and skintight skirt. "I'd like to keep my eyesight and my circulation intact, thank you very much."

Sheri rolled her eyes and walked into the back.

"Seriously. I don't do ruffles, lace, tight, or bright."

Natalia pulled out a purple shirt she had found. "Lexi, you have to broaden your horizons. Ruffles are so in right now." Natalia pointed to the shirt layered in ruffles. "How cute is that?"

"I was thinking more along the lines of"—Lexi flipped through a stack of shirts and pulled out a plain tan camisole—"this."

"That would be perfect." Natalia grabbed the shirt and placed it behind the purple. "Under this."

"Addy, help me out here," Lexi begged her friend.

"You wanted this." Addy smiled.

Lexi groaned. "I'll try it. But I'm not making any promises."

Natalia found a pair of black jeans and sent Lexi into the changing room with the outfit. "Ooh, this too." Natalia handed a long, beaded necklace over the curtain.

"More stuff?" Lexi said. "Aren't the ruffles enough?"

"Of course not." Natalia threw a sundress over her arm and searched for bracelets to go with it.

"You're having way too much fun." Addy sat in a chair by the dressing room and shook her head.

"I love shopping." Natalia tried on a silver bracelet inlaid with jade. "This is how I spent my weekends back home."

The curtain pulled back and Lexi stepped out.

"Wow." Natalia twisted Lexi's shirt and pulled it down to her hips. "You look great."

"These jeans are too tight."

Natalia eyed the jeans. "They're perfect. Any bigger and they would be baggy."

"Exactly."

"Jeans aren't supposed to be baggy."

Lexi turned around and stared at herself in the full-length mirror. "It just feels so weird."

"Are you kidding? Perfect curves, great arms." Natalia stood next to Lexi. "Spencer won't be able to keep his eyes off you."

"Sold." Lexi smiled. "Are we done?"

"That's just one outfit." Natalia handed Lexi the sundress. "You need a whole wardrobe. Then we need shoes and makeup. We'll end with hair."

"Can't we do this in baby steps?" Lexi shut the curtain. "Clothes today, shoes next Saturday, makeup the next—"

"Spencer's back-to-school party is tonight," Natalia said. "You're going to walk in there and wow him."

Lexi sighed through the curtain. "Maybe this isn't worth it."

"Of course it is."

"You're just saying that because you want to keep shopping." Lexi threw the shirt and jeans over the curtain rod. "Just take these to the counter."

Natalia walked the outfit to Sheri, who smiled her approval. Whispering, she said, "Mom and I have been trying to get her to do this for years. I don't know how you managed it, but thanks."

Natalia smiled at Sheri and walked off in search of a casual outfit to replace Lexi's basketball shorts and worn T-shirts.

At the end of the day, Lexi had five new outfits, a bag full of jewelry, red highlights in her brown hair, and she was wearing eyeliner for the first time in her life. Natalia put the finishing touches on Lexi's outfit before walking her to the full-length mirror in Addy's bathroom.

Addy put the camera down, her eyes wide. "Wow, Lex. You look incredible."

Lexi wore a silky floral tank top. The browns and creams in the shirt perfectly suited her new hair. Her makeup was understated but added just the right touch of sophistication.

"Your eyes seem huge," Natalia noted.

Lexi shook her now-tamed curls and smiled. "I never thought I'd wear anything like this." She turned around and gazed at herself in the cream pants and brown heels. "But I sure do look good. Addy, you better take a few more pictures. This is definitely going on my Facebook page."

Addy laughed and did as she was told. "We'd better head out."

"I can't believe we're going to Spencer Adams's back-to-school party." Lexi took one last glance in the mirror before walking out. "We never get invited to this."

"Really?" Natalia asked.

"We're not exactly the 'in' crowd," Lexi said. "Or we weren't until Miss Addy here got herself on TV. And now that we have you and my brand-new made-over self, we may just make ourselves the new in crowd."

Addy laughed as she walked her friends into the garage and clicked the door open. "It's just a party."

"It's Spencer Adams's party." Lexi raised her eyebrows.

"Since when are you so into Spencer?" Addy waited as the girls got settled into her car.

"Years." Lexi buckled up. "But you had a crush on him, so I didn't say anything."

"You liked Spencer, Addy?" Natalia asked.

"Of course she did." Lexi smirked at the blushing Addy. "Not that she ever did anything about it. But it doesn't matter now. She's got Jonathon, and I am finally free to crush on Spencer to my heart's content."

Twenty minutes later the girls pulled into Spencer's circular driveway. The house was enormous. Huge white pillars supported a three-story entryway. A brass chandelier hung above the door. Lights lined the long walkway from the driveway to the entry and music blared from the backyard.

"I don't know if I can do this." Lexi shrank down in her seat.

Natalia reached over the backseat and squeezed Lexi's shoulder. "Your outside matches your inside. Fierce and beautiful. Go show Spencer what he's been missing out on."

Natalia didn't say she wished they would all change their minds and go back home. She loved giving Lexi a makeover. But she didn't love huge crowds, and she hated all the attention she was given for being the new girl.

Not to mention, Brian won't be here. He had invited Natalia for dinner that evening with his family and him. Natalia was relieved to say no. Being around him so much was not good for her. But she hated the disappointment in his eyes when she told him she would be going to this party.

The girls made their way to the large mahogany door and rang the doorbell. Its chime was loud and deep, and the door was opened by a maid wearing the traditional black and white ensemble. Used to fancy parties, Natalia felt at home with the formality that greeted her. Looking to her side, she noted that her friends didn't seem nearly as comfortable.

"The guests are in the back." The maid pointed down the marble hallway. That opened up to a formal living room decorated in so much white, it made Natalia's head hurt. Glass doors opened to reveal a lush backyard and a white tent that covered a dance floor. The DJ stood at the end, his large headphones covering his ears.

"Let's get this party started," the DJ yelled into the microphone. Dozens of teens spilled onto the dance floor and began moving together to a song Natalia had never heard.

"Natalia." Spencer walked over to the threesome. He looked like a model in his striped button-down shirt and expensive jeans. Natalia turned her gaze on Lexi, hoping Spencer would do the same.

"You have a beautiful home, Spencer." Natalia smiled at him.

"This is nothing." His smile widened. "We're renovating a mansion right on Tampa Bay. It's going to be spectacular. It should be ready by homecoming."

"That's where Brian Younger worked this summer, right? He told me about it."

"He just helped with the demolition." Spencer's smile faded. "I think it was good for him to spend his summer doing something constructive for a change."

"You mean other than being involved in ministries at the church?" Addy leveled her gaze at the young man.

"Forget about him. Tonight is about us. Come on and dance." Spencer held a hand out to Natalia.

"No, thank you. I don't know these dances. I'd rather watch. I think Lexi would like to dance, though."

Spencer looked at Lexi. *Finally,* Natalia thought. His eyes widened. "Lookin' good, Lexi."

Her face split into a grin. "Thanks."

"I'd better get back to the party. Sure you don't want to dance, Natalia?"

She wanted to walk out right then. "No, I don't believe I will."

He shrugged and made his way back to his friends. Those boys glanced from Natalia to Spencer and back again.

"I'm so sorry." Natalia saw Lexi deflate beside her. That girl was crushed. But she smiled and grabbed Addy's and Natalia's arms.

"There's a chocolate fountain over there." Lexi pointed. "I love chocolate fountains. Let's go."

"Addy!" Several girls intercepted Natalia and her friends.

"Tiffany." Addy smiled. "Nice to see you."

"So I've never gotten to hear the whole story about your TV show and the president's son, and I have been dying."

A chorus of "me too's" followed, and Natalia could tell Addy felt trapped.

"You guys go ahead." Addy waved them on. "I'll catch up later."

"Ah, the trials of being a star." Lexi laughed as the pair walked to the chocolate fountain.

"Is it very hard for her?" Natalia picked up a strawberry and held it beneath the flowing layers of chocolate.

Lexi took a bite of her chocolate-covered banana. "Hard, yes, but totally a God-thing."

"A God-thing?"

"You know, something you aren't looking for and don't expect but ends up being amazing."

Natalia thought of her move to Tampa. It wasn't something she was looking for and she certainly didn't expect it. The amazing part hadn't come yet, though.

"Lexi?" A boy in jeans and a purple shirt stood over them. His brown hair hung straight over his forehead, and his hazel eyes were wide. "You look great. W-would you like to dance?"

Lexi peered at Natalia, who winked her permission.

"Are you sure? I hate to leave you."

"I've got the chocolate fountain." Natalia smiled. "I'll be fine."

Natalia bit back a laugh as Lexi stood to join her partner. The boy was at least four inches shorter than Lexi. But as he led her onto the dance floor, neither seemed to mind.

"Nobody sits alone at my party." Spencer walked up to Natalia and folded his arms across his chest. "And they sure can't look bored. Come on, I'd like to introduce you to my dad. He's in the library."

Natalia knew she wasn't being given a choice.

Spencer opened the sliding glass door that led back into the white room, then opened a door at the side of the room. The library was just that—wall-to-wall, floor-to-ceiling bookcases, hardwood floors, leather couches and chairs.

"This is lovely." Natalia breathed in the smell of luxury. She missed that smell.

"Thank you." A small Hispanic woman stood up from one of the couches. She was very thin and incredibly beautiful.

Natalia was sure parts of that woman's face and body had been enhanced by a doctor. But that wasn't unusual among the wealthy. Her own mother benefited greatly from the plastic surgeon's "magic," as she called it. "I'm Gabriella Adams, Spencer's stepmother. You must be Natalia. We've heard so much about you."

Mrs. Adams's perfume was sweet and strong, and Natalia's eyes watered as she leaned in to greet the woman. "You have a lovely home. It is very kind of you to host this party."

"Anything for our boy." A man Natalia assumed was Mr. Adams stood. He was almost as wide as he was tall, and Natalia marveled at the disparity between husband and wife. Mr. Adams stuck out his hand and Natalia shook it. "I did a little research on you, Natalia. Your father is Oscar Lopez, correct?"

The surprise on Natalia's face must have shown because he continued immediately. "Don't look so worried. I've been planning to expand my business into Europe. I could use some advice from someone as knowledgeable about international business as Oscar Lopez. He's a legend."

Natalia stood still. She was sure one positive aspect of moving to Florida was that her identity could be her own. She'd spent seventeen years as "Oscar Lopez's daughter." *Five thousand miles away, and I'm still living in his shadow.*

"Who knows." Mr. Adams lit a cigar and sat back down. "Maybe we can even get you over to Spain to do an internship with Mr. Lopez, son. Wouldn't that be impressive on your résumé?"

Natalia gazed over and horror spread across Spencer's

face. She knew that look. That was something her father would say, and something she would hate hearing. Maybe she and Spencer had more in common than she thought.

"I need to get back to my guests." Spencer grabbed Natalia's arm, harder than necessary, and led her back into the white room. Once the door to the library was shut, Spencer stopped. "I'm sorry about that, Natalia. I didn't introduce you to them because I wanted to work for your father. I didn't even know anything about him."

The embarrassment on his face was genuine and, for the first time, Natalia felt sorry for the young man. "It's all right. My father would have probably done the same thing. He used to negotiate business deals when we'd go on vacation." *Back when we actually went on vacation together.*

"With anybody, right?" Spencer laughed. "The guy in the suite next to yours? On the same snorkeling expedition?"

"Exactly."

"I hate it." Spencer sat on the white couch and Natalia joined him.

"I used to wish my father was a postal worker or a bus driver."

"I wanted Dad to be a lawn guy." Spencer laughed.

"Really?"

"Sure." Spencer's eyes lit up. "We have crews come and take care of our yard, and they'd always bring their kids. It seemed like so much fun." Spencer cleared his throat. "Of course, they barely make enough to pay the bills, so it was silly to think that."

"I don't know." Natalia looked back at the library door. Like her father, Spencer's dad didn't come through to make things right or talk about what happened. "I have been reading through Proverbs, and there's an awful lot in there about how it's better to be poor and happy than rich and unhappy."

"I'd like rich and happy." Spencer laughed. But Natalia could see the sadness behind his eyes.

"Hey, man, you gonna come out and join your party?" One of the boys from the senior class poked his head in the open sliding glass door. Noticing Natalia sitting beside Spencer, he smiled. "Oh, excuse me. I guess you're working on a party of your own."

Natalia rose, upset at this boy's suggestion. "I'd better go find my friends."

Spencer's eyes were sad. "Sure. I guess I'd better go too."

Spencer followed his friend out the door. Spencer's life wasn't as perfect as he'd like everyone to believe.

Chapter 24

"So what'd you think about chapel?" Brian plopped his Spider-Man lunch box beside Natalia and opened it.

The cafeteria was buzzing, and Natalia was still trying to take in all she had heard that morning. Students talked about last year's mission trip to Costa Rica. The pictures and the stories were so moving. She longed to be part of what they were doing there. "It was great."

"But?"

Natalia nibbled at her sandwich. "I've never been on a mission trip. I'm a little scared."

"Perfectly normal," Brian said, his mouth full of Fritos. "But don't let that stop you."

Spencer nodded toward her from the other side of the cafeteria. She returned it with a wave.

"He's going, you know." Brian didn't sound excited about that.

"He's not as bad as you think." Natalia watched Spencer sit with his friends.

"You had a good time at his party?"

"Sure."

"Natalia, it's all right if you like Spencer." Brian's eyes searched hers. "Shoot, if I were a girl, I'd probably have a crush on him too."

Natalia's heart hurt at the expression in Brian's eyes. "I don't like him. But we do have a lot in common. I think we could be friends."

"Seriously." Brian played with the lock on his lunch box. "It's okay."

"I'm not interested in Spencer or in anyone. I'm not going to date."

"In high school?"

"Ever."

"What?" Brian's eyes were wide.

"The Bible talks about how some people are called to be single." Natalia's voice sounded more confident than she felt. "I think I'm one of them."

"Why?"

Images of Maureen sprawled out on the couch crying and pictures from e-mails her father had sent with him and Fiancée Number Four parasailing in Fiji filled her mind. *That's why*, she wanted to say. But she couldn't.

"I'm sorry," Brian said. "Nothing wrong with being single."

Natalia gazed at Brian, his crystal blue eyes so caring. His adorable crooked smile and the red curls that always seemed to have a mind of their own. "Nothing wrong at all."

Lexi and Addy sat across the table from Brian and Natalia. Lexi was disappointed that Spencer didn't notice her at the party. When Natalia returned from the library with Spencer, Lexi's face had fallen. Natalia tried to tell her new friend that it meant nothing. And Lexi enjoyed the evening, dancing and joking with the other students. But Lexi's hair was back up in a ponytail today, and her face was once again makeup free. Natalia was sure the new clothes Lexi got were relegated to the back corner of her closet.

"You're going on the trip, right?" Lexi asked, spearing her Parmesan chicken.

"I was just talking to her about that."

"Great minds think alike." Lexi smiled at Brian and stole a roll from his plate.

They would be perfect together. They're both fun, they love God, they're down-to-earth. Natalia had hit on a great idea. *So why do I hate the thought of Brian dating another girl? He's not mine. He can't be.*

"I was too scared to go last year." Addy looked up from her plate. "But I'm stepping out of my comfort zone and going this year."

"It's amazing," Lexi said, her mouth full. "Not to mention we get a whole week off school."

"And the teachers don't give us homework that week." Brian winked.

"But Costa Rica . . . I don't know."

"Says the girl from Spain." Lexi eyed Natalia and everyone at the table laughed.

"Pray about it," Addy said.

"But pray for an answer soon." Brian nudged her shoulder. "The last day to sign up is Friday."

The entire lunchroom turned toward the sudden sound of a door slamming and a teacher yelling.

Maureen.

"I said Friday, and I meant Friday." Maureen's normally soft voice was turned all the way up. The door leading from the cafeteria into the senior hallway was open, making it even more of a spectator sport.

Mumbles rolled out from the offending student.

"I don't care about your volleyball game," Maureen continued to shout. Mrs. Stevenson stood from the teacher's table and rushed into the hallway. "If you don't turn that paper in, you won't even be on the team."

Natalia watched, along with everyone else in the high school, as Mrs. Stevenson put an arm around Maureen and guided her into Maureen's classroom. Karen, the girl Maureen had been scolding, walked into the lunchroom.

Natalia excused herself and headed outside. Too many eyes were on her—some sad, others angry. She had to get away.

The door opened and Spencer entered. "You okay?"

Natalia nodded, willing herself not to cry. "She has been having a hard time lately. She didn't mean it. Maureen is normally a very nice lady."

"I totally know what you mean." Spencer sat next to her at the picnic table. "My stepmom gets really angry when she's stressed. Last week she had a fit at the maid because she washed the sheets with the wrong detergent. You would have thought poor Maribel had committed a crime the way Gabriella was yelling at her."

"I'm sorry."

"It's fine." Spencer waved his hand. "She was just worked up about the party. Whenever we have one, she goes into Nazi mode. But then it's over and she gets back to normal."

Natalia wished things were that simple with Maureen.

They'd been back for over a month, and Maureen's depression had only worsened.

"How about if I take you out for ice cream after school?" He leaned toward Natalia. "To cheer you up?"

"Thanks, Spencer." She smiled. "I have to work on that history paper, though."

"I could help you." His brown eyes locked on Natalia's.

"I had better work on it by myself. I typically don't study well with others."

"That's because you've never studied with me." Spencer's perfect smile seemed genuine. But Natalia knew she would be needed at home.

The bell rang, signaling the end of their lunch period. "I need to get to speech class. I'll see you tomorrow."

As Natalia made her way back to class, she saw Karen sitting with a group of friends. Some were girls from Spencer's party, girls who had made her feel very welcome. Those same girls were now looking at her like she had the plague. She understood. Their friend was hurt. *By my stepmother.*

The walk to class seemed to take forever. *Maybe I should go. School hasn't even started in Spain. I could fly back this weekend and still make it in time for the first day of school. Carmen would be thrilled.*

The more she thought about it, the more right the whole idea seemed. She had come here and helped Maureen make the initial transition. There was nothing more Natalia could do. She obviously wasn't really helping her stepmother. And that was the whole reason she had come.

If I'm not needed either place, I would much rather not be needed back home. Spain, here I come.

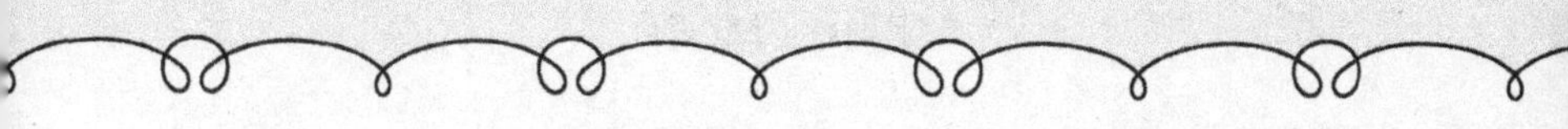

Chapter 25

"Thank you, Brian." Victor placed the hard hat on his head and grabbed a hammer from the toolbox. "This job is very fun. I like to tear down buildings."

Mr. King had offered Brian weekend work gutting an office building in St. Petersburg. With James back at school, Mr. King needed another worker. Victor was still looking for a job, and Brian was glad to put his name in as James's replacement.

"I'm happy to help." Brian pulled a nail from the drywall. "We have to get all of these out, then we get to do the fun stuff."

Victor stood beside Brian and worked quietly. For about a minute. "Natalia, she look very sad last night."

Brian had been trying to get that girl out of his head all day. *Thanks for ruining that, man.* "Her stepmother is having a hard time. Natalia is the kind of person who wants to solve everyone's problems. I think she's frustrated she can't make Mrs. Lopez feel better."

"You think about her a lot?" Victor smiled at Brian.

"Why would you say that?" Brian didn't think he was that obvious.

"You like her." Victor tapped his head. "Victor knows. I was a young man once. Long ago. Pretty girls, they get stuck in your head."

"Natalia is just a friend."

"A pretty friend you like to think about." Victor wrenched a nail from the wall.

Brian shook his head. "She's not interested in me." Brian thought back to yesterday, when Spencer followed Natalia out to the picnic table. Brian had stood to do the same, but he was too late. The pair sat there until the bell rang. Natalia was probably pouring her heart out to Spencer. She didn't need Brian.

"She look at you." Victor turned his brown eyes toward Brian. "I see it. When you don't look, she does."

Brian pulled harder than necessary and fell backward, the nail flying across the room. He landed on the hard concrete with a thud.

"You okay?" Victor held out a hand to help Brian up.

"Got a little carried away."

"Thinking about Natalia." Victor winked.

"All right, men." Mr. King returned from his midmorning coffee run. Brian was sure the man downed a gallon of the black stuff every day. Brian, on the other hand, had given up on it the first day. "Looking good in here. Let's see if we can't get this drywall down by nightfall, huh?"

Brian glanced around the room. There was a lot of work ahead of them. The three worked steadily until lunch, when Mr. King treated them to sub sandwiches and chips. Brian was putting the last bite in his mouth when a familiar voice drifted in.

"Diversify your portfolio. That's the key to wealth management, son." Mr. Adams waddled in, Spencer behind him. Both men were dressed in jeans and button-down shirts.

"Mr. Adams." Mr. King stood, wiped his hands on his pants, and held it out to the elder Mr. Adams. "I didn't expect you here today."

Brian exchanged a tight-lipped smile with Spencer. "I didn't know this building was yours." *Or I might not have agreed to work here.*

"I'm having it renovated as an investment property," Mr. Adams said. "We'll fix it up and rent it out. Great location. I'm sure we won't have a hard time finding a renter."

"Of course."

Spencer walked up to Brian. "Nice hat."

Brian patted the hard hat. "What's under here is priceless. Gotta protect it."

"Priceless. Right. And how'd you do on that English test yesterday?" Spencer knew Brian had gotten a C.

"We don't want to take up too much of your time." Mr. Adams walked around the room. The effort caused him to break out in a sweat. "I just wanted to show my boy here. Got to get him ready to go into business, know the ropes. I'm trying to hook him up with the new girl at school so he can get an internship with her dad's company."

Spencer's face turned red. "Dad, I told you I don't want to do that to her."

Brian's stomach clenched at the plea in Spencer's voice. *He really likes her.*

"It's a great opportunity." Mr. Adams shrugged. "For you and for him. I can bring him a lot of business. I've tried to contact him, but his secretary says he's out of town for an extended vacation."

Brian had never talked to Natalia about her parents. What were they like? What kind of childhood did she have? Did she miss her parents? He felt guilty for not thinking of these things sooner. All he could think about when he was around her was how pretty she was. *But she needs a friend, not another guy drooling over her.*

"Spencer, see if you can get Natalia to give you her dad's cell number."

Spencer's eyes closed.

"He'll thank you." Mr. Adams put an arm around his son. "She may too."

"Dad." Spencer sighed.

"We'll talk about it over dinner, all right?" Mr. Adams guided Spencer to the entrance. "Gary's Steakhouse?"

Brian looked at the door as the pair exited. Gary's Steakhouse was one of the most expensive restaurants in town. *And they go there like it's no big deal. We go once a year—maybe.* Natalia's life had to be like that. She had no idea what Brian's world was like. *What makes me think she'd even really want to be friends? Maybe Spencer is better for her all around.*

Brian was glad to be able to start pulling down the drywall. He surprised even Mr. King with the force with which he tore into it.

Unfortunately no amount of external destruction could calm his internal turmoil.

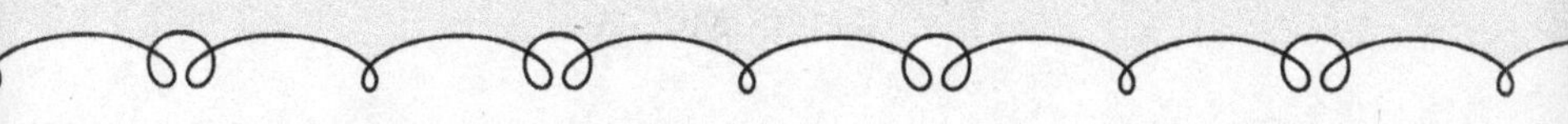

Chapter 26

Natalia stared at the computer screen.

The computer screen. Her father didn't even bother to return her phone call.

Natalia,

My daughter does not give up. Your stepmother needs you. And you need this year. It is good for your résumé. It is much easier to get into an American university when you have a degree from an American high school. Think about your future. Victoria and I are going to spend another week in Australia, then we will come back and we will start our new life at home. She needs some time to adjust to that. I'm coming to New York on business in a couple of months. You can come up and join me. If you still want to come home, we can talk about it then.

Papa

Natalia slammed her laptop shut. She couldn't even go home. Her father didn't want her. Her mother had been offered a more lucrative position at a new television station in Barcelona. She had written to say that since Natalia had moved away, she decided she would too. But Natalia could visit when she came home.

Right. Because Barcelona is right around the corner from Madrid.

Carmen's family would let Natalia stay with them. But where? They had a spacious apartment, but no one left a room open so a friend whose parents had no time for her could live with them.

Natalia threw herself down on the bed and cried. Her parents were too busy for her. Her stepmother was too depressed to notice her. Her friends were moving on. Even Carmen's e-mails and phone calls were slowing down. Her life went on without Natalia in it. And her friends here . . . Addy and Lexi were great, but they already had such a close bond. Natalia felt like she was interfering in their friendship. They were just being nice, letting Natalia hang out with them.

Her phone rang and she wiped her eyes. Brian's name scrolled across the phone's face.

"Hello?"

"Natalia?" Brian's voice sounded unsure. "I'm sorry to bother you. But my dad insisted I call and invite you over to lunch after church tomorrow. I understand if you're busy, but—"

"No, I'm not busy." Natalia tried to convince herself that she was excited simply because she would get to ask the pastor some questions. "I'd love to have lunch with your family."

"Really?" Natalia could picture Brian's smile. "I'll meet you after the service. Maureen can come too, of course."

Natalia swallowed past the lump in her throat before speaking. "I don't think she wants to be seen right now."

"Why?"

"Were you in the cafeteria on Thursday?"

"Oh, that."

"She refused to go back to school Friday, refused to answer Mr. Lawrence's phone calls. She is sure he's going to fire her."

"He's not going to fire her." Brian's tone didn't match his words.

"What are you not telling me?"

Brian's sigh punctuated the silence. "Karen Jordan's parents are the type who get angry if someone looks at their daughter the wrong way."

Natalia recalled the way Maureen screamed at Karen, humiliating the tenth grader in front of the entire high school. "So they are pretty upset, then?"

"That's a nice way to say it. But we all understand Maureen just made a mistake. My dad and Mr. Lawrence are on her side."

"But?"

"But she'll probably get an earful from the Jordans."

"Great." That was the last thing her stepmother needed.

"Maureen really should come tomorrow. We're a lot of fun. She can get her mind off all this. She doesn't need to sit around and feel sorry for herself."

Natalia wanted to tell him that's all Maureen did. But she didn't want to burden him with her sad stories.

"Just ask her." Brian cleared his throat. "So what did you do today?"

"Nothing, really."

"Nothing? On a Saturday. That's terrible."

"I don't have the most active social life, you know," Natalia said. "Addy is visiting her friend Kara, and Lexi went on a weekend trip with her dad."

"You need to do something fun so you have something to tell them on Monday."

"I do have something fun. I'm having dinner with the pastor and his family tomorrow."

"Dinner with my family cannot be the highlight of your weekend." Brian paused before continuing. "Tell you what, how about I pick you up and take you someplace?"

"But it's almost eight o'clock." Natalia looked at her alarm clock. "That's late for you Americans."

"What is that supposed to mean?" He didn't bother to disguise the mocking tone in his voice.

"The malls close at nine. There's nothing to do here at night."

"You live here a month and think you know everything. Just get dressed. Put on some jeans and lots of bug spray. I'll pick you up in fifteen minutes."

Natalia loved the idea of getting out of the house. But she worried about getting out with Brian. Would he get the wrong idea? Would she?

"And I know what you're thinking," Brian interrupted Natalia's thoughts. "But it's not a date. So no funny business, all right? I'm hard to resist, I know. But it's for your own good."

Natalia did not want Brian to know how close to the truth he was, so she played along with his joke. "Very well, sir. If you insist."

Natalia hung up the phone and skipped to her closet.

What to wear for a night out on a nondate with a guy she was far too attracted to for her own good? She rifled through her jeans, trying to find the baggiest pair. Then she pulled out a plain blue shirt. No frills, nothing that could be considered attractive.

"Maureen?" Natalia knocked on her stepmother's door. She had barely come out for the past two days. "I'm going out for a little bit. Is that all right?"

"Sure." Maureen's voice was soft. Tired.

Natalia wished Maureen would at least ask where she was going and with whom. *Sure, she trusts me.* But Maureen's lack of concern went beyond trust. If something didn't change soon, Natalia would have to call for help. Maureen couldn't go on like this.

The doorbell rang right as Natalia was covering herself with bug spray kept in the garage.

"Hi, Brian. Sorry it took me so long."

Brian coughed. "I think you're safe from the bugs. I don't know if I'll even survive being in the same truck as you."

"Those mosquitoes you have here are awful." Natalia folded her arms as Brian pretended to be gasping for air.

"Hey, you're one of us now. They are *our* mosquitoes."

Natalia loved the way that sounded. If only she felt as if she belonged.

"All right, hop in the truck. I promise to have you back by eleven."

"Excellent." Natalia smiled. "Where are we going?"

"Wait and see." Brian walked to Natalia's side of the truck and opened the door for her. She lifted herself into the truck and sat as Brian made his way back to the driver's side. His cologne permeated the air in the vehicle, and it smelled wonderful.

No. We are friends. He's just taking me out because I haven't had anything to do all day. Nothing more.

The door groaned as Brian opened it and sat down. Natalia tried to force her heart not to race when she looked at Brian's profile. So kind. So handsome. *So not for you.*

Brian drove outside of the city, beyond where there were even streetlights.

"Good thing I trust you, Brian Younger."

"I like the way you say that. 'Brian Yung-ah.' So proper."

Natalia wanted to tell him she liked the way he said her name, the easy way it rolled off his tongue. But she couldn't. He might get the wrong idea.

"Almost there." Brian pulled off onto a dirt road that led into the woods.

"All right, seriously. Where are you taking me?"

Brian pointed to a tall structure directly in front of them. "There."

"What is it?" Dusk had set in, so the structure seemed to blend into the surroundings.

"It's an old lookout tower." Brian opened his door and walked around to her side. Natalia had never experienced such gentlemanly behavior. She found it quite enjoyable. She jumped out of the truck, and Brian reached into the glove compartment to pull out a small flashlight. "It'll get dark quick out here."

Natalia looked up. The tower was wooden and very tall. Steps wound around the circular base all the way to the top, which had a walkway all around it.

"Is this safe?" Natalia was sure the structure was several decades old.

"Of course." Brian clicked his flashlight on and shone it on the ground in front of them. "This is the place I go when I need some one-on-one time with God."

"You come all the way out here to pray?" Natalia followed Brian on the steep stairs.

"You'll see why soon."

Natalia felt herself getting winded halfway up. They were already above the tree level. And there were still many more steps to climb.

Brian stepped to the side when they reached the top so Natalia could stand at the rail and look out. The full moon cast a silvery glow on the trees, and out in the distance was a river, its still waters reflecting the moon and framing it with plants Natalia had never seen before.

"This is lovely."

"I know." Brian leaned on the rail next to her. "My dad brought me here for the first time about three years ago. I had just hurt my knee pretty badly. Dad actually had to half carry me up these stairs."

"Oh no." Natalia looked at Brian. "What happened?"

"I was really into martial arts. Used to compete and everything."

"I thought you weren't athletic?"

"Most people at school didn't know. I always said I wouldn't play school sports because I wasn't any good."

"Why didn't you want people to know about your martial arts?"

Brian shrugged. "Being a pastor's kid, I get watched

in everything I do. People are always expecting so much from us. But in martial arts, I was just Brian. No one knew who my dad was or where I went to school. It was nice. I wanted to keep it like that."

"What happened?"

"I blew my knee out, doing something stupid."

"What?"

"I was playing around with some buddies before class, flipped one of them over, and my knee just ripped apart."

"That's terrible."

"You're not kidding." Brian blew out a long breath. "Just like that, my martial arts days were over."

"Couldn't you go back after your knee healed?"

"No." Brian looked out at the river. "Doctor's orders. I was so angry."

"I can imagine."

"That was the one thing in life I really loved, and God had to go and take that away from me too."

"You were mad at God?" Brian always seemed so confident in his relationship with God.

"You bet I was. Furious. I'd sit in church and stare at the baptistery. Refused to listen to the sermons. I told Dad he could ground me, spank me, do whatever he wanted. But I was done with God."

"What did your dad say?"

"Nothing." Brian smiled. "He brought me out here. I thought it was my punishment, that he was going *Survivorman* on me and I'd have to find my way home."

Natalia laughed. "But that wasn't it?"

"No. He took me up here and had me stand right there and said, 'What do you see?'"

"And then what?"

"You have to answer that." Brian turned his blues eyes toward her. "What do you see?"

Natalia forced her gaze away from Brian. "Trees, a river, birds, plants, mosquitoes."

Brian aimed his flashlight down to a path directly below the tower. "See that trail?"

Natalia's eyes adjusted to the light. When they did, she saw the slight trail, snaking its way through the forest and to the river, where it ended at a dock. A small boat was tied to the dock. She leaned forward to see where the river went from there. "Is that the ocean?"

"Very good." Brian smiled. "It's hard to see when it's dark. I'll bring you back sometime during the day. It's much more obvious. But, yes, that's the ocean."

"Amazing."

"But you don't see any of that from down there." Brian once again pointed his flashlight to the trail below them. "When you're there, it's just a bunch of trees. And if you've never been on that trail, you might think it just goes deeper into the woods."

"I doubt I would even get on that trail if I hadn't been up here. It would seem frightening, just walking into the forest."

"That's what I said."

"And your dad?"

"He said our lives are like this. God puts us on paths that sometimes seem very dark and pointless. Sometimes it seems like there's no way out. And a lot of people get upset at that, and so they get off his path and go off on their own."

"But when they do that, they miss what is waiting for them at the end." Natalia thought of her desire to leave Tampa, of Maureen's desire to hide away until the pain was over.

Brian pointed to the ocean. "Through the woods, onto the river, and then into the ocean. From there, you can go anywhere. Possibilities are limitless."

A tear fell down her cheek. "But first, you have to get through the forest."

Brian stepped closer to Natalia so their shoulders were touching. "That's right. And sometimes, getting through the forest seems almost impossible."

"That's why we need to trust God." Natalia looked around. "He sees what we don't."

"You catch on quick." Brian nudged Natalia.

"So you brought me up here to give me a sermon?"

"No sermon." Brian laughed. "Not me. But I did think you might benefit from what my dad taught me that day."

"I did." Natalia took in a deep breath. The scent of the forest was fresh and clean, tinged with a bit of the salty sea air. God knew everything. He had a purpose for everything. She just needed to trust him and keep walking through the wilderness. The end may not be in her sight, but it was definitely in his.

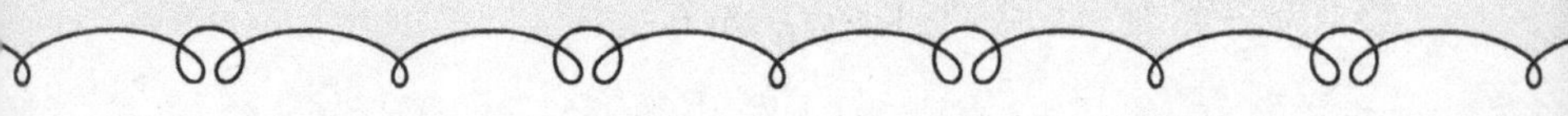

Chapter 27

"And this is Brian when he played one of the wise men in the children's Christmas pageant." Mrs. Younger pointed to a picture in the ornately decorated scrapbook. Five-year-old Brian's red hair was plastered to his head, and he wore a dark blue robe and a deep scowl.

"Mom, please." Brian put a hand over the picture. "Don't you need to work on lunch?"

Mrs. Younger laughed and turned the page. Little Brian was between his two older sisters, standing in front of the church Christmas tree. The robe was off but the scowl was still there. "He hated having his picture taken."

"Seriously, Mom." Brian's face was turning red. Natalia couldn't imagine why he would be embarrassed. His parents adored him. His mother spent hours putting together scrapbooks like this so she could remember every moment of his childhood.

"Brittany and Brigit are working on lunch." Mrs. Younger waved Brian away. "Why don't you join them?"

He sighed and stood, defeated. "At least promise me you'll skip past the bathtub shots."

Mrs. Younger didn't look up. "Go work on lunch, dear. Your sisters need you."

"You have a beautiful family." Natalia gazed at a page with the family standing together on the beach.

"I am blessed." Mrs. Younger smiled.

"Your daughters are both in college, right?"

"Brittany will be a senior, and Brigit is a sophomore."

"What are they studying?"

"Brittany is majoring in elementary education." Mrs. Younger looked at Natalia, her eyes mirror images of Brian's, clear, blue, and caring. "She wants to teach kindergarten."

Natalia marveled at the pride in his mother's face.

"And Brigit?"

"Brigit wants to go into the medical field, but she can't decide if she wants to be a doctor or a nurse."

"I'm sure you and Pastor Brian are hoping she'll be a doctor." Natalia's father would be thrilled if she were considering a career as a doctor.

Mrs. Younger shrugged. "We've always told our kids we want them to do what God wants them to do. If he wants Brigit to be a nurse, then that's what we want for her."

Natalia stared down at the photos. Parents who love each other and love God and who want their children to do what God wants them to do. "Your children are fortunate."

"What about you?" Mrs. Younger smiled into Natalia's eyes. "Do you know what God wants you to do?"

Natalia sighed. "No, but my father expects me to make that decision very soon."

"Really? Why is that?"

"Papa has a five-year plan for everything. He expects me to do the same. He is not happy that I am a few months from graduating and I don't know what I am going to do next."

"Sometimes God only reveals his will one day at a time." Mrs. Younger patted Natalia's arm.

Natalia turned a page in the scrapbook. Pastor Brian's smile beamed as he stood in the baptistery with little Brian. "Unfortunately, my father does not believe in God."

"That must be difficult for you."

Her soft words touched a place in Natalia's heart that she worked hard to keep hidden. She closed her eyes against the tears that threatened to spill out.

Mrs. Younger placed a gentle arm around Natalia shoulder. "We are praying for you, dear."

"Thank you." Natalia hated the weakness she felt, hated needing to be comforted.

"Soup's on." Brian emerged from the kitchen.

"What kind of soup will we be having?" Natalia sat up and pasted on a smile, relieved for the interruption.

He laughed as he led Natalia into the dining room. "Sorry. It's a saying. It just means that dinner is ready."

Natalia sat down at the table. Brian's sisters laid out the meal—roast beef with vegetables, biscuits, and a salad.

"I don't think we've been formally introduced, Natalia," the older of Brian's sisters said. "Of course, Brian talks about you so much, I already feel like you're part of the family."

The glare Brian shot at his sister caused Natalia to laugh. She had never seen him anything but jovial.

"Anyway, I'm Brittany." Winking in her brother's

direction, she held a hand out to Natalia. "It's nice to meet you."

"I'm Brigit." Brian's other sister had a quiet voice and more reserved demeanor, like her mother. Brigit was Natalia's height, with blondish brown hair and Brian's eyes. Brittany's hair was red, but not as vibrant a red as her brother had. Both girls had their mother's fair skin and nose that turned up slightly at the end. They were adorable young women.

"I'm happy to meet you both."

"You're right, Brian." Brittany flashed a smile. "She does have a cute accent."

He pulled out a chair for Natalia, elbowing Brittany in the process. "Oh, so sorry, sis."

"All right, you two." Pastor Brian sat at the head of the table. "Enough fighting. You're going to frighten our guest."

"Please excuse my big-mouthed sister," Brian said quietly.

"I heard that." Brittany leaned across the table. "I'm sorry, but I just can't help myself. You're the first girl Brian's ever brought home."

"Natalia is here because she'd like to talk to Dad about apologetics."

Natalia was sure the glare Brian gave to Brittany would melt the butter sitting in front of her.

"And I am so glad we could finally do that. Most of my students don't want to talk about Bible class outside of school."

"Oh, Pastor Brian, that's my favorite class of the day. I've already learned so much."

Mrs. Younger placed a hand on her husband's shoulder. "Before he gets going, why don't we pray for the meal?"

The pastor held a hand out to his wife on one side and

Brian on the other. Everyone was holding hands. Brian held his out to Natalia.

Natalia closed her eyes but heard none of the prayer, her heart was beating so loudly in her ears. Brian's hand felt so perfect in hers. Its warmth rushed all the way up her arm. She was both relieved and disappointed when Pastor Younger said, "Amen."

The conversation was as delicious as the meal, and Natalia felt incredibly comfortable with this family. They were genuine and fun, and it was obvious they loved to be together. *What would it be like to grow up in a family like this?* Natalia allowed herself to dwell on the possibility of being more closely connected to the Younger family. But she quickly dismissed it.

Brian deserves someone so much better than me. Natalia watched Brian laughing with Brittany, the earlier frustration gone.

Pastor Brian's cell phone rang, and the table grew silent. Brigit looked at her father with her eyebrows raised. "Not at Sunday dinner, Dad."

He glanced at the caller ID and sighed. "It's Mrs. Jordan. I need to take it."

Natalia felt her face heat up. Mrs. Jordan. Karen's mother. She was probably calling about Maureen. Pastor Brian stood and left the room before answering.

Brigit's fork banged against her plate. "Can't he just turn that thing off for an hour while we eat?"

"Hey, Natalia." Brian turned to face her. "Want to see the backyard? It's Mom's masterpiece."

Brian was trying to get her out of the kitchen so Mrs. Younger could speak with her daughter. "Sure, I'd love to."

He led Natalia through the kitchen and opened the blinds to the sliding glass door. She gasped at what she saw. Flowers and plants everywhere, with a rock path leading to a small gazebo. "It's spectacular."

"This is Mom's stress reliever." Brian opened the door, and Natalia breathed in the delicate fragrances.

"Is her job very stressful?"

"She's a pastor's wife." Brian shrugged. "That's not easy. People always have expectations of her. And she is much more introverted than Dad is, so leading Bible studies and women's events doesn't come naturally to her."

"Your mom's job is to be a pastor's wife?"

"Well, it's not a paid position, but, yeah. She's been a stay-at-home mom our whole lives, and she spends her free time helping Dad at the church. And creating a backyard wonder garden."

Natalia sat on the bench. "It is beautiful."

He sat next to her and stretched his legs. "Hey, sorry about Brigit in there. She hates when Dad gets calls during family time."

"No, it was fine."

"And sorry about Brittany. She just has a big mouth. And quite an imagination. Big, huge imagination."

Natalia laughed. "Your family is wonderful."

"Most of the time." Brian smiled. His teeth looked even whiter close up, and the sunlight did amazing things to his eyes. "But we're definitely not perfect."

"You sure seem like it." She blinked. "Your family, I mean. All of you. You get along . . . you love each other."

"We've had our moments." He leaned forward. "Brittany

went through a major rebellion when she was fifteen. She got into some pretty bad stuff. Dad even considered resigning."

"Really?"

"It was bad. Mom was crying all the time. People were constantly calling, telling us what Brittany was doing, where she was, who she was with."

"That's terrible."

"You're not kidding." Brian sat back, his shoulder touching Natalia's. "But she finally came out of it."

"How?"

"When she realized her behavior was going to cost Dad his job. Dad had actually written out his resignation letter. He was reading it to Mom when Brittany walked in. She fell apart. She begged Dad not to quit. She even went to the deacons and apologized for the stuff she did. She started meeting with Pastor Mike's wife once a week, really got back on track. It was pretty amazing."

"Did Brigit ever do anything like that?"

"No, Brigit's rebellion was quieter. She'd go for a while without talking to anyone. Or she'd blow up at little things. Or just stop reading her Bible for a while. We all knew she was struggling, but no one outside of the family knew." Brian smiled. "Kind of like someone else I know."

Brian's eyes were so full of concern. She wanted to tell him everything. How she was homesick, how she was furious at her parents for leaving her stranded. How Maureen's depression was crushing her. How she felt safe and at peace whenever he was around. But none of those thoughts could make their way past the lump in her throat.

"What about you?"

Brian's forehead wrinkled. "What?"

"You told me about your sisters' rebellion. What about yours?"

"I told you about when I was mad at God after I hurt my knee."

"That was it?"

He grinned. "Once, when I was in eighth grade, I snuck behind the bleachers with Tiffany Weaver and kissed her. On the lips."

A laugh burst out. "How terrible."

"No, that's not the worst. The worst was that Spencer Adams had just gotten a brand-new digital camera. He took pictures of the whole thing."

Natalia laughed even louder. "Oh dear."

"I'm not done." Brian stood and acted out what happened next. "He went out and printed the pictures, poster-sized, and put them up all around school. Tiffany thought I had set her up, so she was mad. My dad got all kinds of calls from people at church and in the school, so he was mad. Tiffany was dating another guy at the time, so he was really mad. It was not a good time."

Brian slumped back into the seat.

Natalia looked at him and shook her head. "That was a wonderful story. But that was not rebellion. Don't you have anything better than that?"

He held up his hands in surrender. "That's it. Unless you want to give me a better story."

Brian leaned forward, and Natalia had the overwhelming urge to grab him by the collar and give him a kiss that would make him forever forget Tiffany Weaver. *But I can't. What am I thinking?* Natalia stood to clear the errant thoughts from her mind.

"Hey, just kidding." Brian stood and looked into Natalia's eyes.

"I know. Sorry. I was thinking about something else."

"What?"

Something I can never tell you. Something I need to get out of my head as soon as possible. "You and Spencer have never really gotten along, have you?"

Brian sighed. "That was a long time ago. Like I said, if you like him, that's fine. I wasn't trying to make him look bad by telling you that story."

"No, that's not it." She saw the sincerity in his eyes. "I told you, I am not dating. There is no interest at all."

"Okay, no talk about dating or Spencer." Brian sat back down. "How about Costa Rica? Have you decided whether or not you're going on the trip?"

"I would really like to. But I don't think I can get the money."

"I thought your dad was loaded."

Natalia laughed. "Yes, he is a wealthy man. But he would not approve of me going to another country to help missionaries and tell people about Jesus."

"He hates Christianity that much?"

"He thinks people should be allowed to believe whatever they want and that no one should go around trying to force his beliefs on anyone else."

"So no money from your dad." Brian nodded. "How about your mom?"

"She might say yes, but then she would never get around to sending it to me."

"Scatterbrained?"

"Just very busy."

"I know what the teachers here make, so Maureen is definitely out."

Natalia's laugh lacked humor. "I cannot work anywhere because I don't have the right visa for that."

"Then we'll just have to pray God brings the money in."

"Sure, we'll pray in a thousand dollars. No problem."

"Hey, God's filthy rich. A thousand dollars to him is nothing at all."

Natalia looked at Brian. "You should be a pastor."

"What?" His face drained of color. "Where did that come from?"

"Really. Yesterday you gave me a beautiful sermon. Today you're challenging me to trust God for money for the mission trip. You do a great job teaching the ESL class. They love you. You would make a great pastor."

Brian sat up, his spine stiff. "No way. I grew up in a pastor's home, remember? I'm not doing that to my kids."

"But your family is wonderful."

"Wonderful, but not perfect."

"And yours will be?"

Brian relaxed. "No, but I just don't want to go into ministry. I'll help out at a church. I'll be the pastor's advocate. I'll take his kids out for ice cream, and I'll never call their dad if I see them kissing a girl under the bleachers."

"Can you not do all that and still be a pastor?"

"I don't want to be a pastor."

His voice was louder than Natalia had ever heard it. She put her head down, avoiding his gaze. "I'm sorry."

Brian put a hand on her leg. "No, it's me. I've just been hearing that for years. Everyone thinks I should follow in my dad's footsteps. But I don't want to. And I get tired of hearing it."

"I can understand that."

"You can?"

"My parents are both very successful," Natalia said. "Everyone—including them—expects me to be just as successful. My father asks me constantly if I know what I'm going to study, and he gets upset when I tell him I have no idea."

The sliding glass door opened and Brittany stuck her head out. "All right, lovebirds. Time to come in for dessert."

Natalia laughed as Brian let out a loud growl. "Not perfect, see? My family is most definitely not perfect."

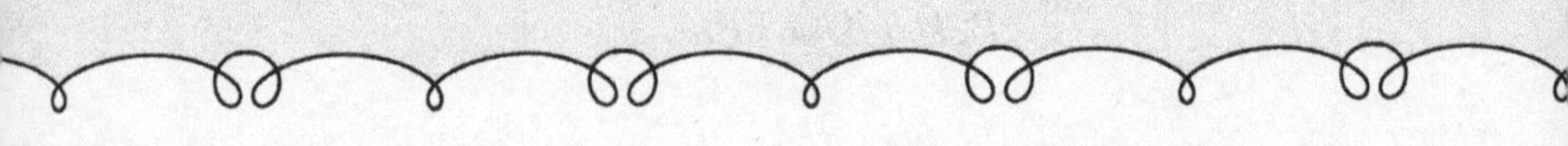

Chapter 28

"Peanut butter pie or red velvet cake?" Brittany's tone left no doubt as to which she preferred.

Brian groaned. His oldest sister was really pushing it today. "Britt, let her pick what she wants."

"I have never tried peanut butter pie." Natalia graciously accepted a generous slice.

"It's Grandma Younger's secret recipe." Brittany winked as she handed it over.

"It's from the four-ingredient cookbook we got you two years ago." Brian rolled his eyes.

"Way to ruin it."

"And you know the reason we got her a four-ingredient cookbook?" Brian was ready to give Brittany a taste of her own medicine. "Because she was dating Bailey Kane, and Bailey loved home cooking. All Brittany knew about home cooking was 'add water and stir.' So we got her this cookbook, and that helped the relationship last an extra, what, two months?"

Brittany blew her bangs away from her forehead. "Not all of us are as lucky in love as you, Junior."

Brian should have expected that, but he was still embarrassed. Natalia would never come over again, he was sure of it.

"Was Mrs. Jordan very upset?" Natalia sat next to Dad and asked quietly.

Brian knew Dad's pause meant yes. He also knew Mrs. Jordan. But he hoped Dad would spare Natalia the gory details.

"She wants to meet with your stepmother tomorrow."

Natalia's eyes widened.

"Don't worry," Dad said. "I'll be in there and so will Mr. Lawrence. I'm sure it'll all be worked out."

Brian wanted more than anything to take Natalia back outside, to ask her how she was feeling about what was happening with her stepmother, with school. *I'm trying so hard to get her to open up, God, but she won't. What am I doing wrong?* But she looked so uncomfortable earlier, he wouldn't ask her again. Maybe she'd rather talk with Spencer.

Natalia finished her dessert and enjoyed more conversation with Dad about sharing her faith.

"I'm going to e-mail my friend Carmen this afternoon and tell her some of what you've told me. I can't wait."

Dad laughed. "Good. But be gentle. Arguments don't win people to Christ. Love does."

She smiled and agreed with Dad. Brian couldn't help feeling that this was perfect—Natalia with his family, sitting around discussing theology with Dad. Looking at scrapbooks with Mom. Even getting teased by Brittany. It felt so right. *Sure, to me. But Natalia is just being nice. No way does she feel anything more than a polite friendship. The sooner I get that through my thick skull, the better.*

But it wasn't his head that Brian was most worried about.

"I'm sorry." Natalia looked at her phone. "I really should go. Maureen will be wondering where I am."

"Just a minute." Mom brought a plastic container out of the kitchen. "Here are some leftovers for her. Please tell her, again, how sorry we were she couldn't come. Hopefully next time."

"Thank you." Natalia took the container from Mom and smiled.

Natalia was silent most of the ride home. Brian didn't want to force conversation if she didn't want it.

"You really do have a wonderful family."

"I know." He pulled into her driveway. "Maureen will get over this. She's a strong lady."

Natalia gripped Mom's container against her chest. "I'm sure you are right."

"You can talk to me, Natalia." Brian searched her eyes, sensing the hurt in them. "I just want to be a friend. You don't have to go through this alone."

Her eyes filled with tears. She blinked them away and opened the car door. "Thanks. You are a good friend, Brian. I just . . ." Natalia got out of the car, then leaned her head back in. "I need to go."

She walked into her town house. Why was she so afraid to talk about what was really going on? Why so closed off?

Brian pulled out of Natalia's driveway and pointed his truck home. *God, help me help Natalia. And, please, God, help me not completely lose my heart in the process.*

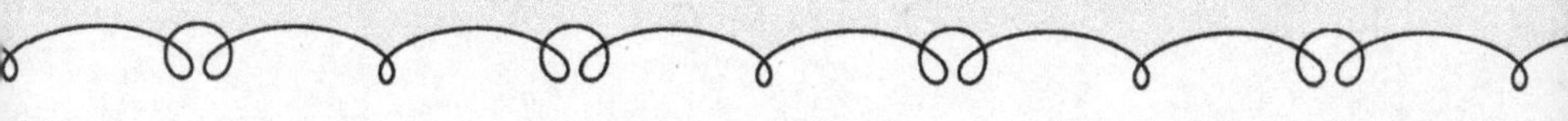

Chapter 29

"So here are some options for the fall semester." Lexi laid four Bible-study books out on the table in Mrs. Stevenson's room. This was the first meeting of the girls' Bible study, and Natalia was amazed to see fifteen girls gathered around the two long tables. "A study of Philippians, one of the fruit of the Spirit, one about 'Girl Issues,' and this one is about dating."

"Dating, definitely." One of the sophomore girls picked up the book and read the blurb on the back. "Wait, maybe not. This is all about waiting to date."

"You're fifteen, Tori." Lexi leveled her gaze at the young woman.

"I'm allowed to date when I'm sixteen," the younger girl answered. "Which is two months away. I need to get ready."

Lexi rolled her eyes. "All right. Any other thoughts?"

"I like this one." Natalia opened up the study of the fruit of the Spirit. She had memorized the passage in Galatians last year. She desperately needed more patience and peace right now. Not to mention joy.

"I liked that one too," Addy said.

The girls spent the next few minutes discussing the four books before finally settling on the fruit of the Spirit study.

"All right, then," Lexi said. "I'll order the books today. They're eight dollars. It usually takes a week or so to get them in, so how about next Monday we just talk about the passage? Read it over this week and take some notes."

The girls agreed, and Lexi asked if anyone had prayer requests. The girls shared several needs, from sick grandparents to science tests. Natalia wanted to tell the group about her need for money to go on the mission trip, but she was concerned. She had never needed money before, and she was embarrassed to admit the fact that she needed it now.

"Natalia?" Addy looked at her. "Anything we can pray about for you? Remember, nothing we say in here leaves this room."

Natalia took a deep breath. "I'd really like to go on the mission trip to Costa Rica. But I'm not sure I can get the money for it."

"I know someone who can get it for you." Lexi pointed up, and Natalia thought again that her new friend and Brian would make a great couple. "Let's ask him."

Lexi led in prayer, and Natalia was impressed at how natural she sounded, conversing with God the way she talked with her friends. When Lexi finished, she walked over and gave Natalia a hug. Natalia couldn't breathe from the force of it, but it felt good.

"You're going on that trip."

"I hope so," Natalia said. "I'd really like to."

With a few minutes left before the first bell, Natalia walked outside and checked her e-mail on her phone. She had written a long note to Carmen the night before, telling her what she learned from Pastor Brian yesterday afternoon. She hoped her friend had responded.

Natalia's heart caught in her throat when she saw a note from Carmen in her in-box. When Natalia opened it, she read: "Glad you are convinced you're right. Just don't let those Americans corrupt you too much. —Carmen."

Natalia punched her phone off. She spent two hours crafting her letter, trying to be loving yet firm, giving Carmen solid reasons why the Bible was true, why Jesus was real, why there is one absolute truth. She was sure Carmen would at least ask questions, open up a dialogue about those thoughts. Instead, her friend just gave her a verbal pat on the head and that was it.

"You okay, Natalia?" Spencer put a hand on her shoulder.

Shoving her phone deep into her backpack, she winced. "I'm trying to share my faith with a friend back home."

"Not going well?"

"She just doesn't care."

Spencer nodded. "My mom is kind of like that. After she and Dad got divorced, she just gave up on God. I try to talk to her, but she doesn't want to listen."

"I'm sorry," Natalia said.

"Yeah, and then I get caught in the middle of Dad's and her arguments. She's always mad at me because I want to spend more time with him. But she's so focused on trying to get another husband that she doesn't have time for me."

"Are things with your dad better?"

"No." Spencer shrugged. "But he doesn't get all dramatic on me the way Mom does."

Natalia could definitely relate. "It's hard for a woman to watch the man she loves move on."

Spencer looked at Natalia, his dark eyes sad. "You're easy to talk to."

Natalia wasn't sure how to respond. Thankfully, the bell rang, giving her a way out.

"Natalia." Spencer held her arm. "Want to hang out after school? There's a great smoothie place around the corner."

"Thanks, Spencer, but I can't. Homework."

Natalia hurried to homeroom, avoiding his gaze. Spencer was interested. That much was obvious. She also knew that beneath the confident exterior he was insecure and lonely.

Why can't he see Lexi? She would be a perfect match for him. She's fun and godly. She could listen to him and help him, make him laugh. Natalia sat in her desk and laughed at herself. Just a few minutes earlier she was thinking of how perfect Lexi would be with Brian.

Why was it that someone so committed to remaining single was also such a romantic at heart? Natalia didn't want to dwell on that thought. Because the answer revealed more than she was willing to admit.

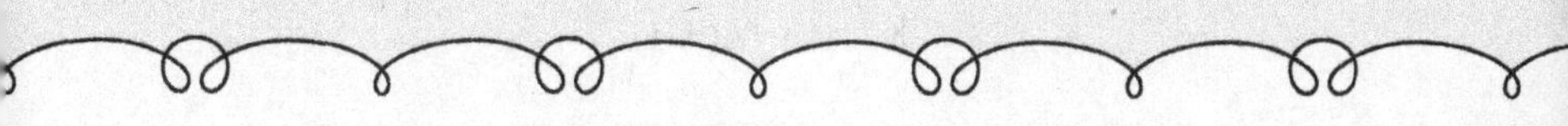

Chapter 30

"You have a package." Maureen dropped the brown box on the couch and retreated to her bedroom.

Since her meeting with Mrs. Jordan on Monday afternoon, Maureen had been brooding. She refused to talk about what happened. Natalia heard Karen telling her friends Maureen would be fired if she even looked at her the wrong way. But Natalia didn't know whether that was true, or if it was just Karen trying to show off. But Maureen had been like a turtle—coming out only when necessary and hiding the rest of the time. Natalia couldn't wait for ESL class that evening just to escape the silence of her house.

"Mamá remembered my birthday." Natalia smiled to herself as she tore open the package. "And a week early." Mamá was usually late with her gifts, and even then it was almost always a card with some money tucked inside. But this time she had sent a package. She had taken the time to buy something for Natalia and get it in the mail before her birthday arrived.

Natalia opened the box to reveal a stack of manila envelopes. She opened the one on top and saw the logo for an Ivy League school.

"College applications?" Her heart sank. As she opened the remaining envelopes, she saw more applications. Harvard, Yale, Duke, Pepperdine. At the bottom of the stack was a note on legal paper from her mother.

"Time to get started," it read. "You need to fill these out and send them out by the end of the month. Your father will put the money for your application fees in your bank account. We're hoping you have decided on your major. Knowing that will help narrow down your choices. —Mamá."

Natalia threw the box down. "Thanks, Mamá. So nice to see that you and Papa are united on something."

Unwilling to stay in the town house any longer, Natalia walked to the garage and grabbed her bicycle. She didn't know where she was headed; she just had to get out. The humidity had not let up even though it was September, and sweat trickled down her back. She turned out of her neighborhood and out onto the main street. She was halfway to the church before she realized where she was headed.

Oh well, I have to be there tonight anyway. I'll just tell Pastor to let Brian know I won't need a ride.

Twenty minutes later Natalia turned into the parking lot at the church. She was soaked with sweat, but she felt better. She walked over to the church offices, hoping to find Pastor Brian before he left for the day.

"Natalia." Mrs. Younger was in the church office, folding bulletins for Sunday. "How are you?"

"I am good."

"You look exhausted. Would you like a drink?" Mrs. Younger walked into the lounge area where she pulled a water bottle from the refrigerator.

"Yes, thank you. I biked here."

"Oh, Natalia, you should have called. We'd have given you a ride."

"No, I needed to exercise to clear my head."

Mrs. Younger's eyes softened. "Is everything okay?"

Natalia sighed. She couldn't lie to this kind woman. But she didn't want to burden Mrs. Younger with her problems.

Brian's mother laid down the bulletin she was working on and pulled out a chair. "Sit down and talk to me."

Natalia did as she was told. "My mother sent me a package today. It was filled with college applications."

"And that upset you?"

"It wasn't the package. Not really. It was just that . . ." Natalia felt foolish.

"Go on." Mrs. Younger's soft eyes broke right through Natalia's barriers.

"My birthday is next week." Natalia spoke softly, her eyes on her hands.

"You thought it was a gift."

The compassion in Mrs. Younger's voice was too much. Natalia couldn't stop the tears. "It is silly, I know. But I was so excited, and when I saw what was really in it . . ." She wiped a tear from her face. "My parents seem more concerned about me choosing what I want to major in than in who I am and how I'm doing."

"I'm sure that's not true."

Natalia knew Mrs. Younger couldn't understand that it

was true, all too true. "They want me to go to a good college, get a good degree, and make a good salary."

"My parents were a lot like that."

Natalia looked up. "Really?"

"Daddy owned a chain of grocery stores in southern Georgia. He didn't have a college degree, but he worked hard and long and ended up very successful. He expected that and more from my sister and me. He taught us from the time we were little that money equals success and education gets us money."

"Sounds like my father."

"Daddy wanted me to be a doctor and my sister to be a lawyer. He had it all planned out, from where we'd get our undergraduate degrees to where we'd go after that."

"What happened?"

Mrs. Younger laughed. "Brian Younger happened. I met him my first year of college. He swept me off my feet."

"Did you know he wanted to be a pastor?"

"He didn't know he wanted to be a pastor. Neither of us really had a relationship with God. My parents were good people, but not really religious. Brian's parents were, and are, some of the godliest people I know. But when I met him, Brian had strayed away from the faith."

"What happened?" Natalia couldn't believe what she was hearing. She assumed the Youngers had been Christians since they were little, that their courtship was like something from the dating book none of the girls had wanted to read.

"Brian's parents." Mrs. Younger closed her eyes. "Brian brought me home and I fell in love with them. They were so warm, and they spoke so openly about their relationship with God. Like he was a friend. I asked Brian why he never talked to me about God. He didn't have a good reason. So I made him take me to church and teach me the Bible."

"Wow."

"By the end of our freshman year, I had become a Christian and Brian started leading Bible studies on campus. By the end of our sophomore year, he had switched to a Bible college."

"What about you?"

"I was still majoring in premed, but my heart wasn't in it."

"What did your parents think?"

"They hated Brian, especially when he transferred to the Bible college. Daddy wanted me to break up with him right then."

"And you didn't?"

"I struggled with it," Mrs. Younger said. "The Bible says to obey your parents, and they were telling me to end my relationship with Brian."

"So what did you do?"

"I prayed about it. I didn't want to make my parents angry, and I certainly didn't want to lose the opportunity to see them come to Christ. But I felt like God was telling me I needed to trust him. He had brought Brian and me together. My parents' reasons for wanting me to break up with Brian weren't grounded in the Bible. Quite the opposite, in fact."

"They wanted you to break up with him because he was a Christian."

"Because he was a Christian going into the ministry." Mrs. Younger frowned. "Not my father's idea of a good job. He thought pastors were just leeches who begged people for money and made them feel guilty for the bad things they did."

"So what happened?"

"I told my parents everything. That I loved God and wanted to serve him, and that I loved Brian and felt God was calling me to help him in his ministry."

Natalia took a deep breath. "Were they very angry?"

"Yes." Mrs. Younger's eyes filled with pain at the memory. "My father refused to speak to me. He told me I was wasting my life. He even cut me out of his will."

"That is terrible." Natalia shook her head. *Would my father do the same thing?* "What about your mother?"

"She would slip me money occasionally, and she'd call me when Dad was at work. I was able to talk to her about what God was teaching me, and she accepted Christ as her Savior a month before our wedding."

"And your father?"

"It took many years, but he became a Christian too."

"That's wonderful."

"It is, but it took half a lifetime to get there." Mrs. Younger looked at Natalia. "I don't know what God has for you, Natalia, but I know it is something wonderful. You just keep trusting him. He's the best father in the universe. And he has a great plan for your life."

Natalia took a ragged breath. "I don't know what I am supposed to do or where I am supposed to go next. I don't want to disappoint my parents, but nothing in me wants to go to an Ivy League school. My parents work all the time. I do not want that."

"What do you want?"

The image that sprang to Natalia's mind was that of Brian giving the devotion at the ESL class and her interpreting. She loved Thursday nights, loved working with the people who came to learn English. She loved talking to them about God and the Bible, hearing their stories. "I'd love to be in ministry somehow. I would give anything to go to a Bible college. But my parents would never allow me to do that."

"You need to trust God to work on your parents. Honor them, respect them, love them. But if their desire for you is opposed to God's will for you, then you have to obey God."

"But they will hate me."

"Never." Mrs. Younger placed her hands on either side of Natalia's face. "They might be angry for a time. But they would never hate you. No one who knows you could ever hate you, Natalia."

Natalia prayed that was true. She didn't want to disappoint her parents. But she knew, like Mrs. Younger, that her parents' dream for her was not her dream. Would she ever have the courage to tell them that?

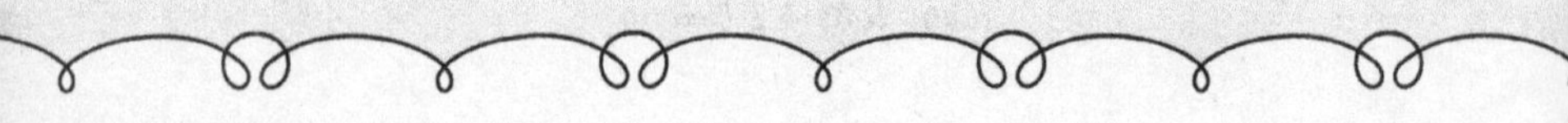

Chapter 31

"Have another churro." Carmen waved the pastry under Natalia's nose. The pair was sitting on their favorite bench in Retiro Park.

Natalia took a bite as she watched people row little boats in the pond.

Rollerbladers sped past, children laughed in the grass.

Natalia sighed. She was back in Madrid. Life was perfect. No questions about the future, no Brian Younger tempting her to forget her vow to remain single, no American clichés or US History research papers. Just life as she had always known it. And Spanish, Spanish everywhere.

Except for an annoying group of Americans singing. Where was that coming from? They were so loud. And so close. Natalia stood to find the Americans, ask them to please stop singing. But she tripped and fell, headed straight for the water.

And landed on the floor in her town house in Tampa. Surrounded by Addy, Lexi, and Brian singing "Happy

Birthday" at the top of their lungs. Balloons hung suspended in the space over Natalia's head, and the threesome didn't miss a beat when they helped her to her feet and ended with an off-key, "Happy birthday to you!"

Natalia smoothed back her hair and looked down at her T-shirt and pajama bottoms. Brian's smile was huge, and she could only imagine how terrible she looked. *What is he doing here?*

"Get up and get dressed, birthday girl." Lexi helped Natalia stand and walked her to the closet. "Would you like me to help you pick out something to wear?"

Natalia's laugh was weak. She wiped the sleep from her eyes and looked at Addy.

"All right, let's give her a few minutes to wake up and get ready." Addy obviously got the unspoken message Natalia had been sending her. "We'll go down and get breakfast ready."

"Breakfast?"

"Of course." Brian's eyes lit up and Natalia's heart flipped at the sight. "Every great birthday begins with a great breakfast."

He led the way out, and Natalia sat on her bed. She tried to remember if she had even told anyone that today was her birthday. Mrs. Younger. She must have told Brian. *Which means he very well may have been the one to orchestrate the whole thing.*

Natalia was embarrassed. How childish was it to want attention on her birthday? Silly. And Brian, Addy, and Lexi were just doing all this because they were kind people. Natalia determined to let them leave after breakfast. *No fuss for me. Well, no more fuss.*

Natalia was putting a dab of lip gloss on when a heavenly

smell greeted her nose. Bacon? And something else, something sweet. Her stomach growled, and she remembered she didn't eat dinner last night. She spent the entire evening trying to compose her two thousand–word essay for English. When she had finished, it was midnight, and she was too tired to do anything but crawl into bed.

"Wow." Natalia walked into the kitchen to find her three friends crammed into the tiny room. Brian was hunched over a small appliance, Addy was cooking eggs on one side of the stove, and Lexi was flipping bacon on the other. "It smells delicious."

"I'm making waffles." Brian lifted the waffle iron and eased the monstrous creation onto a plate. "Secret family recipe."

"The same secret recipe your sister used to make her peanut butter pie?" Natalia laughed.

"No." Brian wore a mock look of horror. "This recipe has *five* ingredients, thank you very much."

"Move over, the biscuits are ready." Lexi pushed Addy to the side and opened the stove. "Keep stirring the gravy, Addy. Don't let it burn."

"I can't stir it with the oven open." Addy laughed.

Lexi shut the stove with her hip and placed the pan of biscuits on the counter next to the sink. "All right, stir."

"Hang on, I need to get these eggs out."

Lexi grabbed a spoon and stirred the gravy in the pot behind Addy's pan as Addy grabbed a bowl and scooped the eggs into it. Natalia sat on a stool and watched the commotion, overwhelmed that her friends would go to so much trouble, just for her.

The small dining room table had been decorated with a festive blue tablecloth and matching streamers hung from the chandelier. Paper plates in blue and red polka dots were on the counter, and clear plastic cups were beside a pitcher of what appeared to be freshly squeezed orange juice.

"Here is your seat of honor." Brian pulled out a chair that had balloons tied to the sides. He handed Natalia a napkin and strapped a huge, pointy hat to her head. Addy snapped a picture, and Lexi laid a plate in front of Natalia.

"Please don't make me eat all by myself." Natalia looked at all the food on the plate and wondered how she'd ever be able to eat it all.

"All right, if you insist." Brian stuffed a long piece of bacon in his mouth and began heaping food on one of the paper plates.

"Hey, save some for the rest of us," Lexi said.

The foursome was finishing breakfast when the front door opened. "Natalia?" Maureen walked into the cramped kitchen.

"Ta da," Brian sang, his arms gesturing toward the stove. "I told you we wouldn't burn anything. Ye of little faith."

Maureen's smile didn't quite reach her eyes. "I never should have doubted. This is very sweet. I'm so glad Natalia has such good friends."

"And this is just the beginning." Lexi put her hands on Natalia's shoulders.

"No, please," Natalia said. "You've done enough. This was very nice. Just go on and enjoy your day."

"Oh, we plan to enjoy our day." Brian sat next to her, his blue eyes dancing.

Addy sat on the other side of Natalia. "Don't worry. It's going to be fun."

"But I have homework . . ."

"There's no homework on your birthday." Brian leaned forward, elbows on the table, his nose just inches from Natalia's.

She sat back and took a deep breath. *Lord, what are you doing to me?*

"Seriously, Natalia." Lexi pulled Natalia up. "It would be really selfish of you not to let us spoil you on your birthday."

Natalia laughed. "I certainly don't want to be selfish."

"Certainly not," Brian echoed.

"I think I have everything on your list." Maureen came back in the kitchen carrying a small suitcase. Natalia never noticed that she had left.

"What's that for?" Natalia took the suitcase from Maureen.

"Patience, my friend." Brian took the suitcase from her, and Natalia's heart skipped a beat when his hand brushed hers. "All will be revealed in time."

Natalia gazed at Addy and Lexi, but they just smiled and motioned for Natalia to follow Brian out the door.

"Relax," Addy whispered as Natalia walked toward Lexi's SUV. "Let us pamper you. We've been looking forward to this all week."

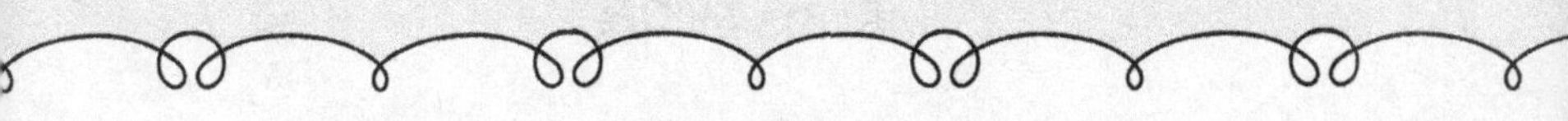

Chapter 32

Natalia stuck her head out of the dressing room. "I can't."

"Natalia Lopez." Lexi planted both hands on her hips. "Show us the dress."

"It's too much."

"My parents own the store." Lexi waved her hands, dismissing Natalia's concern. "They mark these things up like crazy. That dress really only costs about five dollars."

Natalia knew that wasn't true. The cotton sundress was beautiful, coral and yellow, with wooden beads sewn across the neckline. It felt like heaven against her skin, and even though she argued, she'd hate to have to give up the dress now that she had it on. During her lonely moments at home, Natalia had surfed through her favorite clothing websites, dreaming of buying some new clothes. Oh, how she missed shopping.

"Don't make me pull you out of there," Lexi threatened.

"Fine." Natalia slowly opened the curtain. Her three friends let out a communal gasp. "Is something wrong?"

Brian's eyes were wide. "No. Nothing's wrong. Nothing."

Lexi walked Natalia to the three-way mirror. "What Brian is trying to say is, you look fabulous."

Natalia gazed at herself in the mirror. The dress's empire waistline emphasized her tiny torso. The skirt floated down almost to the ground, revealing her hourglass figure without clinging too tightly to it. The bright colors highlighted Natalia's olive skin and made her green eyes stand out even more. "It's lovely."

"You're lovely." Addy wrapped an arm around Natalia. "Now for shoes and accessories, right?"

"Of course." Lexi smiled. "I believe you know where those are?"

"No, this is more than enough." Natalia backed away from the mirror. "I don't need anything else."

"I may not know much about fashion"—Lexi peered into the changing room—"but I'm pretty sure those tennis shoes you wore here would not go well with this dress. Am I right?"

Natalia laughed. "Yes."

"So get some shoes. And some jewelry. And a new purse. And hurry it up because we have lunch plans."

"Lunch plans?"

"Less talking, more shopping, *chica*," Lexi ordered.

An hour later Natalia was led onto the veranda of a seafood restaurant in south Tampa. The hostess seated them at a table against a window that framed the Gulf of Mexico.

"This is beautiful." Natalia loved looking out over the greenish-blue water, seeing boats in the distance and children playing on the sand down below.

"We know it's not as pretty as the Mediterranean, but we hoped you'd like it." Addy unrolled her napkin and placed it on her lap.

"I hardly ever went to the beach." Natalia thought back to her busy life in Spain. "Madrid is right in the middle of the country, so a trip to the beach took several hours."

"We brought our suits." Lexi reached for one of the buttery rolls the waitress had placed in the middle of the table. "Yours is in the suitcase Maureen packed for you."

"This is your day, Natalia." Addy smiled. "We'll do whatever you want."

Natalia caught Brian staring at her. His face turned red and he pretended to be interested in the menu. "What do you think, Brian?"

"I like the beach." He was still looking at the menu.

Why is he being so quiet? This is not like Brian at all.

"Are you folks ready to order?" The waitress stood over the table and the conversation was halted.

Natalia couldn't decide between the grilled salmon and the shrimp scampi. Lexi liked both, so the girls decided to order one of each and share.

"Seriously, Addy," Lexi said as the waitress walked away. "Fried chicken and fries? You could get that at McDonald's."

Addy stuck her tongue out at Lexi and smirked. "Don't mock my food choices. I didn't say anything about you wearing your basketball shorts to a fancy restaurant."

"Uh, I think you just did." Lexi laughed. "Fine. You got me. But you'll be jealous when we're done and I'm relaxing in my stretchy pants."

"I have never had swordfish before, Brian." Natalia wasn't used to being the one trying to make him talk, but she hated that he was so distant. "Is it good?"

"It's great." His eyes were on the water. Was he bored? Spending all day with three girls couldn't be his idea of fun.

Natalia yawned. "I do not think I'll have the energy to go to the beach. This has been a wonderful day, but I should probably head back home after this. I'm sure Maureen is getting lonely."

"She can come with us," Lexi suggested. "We can give her a call."

"No, that's okay." Natalia glanced over at Brian again. His eyes were still glued to the water.

Lexi looked at Natalia, then at Brian. Her frown let Natalia know she saw his boredom too.

The conversation at the table was stiff but enjoyable. Lexi and Addy were trying, but Brian remained quiet, closed off. Very different from the Brian Natalia thought she knew.

As she finished off the last of her rice pilaf, five waitresses walked up to the table with a huge slice of chocolate cake, a sparkler glowing in the center.

"Happy, happy birthday, from everyone to you," they sang. *"Happy, happy birthday. May all your dreams come true."*

Natalia was self-conscious as everyone on the veranda turned to watch her blow out the candles. Lexi stood on her chair and shouted, "This is Natalia's seventeenth birthday.

Her first birthday away from her home in Spain. Let's give her a big Tampa welcome."

The patrons clapped politely, and Natalia looked at Lexi, amazed that she could have so little reserve. *What would that be like?*

Natalia tried to enjoy the cake, but she could not stop thinking about Brian. He seemed miserable. *I'm sure there are a hundred other things he'd rather be doing now.*

"Now for your gift." Addy pulled a powder blue envelope from her purse.

"No." Natalia pushed the envelope away. "You bought me new clothes and a meal. You made me breakfast. This is too much. Whatever is in there, you keep and enjoy. I couldn't possibly take anything else from you."

"Oh, yes, you can." Lexi grabbed the envelope from Addy's hand and patted Natalia's head with it. "This isn't even from us."

"What?"

Lexi forced Natalia to take the envelope. "Just open it, woman, and ask questions later. We've been dying to see you get this all day."

Natalia couldn't imagine what was inside. She carefully peeled away the paper, revealing a plain white card. She opened it to find a note saying the balance for the mission trip to Costa Rica had been in paid in full.

"I don't understand." Natalia flipped the card over. Nothing else. No explanation, no signature.

"You, my dear, are going to Costa Rica." Lexi dipped her finger in icing and grinned.

"But how?"

"That's a secret. We don't even know. Pastor Brian just gave this to us and said someone in the church felt God wanted them to help you go on this trip."

Natalia looked at Brian. "Do you know who did this?"

He shrugged. "Even if I did, I couldn't say. Some people enjoy giving secretly. The Bible talks about how you lose your reward if everyone knows everything you do."

"Okay then." Lexi shot Brian a "lighten up" glare. "Are we ready to hit the beach?"

"No, really," Natalia said. "I should get home."

Addy stood from the table. "We're a mile away. Come on, just for a little while."

"Maureen told us she has a ton of grading to do." Lexi also stood, and Natalia and Brian followed. The group made its way outside. "So you might as well hang out with us."

"It seems as if I have no choice." Natalia opened the car door and climbed in.

"Sure you have a choice," Lexi said. "You can choose to have fun or you can choose not to. But, either way, we're going to the beach."

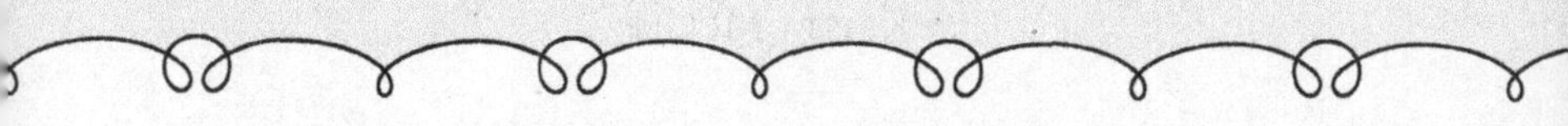

Chapter 33

Brian had never felt so uncomfortable. When Natalia walked out of the dressing room wearing the sundress, it was as if a giant hand had slapped him across the face. *She is so far out of your league, man,* he had thought. *You're peewee tee ball and she's the major leagues. What are you thinking?*

Natalia was easily the prettiest girl he had ever seen, much less been friends with. But that was the problem. He didn't want to be friends with Natalia. And he had been kidding himself by making believe that was all he wanted. He wanted so much more. But there was no chance of that. Girls that pretty didn't want to date him.

So why am I torturing myself by being around her? And at the beach, no less. If seeing her in a sundress knocked me out, seeing her in a bathing suit will kill me.

"What is your problem?" Lexi cornered Brian after the others had left the car. "You act like you'd rather be anywhere else than here, and Natalia can totally tell. You're the reason she tried to get out of going to the beach."

"I'm sorry." He tried to walk away, but Lexi pulled him

back. Brian knew he was in trouble when Lexi put her hands on her hips.

"Not enough. Spill it. What's going on?"

"Nothing."

"Liar."

"It's personal, okay?"

"Fine, don't tell me what's wrong." Lexi crossed her arms. "You know what Natalia's been going through lately. This is her day. You planned the whole thing, after all. The least you can do is act like you're having fun."

"You're right." He hated that he was making Natalia uncomfortable. Everyone would have been better off if he hadn't tagged along. "I'll try to act like I'm having fun."

Refusing to have any more conversation with Lexi, Brian walked quickly to the bathrooms and changed. Suddenly, the SpongeBob swim trunks he had purchased as a joke looked ridiculous and immature. *Spencer Adams wouldn't wear SpongeBob trunks.*

Come on, man. Suck it up. Brian walked toward the row of towels belonging to his friends.

"I still can't get over it." Natalia spread sunscreen on her arms.

Brian resisted the urge to grab the tube from her and do the job himself. *At least she's wearing a one-piece.* He tried not to spend too much time gazing at Natalia's perfect figure in her red Speedo swimsuit. *Thank you, God, for that.*

"Someone actually paid a thousand dollars so I could go to Costa Rica." Natalia's smile was heart-stopping.

"I'm so glad you're coming." Addy took the tube of sunscreen from Natalia. "This is going to be great."

"Speaking of great." Lexi stood. "Let's get out there in the water. The surf isn't great at this beach, but we can definitely boogie board."

"Boogie board?" Natalia's smile faded. "Aren't boogies the word for . . . you know." She pointed to her nose.

Lexi's laugh was loud. "No, those are boog*ers*. Totally different." Lexi reached for her board. "This is a boogie board. Brian, go grab yours too, and we can show her how it's done."

"No problem." *Any excuse to get away.* Brian took his time walking back to the car. *All right, God, you've got to help me here. If you're asking me to be Natalia's friend, then I need some supernatural help to be able to see her as that. Can't you make me less attracted to her? Give her an ugly wart or a really bad habit or something? Does she have to be so beautiful?*

A few minutes later Brian threw himself on his board and paddled out into the ocean. The salt water relaxed him, and for a moment, he was able to think about something other than his pointless attraction to Natalia Lopez.

Until Natalia came to him to ask for help on the boogie board.

"Wouldn't you rather have Lexi show you?"

Natalia pointed to Lexi out on the waves. "I don't think I can pry her off of that thing."

"You're probably right." Brian shot up another prayer for help and handed the board to her. "It's really easy. You just wait for a wave, hop on the board, and let it carry you to shore."

The ocean chose that moment to stop moving. No waves. Not even a ripple. Just Brian and Natalia. Addy was on the shore building a sand castle, and Lexi had drifted to the right, far enough away that conversation with her was impossible.

"This happens sometimes." Brian looked out, willing a wave to jump up.

"Is everything all right?" Natalia's green eyes searched his, and Brian turned his head, hoping Natalia couldn't read his thoughts.

"Yep, everything's fine."

"You just don't seem yourself today."

"Even class clowns have their off days. I'll be funny again tomorrow."

"That is not what I mean." Natalia's voice was soft, hurt.

"I'm sorry." Brian took another look out at the water. Nothing. He needed to get her talking. He couldn't think of anything coherent to say. Not with Natalia so close and appearing so vulnerable. "So what were your birthdays like in Spain?"

Natalia stared out at the still-calm water and smiled. "They were nice. My dad and Maureen usually took me out to a restaurant. My half sister, Ariana, would come along too."

"I didn't know you had a sister."

"Her mom has custody of her, so we don't see each other all that much."

"So you'd go out to dinner." Brian floated on the water. "What else?"

"That by itself was special. Papa works a lot, so family dinners were rare. But on my birthday, he would not only take us out, he'd even turn off his cell phone."

Brian thought of his own father. "You've got me there. We have family dinners all the time. But Dad turning off his cell phone? I don't think that's possible. He's afraid a tragedy might happen to somebody at church, and he wouldn't be there when they called."

"He cares very much."

Brian let his feet dig into the spongy sand. "He does."

"So do you." Her eyes locked onto his.

Brian had the urge to swim away as fast as he could. *Where are the waves?*

"You have a pastor's heart."

"Maybe." He did not want to have this conversation again. "But I don't have the desire."

"So what would you like to do?"

Grab you and kiss you. That's what I'd like to do. "I'm not sure yet. I've enjoyed working demolition with Mr. King. I could just do that. I'm sure Spencer could keep me employed for the rest of my life."

Natalia gazed at him, a hint of a smile on her perfect lips. "There is rebellion in you, isn't there?"

"Working demo is rebellious?"

"Not if that's what God wants you to do." Natalia tilted her face up, her eyes locked on his. "Is it?"

Brian turned his head away, the feelings Natalia sparked in him with just a look were almost more than he could handle. "I don't know. I don't need to make any decisions yet."

Natalia sighed. Mom had told Brian a little of her conversation with Natalia. Her parents expected her to make her career choice immediately. Guilt attacked his conscience when he thought of how flippantly he was treating Natalia's questions.

He started to apologize when a wave appeared on the horizon.

"All right." Brian grabbed the boogie board and positioned it to face the beach. "Just hop on, farther up, lie flat on it with just your legs hanging off. Perfect. Now wait for the wave to carry you to shore."

He stood beside Natalia and laid himself flat, preparing to body surf his way back. The wave was worth waiting for. It broke right before it reached them, and the sound of her laughter rang through the surf as the pair was rocketed back to land.

"That was brilliant," a wet, grinning Natalia announced. "Brilliant."

Brian looked over at Natalia, her smile bright, her eyes full of joy. Brilliant. Yes, she was.

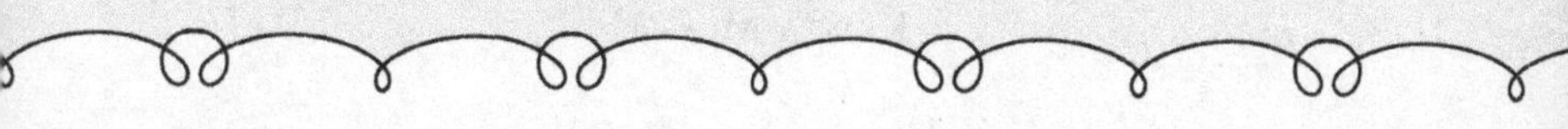

Chapter 34

My brain is going to melt. Natalia sat in her AP US History class, staring at her giant textbook. So many names and dates and events, most of which she was reading about for the first time.

"This is so hard." The girl behind Natalia must have heard her sigh. *She* thought this was hard? At least she had studied some of this before. *What was I thinking, taking this class? And now it's too late to drop it. I'm stuck.*

The week before, the girls' Bible study topic had been peace. Natalia had listened, knowing she was not experiencing that in her life at present. The stress of living with Maureen, keeping up with schoolwork, and trying not to fall for Brian were overwhelming. God was speaking to her in the study to allow him to give her peace. She didn't need to try to handle everything on her own. She couldn't.

The bell rang, and Natalia dragged herself out and into the lunchroom. The tantalizing smell of grilled chicken and sautéed onions had been drifting in the classroom all period. She couldn't wait to get in line for lunch today.

"So how's APUSH?" Lexi grabbed a tray and stood behind Natalia in line.

"APUSH?"

"AP US History. Aka, the toughest class in school."

"So it's not just me?"

"No way." Lexi grabbed a fork and knife from the chrome holder and the pair inched ahead in line. "I barely squeaked by with a C last year. Addy aced it, though. She even got a 5 on the exam."

A 5 was the highest grade you could get on an AP exam. And very few students got one. "Wow."

"I'm sure she'd tutor you. Addy doesn't like to brag, but she's a total brainiac. Probably going to be valedictorian this year."

Natalia hated to ask Addy for help. But she'd need some type of guidance or she would never be able to survive APUSH. Brainiac, she was not.

"Addy, you need to help Natalia in APUSH," Lexi announced as she slapped her tray next to Addy at their table in the cafeteria.

"That's a hard class." Addy looked at Natalia. "I can't imagine taking it without any previous American history classes."

Natalia smiled. Addy was so gracious. "I hate to impose, but if you could just give me some tips, that would be wonderful."

"No problem. I'll come over tonight."

Natalia sighed.

"Peace, right?" Lexi grinned as she stuffed a quesadilla in her mouth. "Just like we talked about. God gives it to us even in the worst of situations—which, in your case, is history."

Natalia scooted over as Tori, one of the girls from their Bible study, sat next to her. "I have to thank you for your advice the other morning."

Natalia couldn't remember saying anything. "What advice?"

"We were talking about getting up in the mornings to have devotions, remember?"

"I remember." Addy nodded. "We were all saying how hard it is to get up, and you said—"

"'Better to be sleep deprived than God deprived,'" Lexi finished.

"Yes." Tori nodded. "So I've been setting my alarm fifteen minutes earlier all week, and it's been amazing. My days are so much better when I make spending time with God a priority."

Natalia smiled at the energetic sophomore. "I'm glad I could be an encouragement. But you are making me feel guilty because I hit the Snooze button this morning and barely had time to get dressed before it was time to leave."

"And that's how the body of Christ works." Lexi squeezed Natalia's shoulder. "We help each other out and keep each other accountable. We'll be checking in on you tomorrow."

Tori winked. "And you better be sleep deprived."

Thank you, God. Natalia loved that she could sit down and talk about God at lunch. No one made fun of her for it or criticized her. Sure, there were kids at this school who wanted nothing to do with God. But they didn't comprise the entire student population.

Taking her tray to the kitchen, Natalia ran into Spencer. "Hey, Natalia. I've been meaning to talk to you. But you're always surrounded by your groupies."

"My groupies?"

"You know, your girls."

She assumed he meant her friends from Bible study. She did gravitate to them most days. "Did you have something in particular you wanted to talk about?"

"I did, actually." Spencer walked toward the row of microwaves at the far end of the cafeteria. Natalia assumed she was to follow. "Homecoming is coming up. I don't know if you've heard much about it. But it's a pretty big deal here. We rent out a nice restaurant, have a gourmet meal, and afterward, everyone is invited to my new mansion."

"It's in November, right? A few weeks after we get back from the mission trip?"

"Yes." Spencer smiled. "Congratulations, by the way. I heard you're going."

"Yes, someone paid for my whole trip."

"I'm sure whoever it was is thrilled to be able to help you."

Natalia wondered, not for the first time, if Spencer's family was the donor.

"But back to homecoming." Spencer looked into Natalia's eyes. "I'd like to take you as my date."

Is he asking me or telling me? Spencer could be incredibly nice one minute and incredibly arrogant the next. The arrogant side was winning right now, and Natalia did not want to encourage that.

"It's very kind of you to want to reach out to a new

student, but I think I am going to go with my friends, in a group."

His eyes widened. He leaned closer. "I really don't like to brag, but I'm probably going to be voted homecoming king. If people know you're my date, you could win queen."

"In that case, my answer is most definitely no." Natalia raised her eyebrows. "I have no desire to be secondary school royalty. But I think Tiffany Weaver would love that opportunity. You should ask her."

Without waiting for a response, Natalia walked away.

Tori pounced on her as soon as she reached the table. "Did Spencer Adams just ask you out?"

"Do you have radar hearing?"

"He did!" Tori squealed. "You are the luckiest girl alive."

Natalia looked over to see Lexi put her head in her hands. "I am not going anywhere with anybody. I am at peace being dateless."

Lexi's eyes widened. "You said no?"

"I don't think I said I was asked anything that would require a yes or no answer." Natalia grinned. "But if I were, then I would have declined."

"She said no." Lexi's smile widened.

"I did not say that."

"You didn't not say that. You're trying to protect Spencer's fragile little ego while not coming out and telling an out-and-out lie. Spencer Adams asked you out and you turned him down."

Natalia turned to Addy. "A little help, please?"

Addy opened her mouth right as the bell rang. "Ever heard the saying 'saved by the bell'?"

Natalia glanced around as all the girls rushed to throw away their trash and get to their sixth-period classes. "No, but it certainly fits this situation."

Addy laughed as she stood with Natalia to leave. "Is tonight around five o'clock all right?"

"Perfect." Natalia walked down the hall toward speech class. "Thank you so much."

"No problem." Addy turned to walk to her locker. "That's what friends are for, right?"

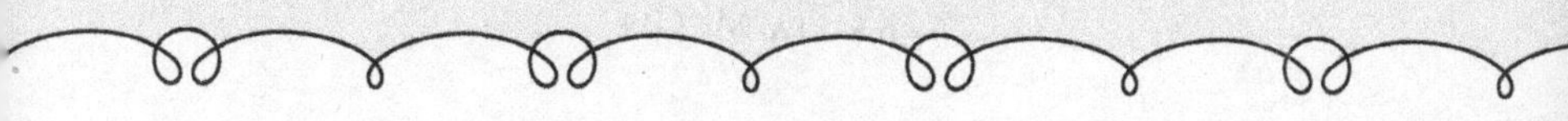

Chapter 35

Natalia checked herself in the mirror. Again.

"How do I look, Maureen?" Natalia twirled around in her floral dress. She had cinched it at the waist with a soft brown leather belt and topped it with a jean jacket. She even splurged on brown cowboy boots at Lexi's mom's store. Papa's birthday money had been well spent.

"Beautiful." Natalia knew Maureen was trying to pull herself out of her depression. She hadn't said anything negative in the last several days. Her eyes, however, revealed the truth. "Where are you going, again?"

"The new teen network, Teens Rock. It's in Orlando. The first episode of their show is tonight, and Addy's friend Kara is one of the stars."

"The one who was on the reality TV show with Addy?"

"Yes." Natalia fished in her purse for her lip gloss. "She and Chad Beacon . . ."

"My students talk about him all the time. The boy who won *America's Next Star* a few years back?"

"That's him—tall, blond, great voice. He and Kara are dating. It's a cute story." Maureen's eyes closed and Natalia needed to move away from that topic. "Anyway, the show is supposed to be like a teen version of *Saturday Night Live*. But instead of a large permanent cast and one host, they have two permanent hosts and several guest cast members. Tonight the entire cast of *Morgan's Road* will be on."

"Oh yes, I've heard the kids talking about that show." Maureen picked a piece of lint off Natalia's jacket. "Several of them have missed homework assignments because they *couldn't* miss an episode."

A month-long "preview" for the new show had been aired on the new network, showing the girls' audition process, the writers at work, the set being constructed. There had been interviews with other teen stars who couldn't wait to be guest hosts. And all the hype worked because teen magazines had Kara's and Chad's faces plastered all over them and thousands had "liked" the show on Facebook already.

"We'll be out pretty late." Natalia heard Addy's car door slam outside. "The show starts at eight o'clock, and there is a party afterward."

"You don't have to give me the details." Maureen waved her hand. "I trust you."

Natalia sighed. She appreciated the trust. But sometimes it seemed more like a lack of concern than a vote of confidence. She opened the door as Addy's hand was raised to knock.

"You look great!" Addy stepped back. "All set?"

"Sure am." Natalia walked over to give Maureen a slight hug. "See you later."

"*Much* later." Addy looped her arm through Natalia's. "Let's go get Lexi and hit the road."

Natalia hopped into Addy's car and buckled up. "I don't think I have ever seen you this excited."

"This is Kara's dream come true." Addy turned out of Natalia's neighborhood and navigated her car toward Lexi's house. "She has always wanted to perform. And this show is perfect. She and Chad get to help write the skits, they get to sing, they help choose the guest stars. And because they're both Christians, they meet together with Chad's parents every morning before rehearsal for Bible study and prayer. Kara is a new believer, and she is just soaking it all up. She calls me all the time, telling me what she's learning. Chad is so good for her. They're perfect together."

Natalia looked out the window. Why was it whenever anyone brought up the subject of romance, Brian Younger's face popped into her mind? *What is wrong with me? God, I know you have to want me to stay single. I want me to stay single. My family is way too messed up for me to think about ever getting involved with anyone. Especially someone as great as Brian. So why do I think about him so much? Get him out of my brain, God.*

"I'll run in and get Lexi." Natalia put the car in Park and opened the door.

Lexi bounded out of her house, screaming her way to the car. "We're going to Orlando! To see a TV show! And hang out with celebrities!"

Natalia laughed as Addy sat back in the car and covered her ears.

"All right, sister, let's go." Lexi leaped into the backseat and slammed the door. "I brought the video camera. This needs to be recorded for my children."

"Your children?"

"Yes." Lexi raised her eyebrows. "Someday I will have children, and I want them to know how cool their mom was when she was in high school." She turned the camera toward herself. "So, kids, this is Mom, back when I was young and beautiful. *This* weekend I am going to see a brand-new television show *O-Town Live*, starring a couple of my friends. Yep, friends. Your mom is cool, and don't you forget it."

The ride to Orlando was fun, with the girls talking and Lexi recording everything. The studio parking lot was full when they arrived. But because their names were on "the list," Addy was directed to a special parking lot—one reserved just for the show's stars.

"I wonder whose car *that* is." Lexi pointed to a shiny red Lamborghini.

"Just be careful opening the door," Addy said. "A dent in that car probably costs more than three of my car put together."

The girls searched for the stage door and were greeted by a stage manager. Once again their names were looked for and found, and the trio was escorted to a special seating area.

"Second row." Lexi jumped up and down. "This is amazing. We're in the second row. I have to record this."

Lexi pulled out her camera and immediately had it snatched from her hand by an angry-looking man wearing a Teens Rock polo shirt. "No cameras allowed."

"I'm sorry." Lexi reached for her camera. "I promise I won't use it."

"No cameras allowed in the theater. You can pick it up in the security office on your way out." With that, the man walked off. Lexi slumped down in her seat and watched him leave.

"Sorry, Lex," Addy said.

"No problem." Lexi reached in her back pocket and pulled out her phone. "I brought back up."

"Are you crazy? Do you want that confiscated too?" Natalia looked toward the door where the man exited.

"It's for the children." Lexi grinned. Whispering into her phone, she said, "Kids, Mom just got in trouble for bringing a camera into the theater. It's against the rules. I don't want you to break the rules, so check this out. Mommy is going to turn her phone off right now . . . as soon as I show you guys the awesome set." Lexi pointed her phone toward the stage.

Seconds later the doors in the back of the theater opened and hundreds of people filed in, their voices filling the theater.

A comedian came out to "warm up" the crowd, then the director entered to thank everyone for coming out to the premiere.

"Joining Chad and Kara tonight are . . ." The name of the first guest hosts had not yet been revealed, so the audience was deathly silent as the director allowed the pause to linger. "The entire cast of *Morgan's Road*!"

The audience stood and cheered. *Morgan's Road* was the most popular teen drama on television.

"Addy." Lexi eyed her friend, who stood and smiled as everyone around her clapped and whistled. "You knew, didn't you? You knew *Morgan's Road* was going to be on and you didn't tell me."

Addy nodded. "I promised Kara I'd keep it a secret."

Lexi pulled out her phone. "Kids, this is the night Mommy is going to meet her future husband, your father. Zach Stone."

Zach Stone was the teen heartthrob who starred in *Morgan's Road*. Lexi pointed her camera to the stage. "He just doesn't know it yet."

A large, angry security guard cleared his throat and glared at Lexi.

Sighing, Lexi pointed the camera toward herself before handing it over. "And this is Mommy getting caught for breaking the rules. Bye, kids."

The director calmed everyone down and continued his speech. "This is a live show, so please, do not distract the actors or yell out. What happens here"—he pointed to the stage—"goes right out there." He motioned to the cameras.

When the last of the instructions were given, the now-familiar theme song for *O-Town Live* began to play. Lights dimmed, and Chad and Kara stepped onstage. The entire audience erupted, with the loudest noise coming from a large group in the front row.

"Kara's family." Addy returned the wave of a large man who, Natalia assumed, was Kara's father.

The show, amazingly, lived up to all its hype. The skits were hysterical, and Natalia was impressed at how versatile the *Morgan's Road* actors were. In the middle Chad sang his signature song, "Freedom," and right after that, he sang a spoof of it in a skit where he played a guy playing Chad Beacon. Kara was his "biggest fan."

"This is great," Natalia whispered to Addy.

Addy nodded her agreement.

Too soon the theme song was playing once again and the entire cast was onstage, dancing and waving good-bye to the cameras and to the studio audience.

Lexi reached into Addy's purse and pulled out Addy's phone. Lexi pointed it toward herself. "Hey, kids. Mom's getting ready to go to a real live after party with my famous friends. And your dad. Don't wait up."

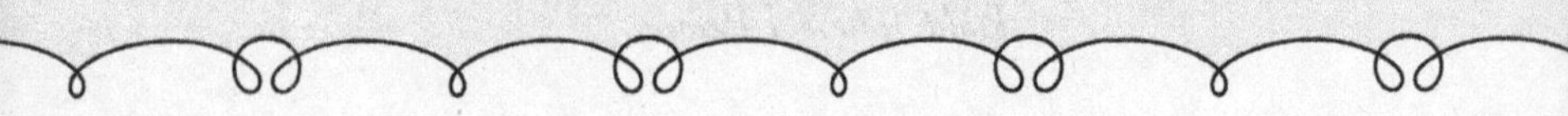

Chapter 36

"It's definitely hard work. But I love it." Kara had pulled Addy, Lexi, and Natalia aside at the after party. Fans and executives had surrounded the young starlet for over an hour. The three friends mingled with the other guests. Lexi had even gotten an autograph, and a covert video, from Zach Stone. But they were all excited to hear how Kara was enjoying her new "job."

"So is Zach as wonderful as he seems?" Lexi looked over to see that young man flirting with one of the VIP guests.

Kara shrugged. "I didn't really spend a lot of time with him. Paige Hanson and I had gotten to know each other a little during auditions, so I spent most of my free time with her."

Natalia remembered seeing the audition episode where Kara and the other girls played guest parts on *Morgan's Road*. Addy told Natalia that Kara was sure that audition was her worst. Natalia wasn't much of a judge of acting, but Kara seemed very natural in all the roles she played.

"And with Chad." Lexi winked.

"Yes, with Chad." Kara's eyes darted to her handsome costar.

"So how is it, working with the man you love every day?" Lexi leaned forward and batted her eyes.

Kara blushed. "His parents don't want us to get too serious yet. So the *L* word definitely isn't in play. But it's great. We have a Bible study every morning. My parents are even coming to that."

"That's great." Addy smiled.

"I know. And they love the Beacons. The four of them will go out to lunch while we're filming or hang out and just talk. My dad is the happiest I've seen him in a long time."

"Kara's dad had a heart attack a few months ago," Addy said. "The doctor recommended he retire and move down here so he could fully recover."

"He goes to physical therapy three times a week," Kara said. "And he's even starting to eat better. Dr. Kara is helping him out there."

"But back to Chad." Lexi raised her eyebrows.

"Chad is great." Kara bit her lip. "I've never known anyone so caring. And fun. To get to work with him every day, doing something I love so much . . . it's amazing."

"God loves to give good gifts to his children." Addy smiled.

"Yes, he does."

"Well, I'd like the good gift of Zach Stone." Lexi watched as he made his way to yet another young woman.

A network executive walked up to the foursome, accompanied by a distinguished-looking man in a suit and his equally distinguished-looking college-age son. "Kara, I'd like to introduce our senator, Gerald Perkins."

"You're from Tampa, aren't you?" Lexi looked down at the man—a good two inches shorter than herself.

"I am." The senator shook hands with all the girls. "And this is my son, James."

James smiled. "We enjoyed the show, Kara."

"Thank you. We enjoyed making it."

Natalia knew Kara meant that. What would it be like to get to do what she loved every day? *But what do I love?* The image of helping in the ESL program popped into her head. *Right, like I could do that for a living. Mamà and Papa would yell at me for even suggesting it.*

"Where do you guys go to school?" James asked.

"It's a small Christian school," Addy answered. "You've probably never heard of it."

"Actually I worked with a guy from a small Christian school this summer. Tampa Christian, I think."

"That's our school!" Lexi grabbed James by the shoulders and shook him. "Who'd you work with?"

"Brian Younger."

Natalia felt her face heat up. Even in Orlando, she couldn't escape him.

"He's our pastor's son." Addy pulled Lexi off the senator's son.

"Great guy. We worked demolition together." James snapped his fingers. "Actually, we worked for the Adams's family. Their son goes to Tampa Christian too, I think."

"Spencer." Lexi sighed.

James grimaced. "Brian is by far the better man."

Addy and Lexi both looked at Natalia.

James looked at Natalia. "Are you two . . . ?"

"No." Natalia wished she were anywhere but here.

"He's a great kid," James said. "Hard worker, fun, mature."

"I don't think this young woman wants you matchmaking, son," the senator interrupted. Natalia closed her eyes in relief. "We just wanted to come by and let you know how proud we are of you guys. A show that's funny *and* family friendly. That's what I love to see. Keep up the good work."

The rest of the evening was a blur of introductions, rich food, and loud music. At midnight, the girls hugged Kara good-bye and headed back to Tampa.

Natalia tried to stay awake for Addy, but her eyelids refused to obey. Thankfully, Lexi was in the front seat and was especially chatty. Natalia gave in to fatigue, her thoughts drifting back to James Perkins's praise of Brian. Too tired to fight off the thoughts, Natalia allowed herself to agree with the senator's son. Brian *was* great . . .

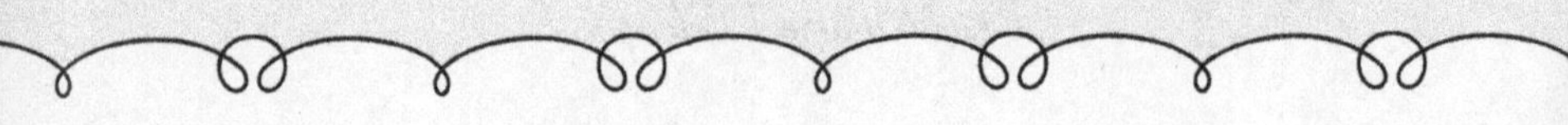

Chapter 37

Brian sat back as Natalia patiently explained the words on the handout. Tonight's ESL class was focused on shopping vocabulary, and Brian had asked Natalia to lead, knowing she would be a much better teacher on that subject than he would.

"Many of these words are similar to our own."

Brian resisted the urge to close his eyes and listen to Natalia speak. Her accent was intoxicating. Combined with her exotic good looks and incredible personality, she was irresistible.

But I have to resist. The whole school had been in shock when word spread that Natalia Lopez had rejected Spencer Adams's invitation to homecoming. *She's made it clear dating is out. God, why can't you make it clear to me too? Being around her all the time is harder than working demolition ever was.*

Natalia flipped through a PowerPoint presentation she had put together. Photos of different stores, with a variety of items, filled each screen. Below each picture was the word in English. She finished a tour of Target by walking through the toy aisle.

Smart thinking. Several of the students had children. This particular vocabulary would be quite helpful.

Confirming that suspicion, hands went up.

"What is the word for *rompecabezas*?" Victor asked.

Natalia thought for a moment. "I'm not sure. Brian?"

"Rompa-what?" Brian snapped out of his daydreams.

"Rompecabezas. It's like a picture that's broken into pieces that you have to fit together."

"Puzzle?"

Natalia's eyes closed. "Yes, of course. Puzzle."

The class tried to say that word—the overload of consonants difficult for Spanish speakers.

Several more hands went up, and Natalia easily identified the words for *skateboard, coloring book,* and *action figure.*

When class ended, several of the students thanked her for the lesson, feeling ready to begin early Christmas shopping now that they knew the words for the items on their children's wish lists.

"You are a good teacher." Brian shut the door as Victor, the last of the students, exited.

She turned off the computer. "I was lucky to have been educated in Spanish and English."

"Yes, but knowing a subject doesn't always mean someone can teach it. You, my friend, have a gift."

Natalia looked at Brian, her green eyes dancing. "I do love this."

"You'll be a great teacher someday."

Her eyes darkened. "My parents wouldn't like that at all."

"Why?" Brian straightened. "Teaching is a noble profession."

"Yes, but my parents expect me to go into a lucrative profession."

He laughed. "Teaching definitely doesn't pay well."

"Exactly."

"But do you think God wants you to be a teacher?"

"I think God wants me to obey my parents and not waste the thousands of dollars they have invested in my education."

The edge to Natalia's voice silenced any further arguments Brian wanted to make.

"I'm sorry." Natalia walked close to Brian, her vanilla-scented perfume enveloping him. "I have been thinking about this a lot. My parents expect me to go to an Ivy League school and become a successful businesswoman."

"But that doesn't appeal to you." Brian was grateful for parents who always encouraged him to follow God's path for his life. "Have you prayed about it?"

"I've prayed for peace to obey my parents." Natalia stepped away, and Brian resisted the urge to pull her close to him.

"God has a plan for your life. If that plan is different from your parents' plan, you need to follow God's."

Natalia smiled. Brian felt his heart lighten.

"Your mom said the same thing."

Brian had forgotten about his mother's earlier struggles. She made her choice to follow God long before Brian was born. "Her dad hated that she married my dad."

"But it was obviously the right thing to do."

"Obviously."

Natalia sat in one of the green cloth chairs. "But they'd be so angry. And what about my testimony? Wouldn't I lose my parents' respect if I disobeyed them?"

Brian pulled up a chair to sit across from her. He could see the struggle on her face and prayed for wisdom to know how to help her. "It comes back to God. Are you more willing to refuse his plans for you or your parents'?"

Natalia closed her eyes. "Why do they have to be different? It isn't fair."

"If your parents gave you a green light to do anything you wanted, what would it be?"

She looked around the room. "This. I'd want to keep doing this. I'd love to go to a Bible college so I could learn more, to help people know him better."

Brian watched Natalia's eyes light up as she talked. Brian leaned forward, his elbows on his knees. "There's a verse in Psalms that says, 'Delight yourself also in the LORD, and he shall give you the desires of your heart.'"

"So God will give me what I want?"

Brian shook his head. "Dad says that verse means that when we are really seeking God, he'll put his desires in our hearts. He makes us want to do what he wants us to do."

Natalia's eyebrows furrowed. "But what I want to do is go to a Bible college."

"And you're seeking God, right?"

Natalia bit her lip. "I'm trying to."

"So that desire is from God. So is the desire to teach. God put those desires in your heart."

"But my parents . . ."

"Trust God with your parents. But obey his voice."

Natalia put her head in her hands. "This is so hard."

The door opened and Juanita, a beautiful Ecuadorian woman in her midthirties, stepped quietly into the room.

"Señorita Natalia." Tears glistened in her eyes. "I had to come back, to tell you thank you. Tomorrow I interview for a job. At Target. You help me. Now I know more words. I can get job, help people. Buy Christmas presents for my daughters. All thanks to you."

Natalia returned the woman's hug. Juanita wiped tears from her eyes as she left the room. Natalia had tears of her own streaming down her cheeks.

"You okay?"

She turned away from Brian and composed herself. "Yes, I've just never . . ."

"You're making a difference." He handed her a tissue. "Feels good, doesn't it?"

Natalia turned to Brian, her green eyes bright from tears unshed. "It does."

She looked so vulnerable, so helpless. Brian reached out for her and pulled her into a tight embrace. Natalia rested her head on his chest and gave into the tears. Brian knew she wasn't just crying over Juanita's words. These tears were for her family, for Maureen, for all the different directions she was being pulled in. He also knew this felt so right. Too right. The only girls he'd ever hugged were his mom and sisters.

This is definitely not the same. Brian's heart raced and his mind went places he knew it shouldn't. *I'm just a shoulder to cry on. That's it. Natalia probably doesn't see me any differently than my sisters do.*

Brian pushed those thoughts from his mind and rubbed Natalia's slender back with his hands. Her tears were slowing and, unfortunately, she pulled away. Her face was red. Was she blushing? Embarrassed?

"I'm sorry." Natalia grabbed her purse and rifled through it. "I'm just . . ."

"Natalia." Brian touched her shoulder. "You don't need to feel guilty for struggling."

Her smile was slow, but Brian could see hope breaking through her despair.

The door opened again. This time Pastor Mike stepped into the room. "You guys done? I'm ready to go home."

Natalia straightened and picked up the last of the night's snacks. "We were just heading out."

Brian's heart sank. *I was just starting to break through. Thanks, Mike.*

"I'm ready." Natalia looked up at Brian.

Any hope he had of just feeling friendship was gone. He needed to stop lying to himself. He was falling for this girl and falling hard.

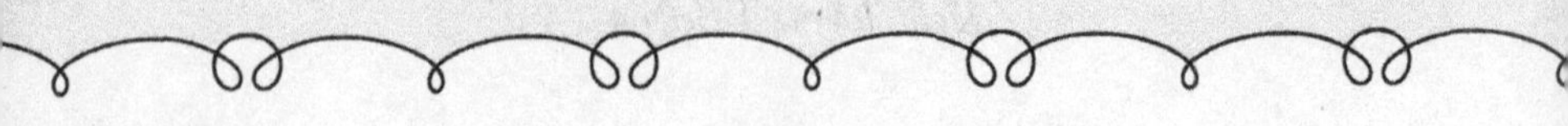

Chapter 38

"I've been trying to stay out of my sister's hair. But I think I need to step in." Carol sat across from Natalia at a picnic table outside the school cafeteria. She had taken the day off and, after dropping her girls in their classes, came and asked if Natalia could miss part of first period.

"I'm so glad you feel that way." Natalia had tried to encourage Maureen to speak to her sister, but that woman refused, barely even speaking to Carol when they saw each other at church. "I leave for Costa Rica tomorrow. Maureen will be all alone for a week."

Carol shook her head. "I shouldn't have waited so long. It's just that . . ."

Maureen and Carol's relationship was strained. Maureen resented Carol's "perfect" life. "Maureen thinks you're waiting to tell her you were right about her marrying my father."

"I would never say that to her. She's grieving. I don't

need to make life harder for her. I want to help her. I just don't know how." Carol shrugged. "Maureen was always the strong one, always in charge. She knew what she wanted and she made it happen."

Natalia thought how different Maureen was from that description. "The divorce has changed her."

"But not forever." Carol's eyes shone. "God doesn't want her to be defined by this."

Natalia thought of the times she had begged Maureen to seek help, to forgive, move on. "I don't know how to help her."

Tears fell down Carol's cheeks and she held Natalia's hand. "You should never have been put in the position where you felt that was your job. I'm so sorry, Natalia."

Natalia looked down at the wooden table, fighting her own tears. "She won't go to a counselor."

"Maybe not." Carol smiled. "But she can go and have fun. Get away. I'll talk to Jack. While you're gone to Costa Rica, we can go on a girls' weekend. Reconnect. Relax." Carol's smile broadened. "Maureen needs to be reminded that life goes on, and she needs to enjoy it."

"I don't know if she'll agree to that."

"Then I'll kidnap her." Carol laughed.

"What?"

"I'll just grab her and throw her in the car. We'll go to the beach, have a spa day. We used to do that all the time before she moved to Spain." Carol folded her arms, lost in thought. "I can't believe I haven't thought of that before now."

Natalia prayed God would use this to help bring

Maureen out of her depression. The knowledge that someone else was helping work toward that end was a relief to Natalia's struggling soul.

The bell rang and Natalia, not wanting to miss Bible class, hugged Carol and made her way out of the courtyard.

"Natalia." Spencer walked toward her. "Ready for Bible?"

"My favorite class of the day."

He raised his eyebrows at her. "You're probably wondering why I was coming from the main office."

She chose not to offend the young man by stating no, that thought hadn't crossed her mind.

"I was called out of first hour because the school is putting together a promotional video, and they wanted to interview me for it." Spencer's smile spoke volumes. "I guess they think I'll be a good face for the school."

"That's quite an honor."

He laughed. "Well, I guess there's not a lot to choose from. I mean, who else would they pick? Acne-faced Derek Harris? Or Brian the Friendly Ghost?"

Natalia's face heated at Spencer's tone. "Brian is one of the nicest, most selfless guys on this campus. He'd be a wonderful choice to represent the school."

Spencer raised his hands in surrender. "I was just kidding. Brian's a nice guy. It's just that . . ."

"You're better looking?"

"You think?" Spencer laughed.

What happened to the nice guy who struggles with his parents just like I struggle with mine? "I think I don't want to be late for Bible class." She walked into the senior hallway.

Spencer walked right behind her. His overpowering

cologne made Natalia's eyes burn. "You can keep running, Natalia, but I'll catch you eventually."

"What?" Natalia spun around.

"Come on." His grin never wavered. "Everyone expects us to date. We might as well give them what they want."

"I don't date." *Can this guy not take no for an answer?*

"Okay, so let's not date. Let's just hang out and have some fun." Spencer shrugged. "It's our senior year. You need some better memories than sitting at home with your step-mom and helping translate Spanish at church."

The bell rang as Natalia opened her mouth to respond to his ludicrous remarks.

"We'll talk later." Spencer slid into his desk and winked at Natalia.

She caught Brian's gaze as it went from her to a very smug Spencer. She hated the sadness she saw there, hated that Spencer's confident air led Brian to believe there was something between Spencer and her.

Pastor Brian opened his Bible and all thoughts of boys were gone. Today they were starting their discussion of worldviews. Natalia had read several chapters ahead in their textbook and was thrilled at what she learned.

"How we view the world affects everything we do." Pastor Brian flipped on the projector and revealed the first slide of his PowerPoint. Two huge pairs of glasses were side by side. One pair looked like a Bible with rims and ear-pieces. The other pair was made from a globe. "Do we view life through the perspective of God's Word? Or do we see it from the world's perspective?"

The hour went by far quicker than Natalia wanted. She

took so many notes, she was writing on the margins of her paper. Everything she heard made her want to know more, made her question if she was really seeking to understand her purpose from God's perspective or using human wisdom to make decisions.

Decisions like dating?

Natalia jumped as the bell rang.

Where did that thought come from? Natalia was sure she shouldn't consider dating. Of course that's what God wanted her to do.

Right?

Natalia gazed over as Brian walked to the front to talk with his dad. Her heart pounded as he turned and caught her eye. In less than twenty-four hours, they'd be leaving for Costa Rica, spending a whole week together. Natalia hated how excited that thought made her.

"All set for our week in paradise?" Spencer's cologne greeted her before he did.

"I was just thinking about it, actually." Of course, Natalia wasn't about to tell him who she was thinking about. Although it might do Spencer good to know she wasn't thinking about him.

"We can have a lot of fun down there." Spencer's smile was big. He was certainly growing bolder in the last few days. "Think about it."

He walked off before Natalia could answer.

I'll think about it, all right. I'll think about how I'm going to avoid you for those seven days.

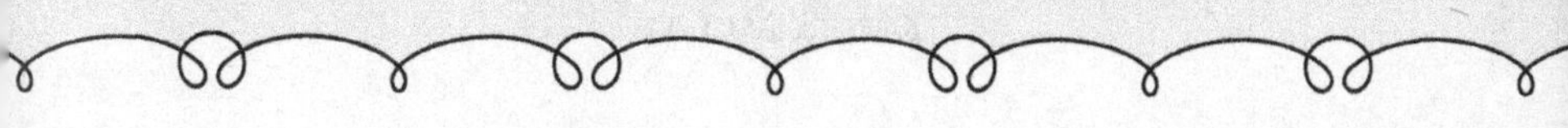

Chapter 39

¿Qué?" Natalia asked. Again. Since they'd departed the airplane in San José, Natalia had had to ask the Costa Ricans to repeat themselves several times. Once, while going through Customs, the official actually switched to English so Natalia could understand what he was saying.

"Their accents are so different." Natalia rubbed her temples. Pastor Brian was beside her, helping to organize the group.

"It's all right, Natalia. You're doing fine."

After a few more difficult conversations, Natalia was able to find a phone and call their contact in the city. Luis would pick them up and drive them to the house where they'd be staying.

"He's on his way." Natalia hung up the phone and looked at the group. "We're supposed to wait outside and he'll be by in a large blue van."

Natalia followed the signs to the exit. The glass doors

opened and the smell of exhaust fumes filled her nose. *This is* not *paradise.* She looked at the dirty sidewalks and far-as-the-eye-could-see pavement. *Where's the rain forest? The monkeys? The waterfalls?*

"Isn't it wonderful?" Lexi's grin filled her face as she stood beside Natalia. "I've missed this place."

"It's . . . not what I expected."

"I was thinking the same thing." Spencer scooted next to Natalia, his shoulder touching hers. "I hope the place we're staying is decent. If it isn't, I have my dad's credit card and his permission to stay at a hotel."

"We're all staying together," Pastor Brian spoke up. "This is a mission trip. We are here to serve, to get out of our comfort zones."

Lexi turned to Spencer. "I felt the same way when I got here last year. But this place grows on you. It's amazing."

He rolled his eyes and turned his attention back to Natalia.

"Is that our van?" Pastor Brian pointed to what looked like a cross between a minivan and a school bus. It had a high roof and a rack on top.

The van pulled up beside the group and a muscular Costa Rican stepped out.

"Luis." Brian grabbed the man and hugged him. "I missed you."

Luis patted Brian's back. His English was much better than Natalia had expected. "Good to see you, little Brian. Ready to work?"

"Of course." Brian grabbed a suitcase and hefted it on top of the van.

"Hey, what are you doing with that?" Tori yelled. The petite sophomore put her hands on her hips.

"All the luggage goes on top." Brian lugged another bag on top.

Spencer put a hand on Brian's arm as he reached for Spencer's designer suitcase. "No. Mine goes with me. The bag alone is worth four hundred dollars. What's inside is worth three times that. It does not go on a roof."

"There's no room inside for luggage." Pastor Brian lifted Spencer's bag. "But don't worry. It'll be fine. We tie it down with bungee cords and put a tarp over it in case it rains."

"At least put mine on the bottom," Spencer grumbled. He sat on a bench as Brian, his dad, and Luis loaded all the luggage on the van's roof.

"All right," Luis called out as the last bungee cord was secured. "Everyone in."

Natalia stepped into the van. The bench seats were clean but faded from the sun. The faint scent of pine cleaner lingered in the air. She sat by a window and Spencer squeezed in beside her.

"It'll get tight in here." He put his arm around the back of her seat. "We'll have to sit pretty close."

Every seat was needed, so Spencer's unwanted proximity only increased when three more were added to their row. His side was plastered against hers, from shoulder to ankle. "Maybe Costa Rica isn't so bad after all," he whispered in her ear.

Natalia refused to answer, choosing instead to look out the window as the van lurched out of the airport. Poverty competed with luxury as slums existed on one block and high-rise apartment complexes on the next.

Farther in, the streets were lined with houses that shared walls. Tall gates stood sentry in front of each.

Lexi leaned over from the end of their row. "People have gates in front of their houses for safety. Look at the top. Folks plaster broken glass up there so no one will try to climb over the gate and get in."

Lexi was right. Some places had razor wire instead of broken glass. "So are robberies common?"

"I don't know if they're common." Lexi shrugged. "But they happen. A lot of streets have guards on them for added security." She pointed to a tiny "house" on the corner as they were stopped at a traffic light.

"Is that guy holding a gun?" Natalia saw a huge rifle slung over the guard's shoulder.

"Yep."

Natalia glanced at Spencer. He seemed to be growing paler by the second. "Are you okay?"

Spencer straightened. "Of course. I just thought . . . this is supposed to be a more developed country. We're working with missionaries."

"It is more developed," Lexi said. "Ever seen pictures of Haiti? This place is like the Taj Mahal compared to that."

"Whatever." Spencer's eyes were glued to the window. Natalia got the impression that he was more upset than he was letting on.

Half an hour later Luis pulled up in front of their house. The bottom floor was the headquarters of a local ministry. The second floor could be reached from the interior or exterior. Natalia chose the latter, walking up the narrow concrete steps behind Mrs. Younger.

The door opened into the living room. It was fairly large and sparsely furnished. Three mismatched couches sat on a brown tile floor, and a large wooden table filled the side of the space.

"There's no TV?" Spencer moaned from behind Natalia.

"No, I'm afraid not." Mrs. Younger pointed to her left. "The boys' room is down that hall."

"Room?"

"Yes." Mrs. Younger laid her suitcase on the floor. "There are several bunk beds in there. Looks like you get first pick."

Spencer, not appearing terribly thrilled with the arrangement, made his way down the hallway.

"Natalia, the girls have two rooms, over to the right," Mrs. Younger said. "I'd like for us to head out to the grocery store once everyone is in. We have the van for a few more hours, then Luis has to leave."

"All right."

Natalia walked into the room and claimed a bottom bunk. *Not the Ritz-Carlton.* She surveyed the room. *But it's very clean. And we have our own bathroom.*

Addy and Lexi joined Natalia and Mrs. Younger on the grocery run. The store was different from what Natalia expected. It was quite large and sold everything from hamburger meat to hardware. There was even a shoe store and a pizza place on the property.

"Each of you should grab a cart. We have twenty people to feed, after all. And the more we can get this time, the easier it will be."

The girls did as they were told and followed Mrs. Younger down the aisles. Natalia had to interpret the names of the items on the list as Mrs. Younger called out what she needed.

"Wait a minute." Addy put a hand on Natalia's arm as she reached for the milk. "This isn't refrigerated."

"So?" Natalia looked at the box. It was perfectly fine. Not too different from what she used back in Spain.

"Milk in a box?" Addy grimaced. "That can't be healthy."

"Says the girl who spent the first six years of her life *in a jungle*." Lexi rolled her eyes and grabbed two more boxes from the shelf. "It tastes really good with cow tongue."

"What?" Natalia and Addy said at the same time.

"You heard me." Lexi grinned. "Costa Rican specialty. Almost as good as my grandma's specialty."

"Don't tell me." Natalia closed her eyes.

"Mondongo." Lexi licked her lips.

Natalia groaned.

"What is that?" Addy asked.

"Cow stomach."

"We won't be having any of that." Mrs. Younger shook her finger in Lexi's face. "Unless you choose to order it on one of our out-to-eat nights."

"Oh, you're eating it," Lexi said.

The girls continued to have fun as they filled each of the four carts with food, drinks, toiletries, and snacks for their week.

When the total came to over two hundred thousand, Natalia's breath caught in her throat.

"It's all right." Mrs. Younger pulled out her credit

card. "That's in *colones*. It is actually about four hundred American dollars. Pretty cheap for all this."

Luis was waiting outside to help them load all the groceries. The sky was dark by the time they arrived back at the house. Empty pizza boxes were scattered around the vacant living room.

"Where is everyone?" Natalia asked as Lexi brought in the last of the grocery bags.

"Brian probably took them out for a walk." Mrs. Younger placed a large watermelon on the counter. "He likes to get a look around and prepare them for the walking we'll be doing the rest of the week."

"We probably walk, what, twenty miles every day?" Lexi put a box of cereal in a cupboard.

"Not quite that much." Mrs. Younger laughed. "But we do walk a lot."

Natalia heard yelling from the first floor. Spencer's voice carried up the stairs. His word choices were not ones she would expect to hear on a mission trip.

"No way am I staying here," Spencer was saying. "I either get a hotel room, or I'm on the first flight home. I did *not* sign up for this."

A horrible smell followed Spencer to his room. Brian, his face red and his eyes dancing, came up behind Spencer.

"What happened?" Mrs. Younger whispered.

Brian walked out the door to the front stairs and began laughing hysterically. The women joined him on the small landing and shut the door so Spencer wouldn't hear.

"Spill it," Lexi said.

"Spencer jumped into this soccer game at the park,"

Brian began, once he stopped laughing. "All these guys are playing. And they're good, you know? I mean, soccer is their sport. But Spencer is sure he can teach them a thing or two. He gets out there and they just run circles around him. So he gets mad and starts to stalk off. But he walks right into this huge pile of . . ." Brian's laughter took over again. But having smelled Spencer, Natalia had little doubt what the rest of the story was.

"He stepped right in it?" Lexi asked.

"And it was a big dog." Brian wiped tears from his eyes. "I mean *big*."

"These are three hundred dollar designer leather shoes." Spencer looked out at them from a window they did not realize was just down from where they were standing. "It is no laughing matter."

The rest of the group came through the gate, most laughing. Spencer disappeared back into his room.

"Oh yes." Lexi shook her head. "This is going to be a great week."

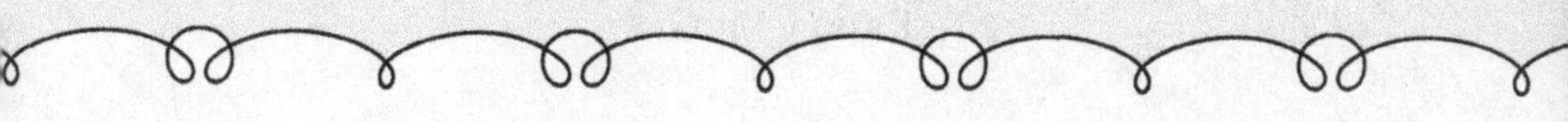

Chapter 40

"What do you miss most about the States?" Addy asked the group of elementary-aged missionary kids. She, Lexi, and Natalia sat at the lunch table with them, taking a break from their morning of preparing for the Vacation Bible School lessons they would begin the next day.

"My Aunt Jeannie." A fourth grader named Alayna pulled out an iPod and showed the girls a picture. "We used to go to the park every Saturday."

"I miss my dog," Cassie, in third grade, said. "We had to leave her with some friends when we moved here."

Natalia wanted to join in the conversation. *I miss Jamón Serrano. Carmen. History that makes sense.*

"Where will you go when your parents are done with language school?" Addy asked.

Cassie sat up straight. "Buenos Aires, Argentina. It's called the 'Paris' of South America."

Natalia smiled. "I've heard that. Are you excited?"

"Yes." Cassie leaned forward. "I'm already Skyping with a girl my age who lives there. Her parents are missionaries too."

"That's great," Lexi said.

Natalia noticed Alayna was staring into her lunch box. "What about you, Alayna?"

"We're moving to Ecuador. Next month."

"Are you not looking forward to it?"

Alayna's eyes were sad. "I have to leave all my friends here. And I don't know anyone there."

"What about Karla Cotter?" Cassie asked. "She moved to Ecuador this summer."

Alayna shook her head. "She's in Quito. We're moving to the Loja Province. That's really far away from Quito."

"I'm sure you will make friends there, Alayna." Natalia hated the sadness on the little girl's face.

Alayna's hazel eyes filled with tears. "But they all speak Spanish. I'm not very good at speaking Spanish. I try, but . . ."

Natalia put a hand on Alayna's shoulders. "How about if I give you some lessons?"

"You know how to speak Spanish?" Cassie asked.

"Sí. Soy de España," Natalia responded.

"You're from Spain?" Alayna wiped her eyes.

"Look at that." Natalia put her hand up to give Alayna a high five. "You know more than you think you know."

"Will you give me lessons too?" Cassie asked.

The other girls in the group echoed Cassie's request. Natalia promised to meet with the girls after Vacation Bible School the next day.

She wanted to begin right then. Ideas for lessons and games were flying through her brain, but a teacher stood and announced lunch was over.

"Will you guys eat with us again tomorrow?" Alayna asked, her voice soft.

"You better believe it." Lexi gave Alayna a hug. "And I want to hear all about the Loja Province, okay? Tell me something cool about it."

Alayna's eyes lit up. "All right. I'll ask my mom."

Natalia, Lexi, and Addy walked to the gym. The rest of the group was there, putting together the pieces for the week's crafts.

"Nice of you to join us." Spencer had been cranky all day. Being in charge of the glittery "Jesus Loves Me" door hangers was probably not helping his mood.

"We were having lunch with some of the kids." Lexi put her hands on her hips. Natalia suspected her friend's infatuation with Spencer was beginning to fade. "You were invited."

"I'm not exactly a kid person."

Pastor Brian walked over to the foursome. "A few more minutes and we need to head out to the church where we'll be working."

"More work?" Spencer stood.

"We're going to meet the pastor and see what supplies we need to get."

"Is Luis taking us?" Lexi asked.

"No." Pastor Brian waved to a group of children walking to the playground. "We're taking the bus."

"Public transportation?" Spencer groaned. "This just gets better and better."

"Give it a rest, Spencer," Lexi said. "We're here to serve."

"All right, guys." Pastor Brian placed a hand on Spencer's shoulder. "Just think of it as an adventure."

Two hours later even Natalia was exhausted by the "adventure." Maps of the bus routes only helped so much. Natalia tried to translate and help navigate, but the latter was made more difficult because most Costa Rican streets had no names. The church they would be helping was located twenty meters north of the pharmacy by the Japanese Park. Parks were as abundant as pharmacies in San José, so locating the right park with the right pharmacy wasn't easy. To compound the difficulties, the sky opened up and dumped water on their heads. Florida had heavy rain, but this downpour was unlike anything Natalia had ever seen.

Finally finding the right park, the group exited the bus and began the twenty meter walk to the church. Natalia soon found the flimsy poncho she pulled out of her backpack was no match for the storm.

"I'm singing in the rain." Brian kicked the water from the puddle up into the air as his surprisingly good tenor voice sang loud enough for the locals to look out their windows at the odd *gringo*.

Lexi joined in, her voice not quite as pleasing as Brian's. Spencer stepped in beside Natalia. "Just when I thought this trip couldn't get any worse."

Natalia's Bible study had focused on gentleness the week before. She bit back a sharp reply and tried to remember what she had learned. "I have always taken having a car for granted. So I'm kind of glad to go through this. God is showing me more ways I can be thankful for what I have."

Spencer stuffed his hands in his pockets. "I guess. But I still say we go find a nice hotel and a driver."

"And miss out on this?" Natalia pointed to Lexi and Brian, now dancing arm in arm down the road.

"I think that's it." Pastor Brian pointed to a sloping dirt driveway that ended with a small concrete building.

"Iglesia de Nueva Esperanza." Pastor Brian's Spanish was almost as bad as his son's. Almost. "Yep. New Hope Church. This is us, guys."

Spencer tried to avoid the mud as he walked down the hill. In her cheap sneakers and old jeans, Natalia ran quickly, slipping and sliding all the way down. "This is fun."

Brian grabbed her arm at the bottom of the hill. "Whoa there. That's concrete." He pointed to the steps leading up to the building.

"That would have hurt." Natalia laughed, hoping to mask the pleasure of having Brian's arm in hers.

"Natalia." Pastor Brian motioned for her to come to the door. "Will you help me? I believe the pastor is in here."

She walked in the church, wiping her feet on the mat to avoid carrying in souvenirs of her trip down the hill.

The church was just a rectangular building with concrete walls, a concrete floor, and several windows—some with glass, some without. Wooden pews filled the center and a small wooden podium sat at the front. The back wall had a large cross hanging on it. That was the only decoration in the room.

The pastor entered from a room in the back. He greeted Natalia and Pastor Brian and introduced himself as Pastor Guillermo.

"He says many thanks for your help. The people of the church are so grateful. They will be coming out tomorrow to bring breakfast."

"It is our pleasure." Pastor Brian waited for Natalia to translate. "We had planned on painting the inside and outside. Is there anything else we can do?"

Natalia swallowed hard as the pastor explained that was more than enough, that he and his people were just happy to have a building. Another church had built it the year before. Having a building that was painted was exciting for his small congregation.

"What color would you like?" Pastor Brian asked.

"Any color is fine." Pastor Guillermo shrugged. Natalia thought back to the debate at school over how to decorate the gym for the upcoming homecoming festivities. *We could learn a lot from Pastor Guillermo.*

The pastor insisted that the group come inside. He had coffee, juice, and pastries in his office—a room the size of Natalia's closet, with a desk, a bookcase, and two chairs. The group filed in one by one to get a drink and a snack.

"This juice is amazing." Lexi held up her glass.

"What's in it?" Natalia asked the pastor.

"It's orange-carrot juice."

"Who knew?" Lexi laughed. "It beats anything I've ever had before."

"Probably because it's fresh squeezed."

"This is pretty good." Spencer finished off his glass.

"See, I knew you'd come around." Lexi lifted her cup in a toast.

"I just said I like the juice."

"It's a start." Lexi grabbed Spencer's cup. "Let me get you some more."

Mrs. Younger walked over to the group. "I want to bring in flowers and pictures and curtains."

"I was just thinking that," Addy said. "And some cushions for the pews."

Natalia thought of the pastor. "Pastor Guillermo is just grateful we are painting. He doesn't expect anything more."

"I know." Mrs. Younger sighed. "But I think of all we have—the flower arrangements in the foyer, carpet everywhere, chandeliers. And ours isn't even a fancy church."

"Not in America." Addy nodded.

"I'm going to ask Brian if we have enough money to get some extras for them." Mrs. Younger walked toward her husband.

The rain stopped, so the group made their way back to the bus stop. Natalia bid the pastor good-bye and expressed the group's enthusiastic desire to return the next day and get to work.

"You're being awfully quiet." Brian leaned forward in the bus to whisper in Natalia's ear. His breath sent tingles down her spine.

"I'm tired." Natalia closed her eyes. "Translating is hard work."

Brian began rubbing Natalia's shoulders, and she relaxed into his hands, too exhausted to fight the pleasure she felt at his touch.

Tomorrow she would remember that she wanted nothing to do with boys. No feelings interfering with her plans, whatever they were. Tomorrow.

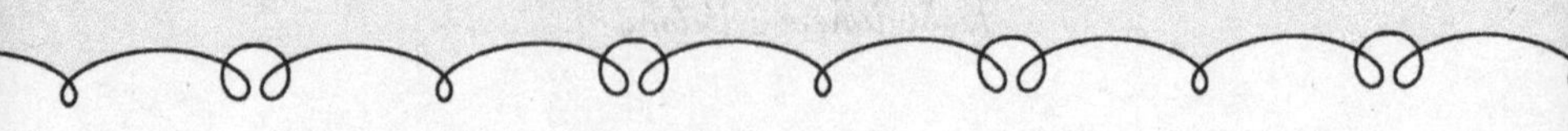

Chapter 41

"You walked five miles to get here?" Natalia asked the young Costa Rican woman serving her *gallo pinto* at breakfast the next day. The church was filled with men and women. The smell of seasoned black beans and rice was unusual for the morning, but she was humbled by the people giving up their time and money to serve them.

"*Sí,* but that is nothing." The woman's deep brown eyes were shining. "We *Ticos* walk a lot."

"Ticos?"

"Costa Ricans," the woman answered. "Walking is good for you."

This woman didn't walk for the health benefits. Judging from her worn clothes and shoes, Natalia guessed that the woman walked because even the public transportation was too expensive for her to take every day.

"Thank you so much for breakfast."

"It is our pleasure."

Natalia finished her breakfast and found the supplies

that were brought in a van with their driver. A luxury for most people here.

The group had decided on a medium blue to paint the outside and beige for the inside. The folks at the church were thrilled with the choices. Natalia marveled at their excitement. Had she ever been excited about a coat of paint before?

While she was painting, ideas for her Spanish lesson with Alayna and the girls ran through her mind. She would teach them a song to learn the days of the week and months of the year, and play Simon Says to teach them the parts of the body. She was so engrossed in her plans she didn't hear Pastor Brian call an end to the morning's work.

"Don't go crazy on us yet, Natalia." Lexi pulled the paintbrush from her hand. "We need you to translate. I can only do so much, you know."

"I'm not going crazy." Natalia hopped down from the chair she was standing on.

"You were totally singing to yourself just then. And smiling." Lexi made "crazy" circles with her finger.

Natalia felt herself blush. "I was thinking about the little girls we had lunch with. I promised to give them a Spanish lesson."

"Whatever you say." Lexi raised her eyebrows. "But tomorrow you might want to lay off the *gallo pinto*."

Spencer, on Natalia's right, was quiet on the van ride back. She had noticed him talking with one of the men—using fairly impressive Spanish—back at the church. *I did hear his mother is Cuban. I wonder why he never used his Spanish before.* Natalia didn't know what they talked about, but she guessed whatever it was had Spencer thinking.

Brian turned around in the seat in front of Natalia. "You've got beige in your hair."

"At least I don't have blue fingers." Natalia pointed to the hand that lay over the seat back.

"I think it's Smurf-tastic." Brian smiled. Having watched him in action today, looking out for the group, trying to speak to the Ticos, Natalia knew she was fighting a losing battle with her heart. "So what do you think?"

"About what?"

"Costa Rica? The mission trip?"

"I love it." Natalia felt Spencer turn away from her, looking out the window at . . . what?

"I knew you would." Brian's smile was quite self-satisfied. "Just like I knew you'd like helping with the ESL class."

"At least you're humble about it all." Natalia rolled her eyes.

"I know." Brian's grin widened. "I'm just about the most humble person I know."

"Will you guys stop it?" Spencer's voice reverberated through the van, silencing everyone.

"Sorry, man," Brian said.

"A guy in there has three jobs, trying to support his family. He brings in seven hundred dollars a month. He comes home to sleep and that's it. And what does he have to show for it? Nothing. And no hope of getting anything better." Spencer punched the seat in front of him. "And he wasn't asking for help. Wasn't complaining. He was telling me how lucky he is. He has electricity and a tin roof. Some of his friends don't even have that."

"Why are you so angry?" Natalia looked at Spencer, his face tense.

He rubbed his eyes. "I don't know. It just doesn't seem fair. He's thankful to be living in poverty."

"And we're ungrateful for living in wealth," Natalia finished softly. The rest of the van had returned to their conversations. Brian turned around in his seat as well.

Spencer looked at Natalia, his brown eyes softening. "I was listening to that guy, and I just wanted to bolt, you know? I didn't even know what to say. And he was so happy. He was thrilled to do what he's doing, to live where he's living."

"He is rich," Natalia said.

"What?"

"He has the riches of God's grace and peace in his life. That's worth a whole lot more than anything the world can offer."

Spencer sighed. "It's making me rethink stuff, you know?"

Natalia prayed that Spencer would open his heart to God's truth. She wanted to talk to him more, but the van stopped in front of a food court.

"Lunchtime," Pastor Brian called out. "We've got forty-five minutes, then we're headed to the language school for VBS."

From the poor little church to a large food court that housed several familiar fast-food chains. Would she ever fully understand the complexities of this small country?

Natalia stood by the registers and helped translate the group's orders. To her relief both Lexi and Spencer helped.

"Your Spanish is good, Spencer."

"Not really." His reply was quiet, and Natalia could tell he was still thinking about his encounter at the church. "My mom tries to get me to speak it with her, but I hardly ever do. It's just so much easier to speak English. That's going to change when I get back."

"Gram and Gramps do the same with me," Lexi piped in. "Maybe we can all practice together when we get back."

There was no time for a response. More of the group needed to order. They were all seated in record time. Lexi, Addy, and Natalia went to the upstairs seating area.

"This is nice." Addy looked around.

"Wait until you see the mall." Lexi dipped a fry in the *salsa rosa*—a mixture of ketchup and mayonnaise.

"That looks disgusting." Addy eyed the salsa rosa.

"I swear, Addy, you're the biggest food wimp on the planet." Lexi held out a fry with the mixture dripping off the end. "Just try it."

"No way." Addy held a hand up.

"It's this or cow tongue."

Addy looked at Lexi. Natalia knew her friend was trying to determine whether or not Lexi was serious about that threat.

"Girl, don't test me." Lexi moved the fry closer to Addy's face.

Addy opened her mouth to take a small bite and Lexi shoved the whole thing in.

Natalia handed Addy a napkin. "You got a little salsa on your chin."

Addy swallowed. "Thanks."

"And . . . ?" Lexi leaned forward.

"It wasn't the worst thing I've ever tried."

"Wait until you taste the cow tongue." Lexi crumbled up the paper from her burger. "It'll surprise you too."

Addy didn't have time to respond because Pastor Brian was calling everyone back to the van. "Time for VBS!"

Natalia couldn't wait to begin. She had spent most of the morning thinking about that afternoon.

"I need a nap," Lexi said.

The group arrived at the language school with just thirty minutes to spare. Natalia, Lexi, and Brian had been put in charge of game time. Natalia laid out the blindfolds for the first game while Brian pulled hula hoops from a storage closet in the back.

"I've got the Smarties and straws," Lexi called out.

"Lay them on a paper plate, with an empty plate beside them," Brian said.

The kids would use the straws to carry each Smartie from one plate to the other. The threesome had fun the day before trying that game out.

"I promised Toni I'd help her set up the crafts." Lexi looked at her phone. "I'll be back in ten minutes."

Lexi skipped out, and Natalia surveyed the room. "Looks good."

"It sure does." Brian's eyes were locked on Natalia, and her face warmed. "The room. The room looks good. The kids are going to love it."

Natalia wanted to laugh at Brian's cover-up. *I know he's interested. I'm sure he knows how I feel. Why am I fighting this again?* The latest picture of her father with fiancée number four popped into her mind. *Right. That's why.*

"All set?" Mrs. Younger walked in the gym.

"Yep." Brian stretched. "Thanks to me. I have worked my fingers to the bone, but we are ready."

Natalia popped Brian in the arm with a blindfold. "And what have I been doing?"

"That's exactly what I've been asking myself."

Mrs. Younger hugged Natalia. "You, my dear, have been doing triple duty—helping here, helping at the church, and translating. I don't know what we'd do without you."

Natalia felt the compliment all the way to her feet. "I love it all. I just wish we could stay longer."

"Let's see if you still feel that way at the end of the day." Brian motioned to the screaming kids pouring into the gym.

Two hours later, with ears ringing, Natalia swept up the last of the Smarties.

"Those kids are loud." She poured the contents of the dustpan into the trash. "But they're cute."

"Loud, yes." Lexi put the last of the hula hoops away. "Cute? Not so much. I don't think I'm designed to be with kids for long periods of time."

Natalia looked at her phone. "I promised the girls I'd give them a Spanish lesson. Do you guys mind if I run over to the chapel? I should be able to catch them before they leave."

"Go right ahead." Lexi gathered the blindfolds in a heap. "I'm going to lie down right here and take a nap."

Natalia ran up the steps to the chapel. She spotted Alayna through the window. The little girl smiled and waved. When Mr. Younger finished his Bible lesson, the kids filed out. Alayna ran to Natalia.

"You came." She hugged the older girl.

"Of course I did."

"I invited some other friends. Is that all right?"

Natalia looked at the eager faces. "Are you girls ready to learn some Spanish?"

"Yes," they all squealed.

"Excellent." Natalia felt her hands being grasped by two of the girls. They dragged her to a covered patio with plastic tables and chairs.

Natalia was surprised at how much Spanish the girls knew. Some had only been in Costa Rica a few months, but they were soaking in the language. They moved past the simple songs Natalia taught them and begged for more. They loved performing, and when Natalia suggested they sing some of their songs on the last day of Vacation Bible School, the girls clapped with joy.

"Yes, yes, yes!" Cassie twirled around.

"Miss Natalia." Alayna tapped Natalia's shoulder excitedly. "Guess what? I asked my mom about Loja, and she said it's the music capitol of Ecuador."

Natalia's heart warmed at the excitement in Alayna's voice. "How exciting. Maybe you can teach your new friends some of these songs."

Alayna's eyes grew wide. "I could!"

Natalia didn't even feel her feet touch the ground as the group walked back to their house. She had never in her life enjoyed anything as much as she enjoyed being with the kids today. It was even better than helping with the ESL class, and she loved that.

Mrs. Younger put a hand on Natalia's shoulder. "I saw

you with the little girls today. I think you've found your calling."

Natalia stopped on the sidewalk and stared at the pastor's wife. "My calling?"

"You are a teacher." Mrs. Younger nodded. "And a very good one. God has given you a great gift."

A teacher? The thought was as terrifying as it was thrilling. She couldn't imagine anything as rewarding as working with children every day. But there was no way her parents would ever agree to that. She was raised to be a successful businesswoman. That's what her parents expected.

"I think you've found your calling." Mrs. Younger's words replayed in her mind. *Your calling.*

Could it be?

Natalia remembered Brian's words, *"God gives you the desires of your heart."* She remembered the Ecuadorian woman she was able to help. Little Alayna's face lit up when she learned songs she could share with her friends.

God, this is my desire. To teach. But how will I ever be able to convince my parents of that?

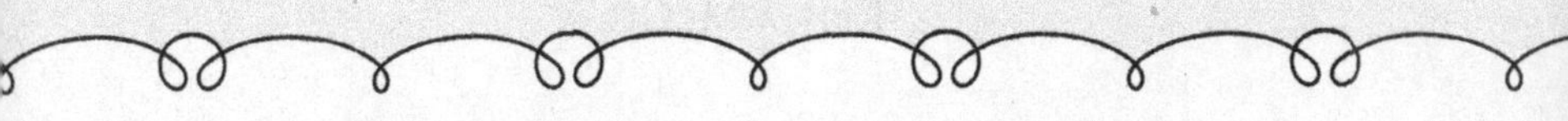

Chapter 42

Brian watched Natalia and Spencer deep in conversation. Again. Ever since Spencer's blowup on the van three days before, he had been monopolizing Natalia's time.

Is this just a trick? Brian's gut clenched as Natalia leaned over, her hair brushing Spencer's shoulder. *He couldn't get her with his looks and charm, so he tries to manipulate her by acting like he's suddenly interested in spiritual things.*

Brian moaned. How big of a jerk was he? *I fly thousands of miles to tell people about Jesus and get mad when a guy from my backyard wants to know him?*

"She's just being a good friend." Mom put a hand on Brian's knee. How did she know what he was thinking?

"No." Brian stared out the window. "I wasn't looking at them. I'm just zoning out. Tired."

"Brian." Mom squeezed his knee. "You're not fooling me. I know you're jealous. It's better to admit it and deal with it than live in denial."

"Not in the mood for one of your shrink sessions, Mom." He turned away.

His mother sighed. He hated hurting her. But this was his problem. And admitting—out loud—that he was in deep like with Natalia would do no good for anyone. If Spencer became a Christian, any hopes Brian had with the beautiful Spaniard were out the window. *Spencer has a whole lot more in common with Natalia than I ever will.*

Dad stood at the front of the van. "Remember, folks, this is our last day at the church. Let's get everything done and leave them with a beautiful surprise on Sunday."

Brian looked out at the church. Being here had been fun. He really connected with the pastor—despite Brian's terrible Spanish. Guillermo had enough English that, between the two of them, conversation could happen.

Guillermo was just eight years older than Brian. His father was a pastor too. They had great conversations about that life. Even in different countries, expectations of pastors' kids remained the same. His dad's church was large and fairly affluent. Brian was surprised to learn there were churches like that in San José. But when a man from this church contacted his father about their need for a pastor, Guillermo felt called to take the position. He was finishing his degree in engineering at the time. Because the church was so poor, he worked for the government and preached for free.

"Brian." Guillermo pronounced his name the same way Natalia did—BrE-ayn. "My friend, I was thinking about you all night. God has a message for you."

Brian stopped what he was doing. "A message?"

"Is that not the right word?" Guillermo pulled out a pocket Spanish-English dictionary the men had used to help communicate.

"No, that's the right word. But it just sounds weird. A message from God? Isn't that what the Bible is?"

"Come with me." Guillermo walked toward the back of the church. Exotic plants and trees with fruits Brian couldn't name spread out before him. "You have a calling."

"I know." Brian plucked a fuzzy green fruit and turned it over in his hands. "I'm a pastor's kid, remember? We're all called to serve God and honor him."

"That is . . . how do you say?" Guillermo flipped through the dictionary. "General. I am speaking of a specific calling."

"You know what I am supposed to do?" Brian didn't like where this was going.

"God has designed you to be in ministry."

Brian threw down the fruit in his hand. "Come on, Guillermo. You, of all people, should know how annoying that is. My dad's a pastor, so I should be too?"

"I no say you should be pastor." Guillermo's English got worse as he grew more passionate. "But ministry, yes. You have pastor's heart. You care for people."

"I can do that in any job."

"Trust me." Guillermo motioned to the church. "You unhappy in another job. I know. I tried. I no take this church right away. I no want it. Pastor. Me? So I work. Good job, good money. But I was *muy* miserable."

"Muy miserable?" Brian grinned.

"You laugh at my English?" Guillermo slanted one eyebrow. *"Señor 'No hablo Español.'"*

Brian laughed at Guillermo's impression of his terrible Spanish. "I really sound like that?"

"No changing subject." Guillermo shook a finger in Brian's face. "Do not run from God's calling. To run only makes the time spent doing his will shorter. Many regrets in that."

"I don't want to be in ministry."

Guillermo breathed deeply. "Yes, you do. But you are scared."

Brian tensed. "It isn't fear. It's . . . I don't know. I don't want people criticizing me all the time. I don't want my phone to always be on or my door always open. I want a normal life."

"What is normal?" Guillermo spread his arms wide. "There is no normal. There is God's way and your way."

Brian hated how right this man sounded. "But if I'm not a pastor, then what?"

"Missionary?" Guillermo smiled. "Many churches like this need pastor."

"Right. You've heard my Spanish."

"Language school."

Brian thought about working at a church like this one. He hated to admit it, even to himself, but the idea was appealing. He loved being in Costa Rica. Loved working at the church. But could he live here? Or in another country? Away from his family? He looked across the grassy yard to where Natalia was helping his mom pull out the decorations they purchased the night before. *If I had someone to work with me. Someone like . . .*

"Natalia has a calling too." Guillermo smiled.

Can everyone read my mind? "Natalia is way out of my league."

"Out of your league?" Guillermo began flipping through the dictionary.

Brian shut the book. "Never mind. I need to get back to work. But . . . thanks. I'll think about what you said."

"I pray for you."

Brian hugged the man. He spent the morning painting the outside of the church and thinking about what Guillermo had said. The more he thought about it, the more excited he got. Was it a coincidence that he'd been working with the ESL ministry? That he felt more at home with them than with his own friends?

A missionary? Brian had met a few as they had come through church. Some had lived in jungles and eaten strange foods. That didn't appeal to him at all. But living in a place like Costa Rica, pastoring a church and maybe doing something else on the side?

Surprisingly, the thought wasn't nearly as repulsive as he thought it would be.

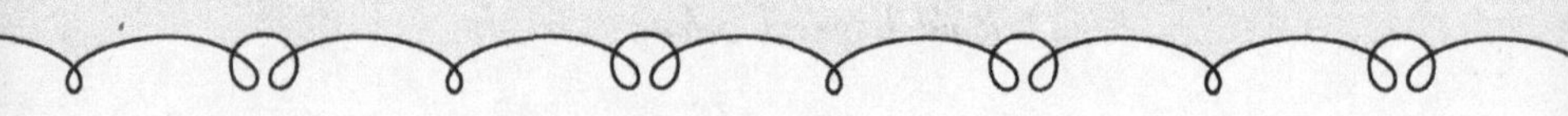

Chapter 43

"And now we have a very special presentation." Pastor Brian stood on the stage in the gym and motioned for Natalia to bring up her group of girls.

Cassie and Alayna led the way with six other girls following behind. Natalia wiped tears from her eyes as she stood to the side and led them in their first song. "La Cucaracha" was a favorite, and many in the audience joined in. After that the girls sang a jump rope song, complete with jump ropes. Natalia thought she would burst with pride. The girls had worked so hard, and their pronunciation was perfect.

They will be just fine in their new countries. Alayna, especially, had come a long way. Natalia had taught her several phrases to help her get to know girls in Ecuador. The eight-year-old practiced them everywhere she went, and she told Natalia that morning that she couldn't wait to get to Loja and meet her new friends.

When the girls finished, Natalia led them down the stairs and back with their group. Pastor Brian began to dismiss the crowd when one of the teachers at the school stepped in.

"Boys and girls, we want to give a big thank-you to the folks from Tampa. How about a round of applause for all their hard work?"

The room erupted in cheers and clapping. The children stood, as did their parents. The teacher at the front waited for a minute before urging the children to sit back down. "As you can see, they are very appreciative of all you've done. And during class the last few mornings, we have been working on something very special."

One of the fourth graders handed a stack of construction paper, tied with ribbon, to the teacher. "These are notes from every boy and girl in here. Please take this back to your church with our gratitude, and know that we will never forget you."

Pastor Brian accepted the papers and wiped his eyes with the sleeve of his shirt. "Thank you all. We have been the ones blessed by this trip. We are so proud of all of you. You are going out into the world to spread the gospel, and we are honored to have been a small part in helping to encourage you in that ministry. Each one of you is treasured by God and treasured by us." Pastor Brian couldn't go on. Natalia cried with him, and the children, urged by their parents, ran to hug the nearest member of the Tampa team.

The walk back to the house was the quietest it had ever been. Everyone was thinking about their good-byes.

"Do we have to go sightseeing tomorrow?" Lexi, of

course, was the first to break the silence. "Can't we spend another day at the language school?"

Pastor Brian shook his head. "I am not going through that again."

"They are such sweet kids." Mrs. Younger nodded.

"Most of them." Addy cocked her head.

A few of the kids were unruly—running out of lessons and talking back to the teachers. Addy had an especially difficult first grader in her Bible story time. Little Jacob would stick his tongue out every time he saw her. When she tried to teach, he would grab the papers from her hand, crumble them up, and throw them at her. Pastor Brian had to be brought in to sit with the boy.

"It was amazing," Addy said. "But I'm ready to get back."

"Tomorrow will be amazing too." Brian pointed toward the mountains in the distance. "Wait until you see the rain forest. And the volcano."

Natalia could see that Brian was falling in love with this country. She had seen him speaking with Guillermo the day before. She didn't know what they had discussed, but it had kept him thinking the rest of the day. Being here had affected Spencer too. Natalia couldn't believe the changes that took place in him in just a few short days. He had worked harder than anyone at the little church, and he even played with the missionary kids on the playground, giving them piggyback rides and playing soccer—not even caring that his expensive shoes were caked with Costa Rican mud.

"I'm with Lexi." Spencer's quiet voice was at Natalia's ear. "But I'd like to go back to the church. There's so much more we could do."

"I know." Natalia regarded Spencer as they made their way down the cracked sidewalk. "But I must admit I am looking forward to being a tourist. I've never seen a volcano."

Spencer slowed, letting the rest of the group go ahead. Natalia stayed back with him. "I need to apologize to you, Natalia, for being such a jerk back in Tampa. And here. You've been a good friend despite my behavior. Thanks for that."

"It has been exciting to see God work in you these past few days, Spencer." And Natalia meant that. His eyes had been opened to the joy of serving God, and his joy had been contagious.

"I need your help, though." Spencer's voice was quiet, and Natalia knew that admission was difficult for him. "I need to change, but it's going to be hard when we get back home. Here, it's easy. We're on a mission trip, and most of my friends aren't here. They're not going to understand when I get back. It'll be easy for me to just go back to the way I was."

Natalia thought of Spencer's friends—the ones who mocked her and her friends as they were going to Bible study or who texted beneath their desks during Pastor Brian's apologetics class. It would be hard for him.

"Of course I'll help you, Spencer. We'll all help you. That's what the body of Christ is for." The pair walked faster, catching up with the group as they made their way into the house.

Brian glanced her way, his expression hard to read. He had been different this week too. More distant. He didn't talk to her nearly as much as he usually did. That should make her feel relieved, but it didn't. She missed his conversations, his friendship. Too much.

And then there was Spencer. He was changing. Much kinder. Hungry to know God more and serve him. He wasn't the same rude rich boy she knew him to be. Was she developing feelings for him?

No. Natalia shook her head to clear those thoughts. *What am I thinking? He's just being vulnerable right now, and that is endearing. But this is not attraction.* And as she examined her feelings, she knew what she felt for Spencer was not what she felt for Brian. *I don't think about Spencer all the time. I don't wish Spencer would sit next to me on the van. I don't worry about how I look first thing in the morning because of what Spencer might think.*

"Girl." Lexi bumped Natalia's arm, following Natalia's gaze to Brian, who was helping his mom pull out the ingredients for the evening's snack. "You've got it bad."

Natalia quickly walked away, refusing to admit just how right Lexi was.

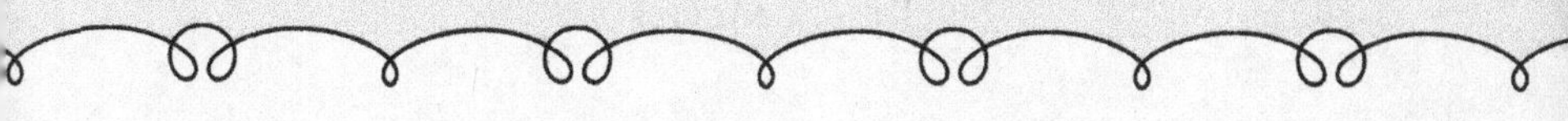

Chapter 44

"Unbelievable." Natalia stood on a bridge looking down at the rain forest. Monkeys lay in the trees, colorful birds flitted past her. And there were so many shades of green.

"I grew up in a place like this," Addy said, her voice soft. "I'd forgotten how beautiful it is."

"Do you miss it?" Natalia had never heard Addy mention her life growing up in the jungles of Colombia.

Addy shrugged. "I know more about it from my mother's journals than from my own memories. But she loved it."

"What made her want to be a missionary?"

Addy looked at Natalia. "She and Dad just knew it was what God wanted them to do. It was a desire he put in their hearts."

"They were killed, weren't they?" Natalia hoped she wasn't prying.

Addy bit her lip. "Yes. But so were most of Jesus' disciples and many Christians throughout the years. Obedience comes at a cost. But I don't think my parents would say they regretted that cost."

Natalia thought about that. *Obedience comes at a cost.* "I think your parents would be very proud of you."

"I hope so." Addy sighed. "I know I'm proud of them."

"This is so different from San José." Lexi interrupted the girls' conversation. "Don't you think, Spencer?"

He was quiet, taking it all in. Hope flared in Lexi's eyes. Her attraction to the young man had certainly not died. Natalia feared, however, that Spencer didn't return those feelings.

"What?" Spencer turned to Lexi. "Sorry. I was thinking."

"About how amazing God is to have created all this?" Lexi smiled at Spencer.

"Actually, yes." His eyes locked on Lexi's. "How did you know?"

"Spence, that's what we're all thinking."

His look of surprise faded to one of conspiratorial understanding.

"Enough standing around." Lexi began walking. "I want to get to the waterfalls. Who's with me?"

The group hiked farther, up steep stairs and past more monkey-laden trees.

"My camera." Natalia remembered that she left it lying on a log before the hanging bridge. She had taken a picture of the group and then continued on. "I need to go back."

"Not by yourself." Pastor Brian's "dad" voice took over. "Bri, go with her."

Brian looked like he would argue, but a glare from his father caused him to shake his head and keep going. Natalia hurried to keep up with him. Halfway across the bridge, she said, "Slow down. Don't forget I'm about a foot shorter than you are, Goliath."

Brian slowed. "Sorry."

"I'll go as quickly as I can." Natalia felt his frustration, but she didn't understand the source. "I know you want to be with the rest of the group."

Brian turned around, and the bridge swayed beneath their feet. He stood still for a moment, his eyes locked on Natalia's. Then he stepped toward her, his blue eyes never leaving her face. The sun chose that moment to peek through the foliage, and his whole face lit up, golden sparks jumping off his red hair. A day's stubble lined his jawline and a thin sheen of red covered his nose, evidence of four days working outside on the church.

He stopped just inches from Natalia, bending his head down so she could feel his breath on her face. "No, Natalia. I don't want to be with the rest of the group."

Natalia's heart beat so fast, she could hear its echoes drumming in her ears, almost feel her blood pumping from her head to her toes. Brian had never looked at her like that. There was no mistaking his meaning, his feelings.

Natalia wanted to say something, to do something. But she was frozen. She couldn't move, could barely breathe. Both stood on the bridge, staring at the other.

Brian groaned and stood up straight, backing up a few steps. "Sorry. Forget that. I'm tired and stressed and not thinking clearly."

Brian walked to the end of the bridge, found Natalia's camera, and returned, dropping the camera into her hands.

She resisted the urge to stop him and jump into his arms, tell him she never wanted to forget that moment. But she couldn't. They were both silent as they made their way back to the group.

"What took you guys so long?" Lexi's smile quickly changed to a curious stare. "Um-hmm. And just what happened back there in the rain forest, Juliet?"

"What?" Natalia's face heated. "We got my camera and came back."

"Then why does Brian look all serious? Brian Younger Jr. never looks serious." Lexi leaned in. "The rain forest would be a great place for a first kiss."

"We barely even spoke," Natalia said, louder than she intended. "And I don't date. Or kiss. You know that."

"I know that's what you keep saying." Lexi shrugged, obviously undaunted by Natalia's arguments. "But your eyes tell me something different."

"Please." Natalia rolled her eyes.

"'Please kiss me, Brian.'" Lexi laughed.

Natalia didn't want to hear any more. "Which way to the waterfalls?"

Lexi pointed to her right. "But when it happens, let me just go on record as saying I called it."

Natalia walked faster, meeting Spencer at the parapet overlooking the most beautiful waterfall she had ever seen. "Wow."

The spray from the falls misted over the pair. "Amazing, right? We sure don't have anything like this in Tampa."

"Or Spain."

"I have taken creation for granted, you know?" Spencer's

eyes never left the waterfall. "I used to think of everything as just what we needed or what we could use to make money. But this—it's just beautiful. God made it to be beautiful."

"Like he's showing off." Natalia smiled.

"I've always heard people talk about God giving good gifts. But I never thought about what that meant. Now I get it."

"What do you mean?"

"This." Spencer motioned to the waterfall. "This is a good gift. God is showing us that he loves us by creating a world that isn't just functional. It's beautiful."

"God delights in giving his children good gifts." Natalia remembered having that conversation with Addy. She was referring to dating. She would, being head over heels in love with Jonathon Jackson. At the time, Natalia didn't want to think about dating as a good gift. It was a curse she was trying to avoid. But maybe Addy was right.

"What are you thinking?" Spencer asked.

Natalia sighed. "I'm thinking that you are right. Maybe I do underestimate God's goodness."

Brian Younger Jr.'s face popped into Natalia's mind and, for the first time, she let it linger.

Chapter 45

"You okay?" Spencer sat next to Natalia on the plane. But this was a different Spencer than the one who got on the plane just a few days before. Being in Costa Rica had changed him. No, God had changed him. Natalia was pleased, rather than annoyed, to have him as her seatmate.

"No." Natalia wiped her eyes. "I'm not okay. I want to stay here."

"I know what you mean."

"The girls in my little group begged me to come back."

"So go back—maybe during Christmas or spring break."

Natalia thought about how much she'd love to do just that. But where would she ever get the money? The only reason she was able to come this time was . . . "By the way, thanks."

"Thanks?" Spencer buckled his seat belt as the stewardess began her preflight speech.

"I know your family provided the money for me to come on this trip. I can't thank you enough."

"No." Spencer hung his head. "I'm so embarrassed. It wasn't my family. I just wanted you to think it was."

"Oh."

"I was such a jerk." Spencer watched the flight attendant demonstrate the proper way to use the oxygen mask.

"I was just thinking of how much you've changed. God is really working in you."

Spencer smiled. "I wish I'd listened to him before. This is amazing—talking to God, reading his Word. I used to laugh at you guys for your Bible studies. Now I get it."

"I'm proud of you, Spencer."

"What do you mean?"

"God spoke to you, and you listened." Natalia felt the plane back away from the gate.

Natalia thought of Carmen back home. She prayed her best friend would find Jesus like Spencer did.

But Spencer didn't find Jesus because he heard great arguments or read three-page e-mails filled with lessons from Bible class. It was God's love and grace that broke through to his heart. *God, help me show that to Carmen, to love her to you. And thank you for showing me that with you, anything is possible.*

Natalia looked out the window as the plane raced down the runway and shot into the sky. She was leaving a piece of her heart in Costa Rica. She didn't know if she would ever get it back.

"Want to talk about it?" Dad asked as Brian stared at the backs of Natalia's and Spencer's seats.

"No."

"Can I talk about it, then?"

"No." Brian pulled a book out of his backpack and pretended to read.

"*Wuthering Heights*? Really?"

Brian moaned. "It's for English. I need to get a head start."

"If I remember my British literature correctly, that story is about a young man who pines for a girl for so long that he eventually becomes angry and reclusive."

"I'm not angry and reclusive." Brian turned the page. "And I'm not pining for a girl. Who says *pining* anyway? What are you, eighty?"

"Right, you're not angry or pining." Laughter laced his father's voice.

Brian slammed the book shut. "She says over and over again that she doesn't date. And I respect that. I try to be her friend. And Spencer—who always gets everything he wants—has a spiritual awakening and gets Jesus *and* Natalia."

"How do you know she's interested?"

Brian sat up and motioned to the couple with his head. "Look how close they're sitting, Dad. We're not sitting that close. Nobody else is sitting that close. And she keeps leaning her head toward him."

"The plane is loud, son." Dad patted Brian's knee. "She's just trying to hear him. And be a good friend."

"Right, a good friend. That's exactly what she's being." Brian closed his eyes. He didn't want to talk anymore, didn't want to see what was going on.

Come on, God. I try to do what's right and what do I get? I don't get the girl. I do get a "message" from you telling me I should do what I most want not to do.

The more Brian thought about being a missionary, the less he wanted to do it. In fact, just about everything was annoying him right now.

"I hate turbulence." Natalia gripped the armrest as the plane bounced up and down. The sky outside her window had grown dark. She knew the pilot was trying to get the aircraft above the storm, but the trip up was not enjoyable.

"Think about something happier." Spencer put his hand on Natalia's. "The girls you worked with. The waterfalls."

Natalia pulled her purse out from under her seat. The girls in her group had made her a card. She read it again. "That just makes me sad. Look how sweet these girls are."

"Sad is better than scared." Spencer took the card from Natalia's hand.

"Perhaps." She pointed to the card. "Cassie drew a picture of us singing. Isn't that cute?"

"You really loved being with them, didn't you?"

"So much."

"I think you'd make a great teacher."

Natalia sighed. That thought had hardly left her mind all that week. "You, of all people, know how that would sound to my parents. A teacher? At a missionary school?"

Spencer returned the card. "A waste of your talents."

"Not to mention the thousands spent on my education." Natalia mimicked her father's baritone voice.

"I guess I'm lucky. I actually want to do what my dad wants me to do."

"Lawyer?"

"Yes. Ever since I was six years old and went to court with my dad for the first time." Spencer smiled. "I knew that's exactly what I wanted to do."

"You don't feel like you were pressured into it?"

He raised his eyebrows. "Dad would probably kill me if I didn't want to be a lawyer. But I do, so we're good."

Natalia sighed. "What would you do if you didn't want to be a lawyer?"

Spencer shook his head. "I've been a Christian less than a week. Don't ask me. The Youngers could probably give you some good advice."

"I'm sure they could." Natalia thought back to the conversation she had with Mrs. Younger, when she explained how she married Pastor Brian despite her parents' protests over his chosen profession. "I don't think I'm ready to hear it, though."

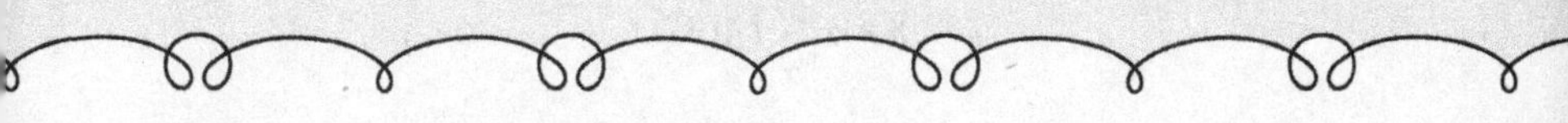

Chapter 46

"Welcome home!" Calla and Nora sang out in unison.

Jack had picked Natalia up from the airport, assuring her that "big surprises" were waiting at home.

Natalia just hoped those big surprises did not include another helping of her stepcousins' crunchy flan.

The house was filled with balloons and streamers. The girls had made a cake with "Welcome Back, Natalia" written on it. She guessed the girls had misspelled her name a few times because that part of the cake matched the blue lettering more than it did the white frosting.

"I've only been gone a week." Natalia laughed. "But thank you. This is all very sweet."

"I helped make the cake." Nora's blue fingers attested to that fact.

"Me too." Calla jumped up. "I cracked the eggs, and I only got a little bit of the outside in there. But I cleaned it all out."

Hmmm, crunchy cake? At least these girls have culinary consistency. "You girls are the best. I can't wait to try it."

"Can we have it now, Mommy?" Calla batted her big blue eyes at Carol. "Please?"

Carol looked at Maureen. "I think that's fine. Aunt Maureen and Natalia have a lot of catching up to do, so we'll eat our cake quickly and let them talk."

What did that mean? Maureen seemed very happy. Natalia was relieved to see a genuine smile on her stepmother's face when Natalia walked through the door. Maybe Carol had been able to make some progress while Natalia was gone.

Before Carol and her family left, Natalia fished through her suitcase for the bracelets she bought for Maureen's nieces. "These are made from trees grown right in Costa Rica."

"Wow." Nora put the bracelet on very slowly, her eyes wide.

"Thank you, Natalia!" Calla hugged Natalia's legs. "I love it."

"I'm glad you love it." Natalia kissed the top of the girls' head.

"So . . . ," Natalia asked Maureen as soon as their guests had left. "What do we have to talk about?"

Maureen sat on the couch and motioned for Natalia to sit beside her. "Let's talk about your trip first. We've done enough talking about me lately."

Natalia didn't need any prompting. She told Maureen everything she could remember about the school, the church, the girls in her group, the food, the sights and smells. "It was wonderful, Maureen."

"It sounds wonderful." She clicked through the pictures on Natalia's cell phone. "Most of your photos are of the girls in your group."

Natalia looked at the picture on the screen—Alayna's mouth was wide open, singing "La Cucaracha" at one of their rehearsals on the patio. "They asked if I could come back."

"When?"

"Whenever I can," Natalia said. "But sometime before the summer, or all of these girls will be gone. Their parents are only at the language school for a year at most. Then they go to the country where they'll be serving."

"Maybe I can go with you next time." Maureen wiped Natalia's hair from her face. "I could even see if we could make it a ministry for my Spanish classes. Wouldn't that be exciting?"

Natalia sat back. "Who are you, and what have you done with Maureen?"

"You sound so American." Maureen laughed. "But you're right. I'm not the same person I was when you left."

"Carol?"

Maureen cocked her head to the side. "Actually, Natalia, it was you."

"Really?"

"The day you left, I sat here feeling sorry for myself, moping around as usual. And then I saw your note."

In all the excitement of the mission trip, Natalia had forgotten she had left a note for her.

Maureen pulled the note out of the side-table drawer. "'Dear Maureen, I know you are struggling now, and you are questioning your decisions. But I will always be grateful that God allowed you to come into my life. You introduced me to him, and you taught me about him. Thank you for that. I am praying God will help you see how special you are, how loved you are by him and by me.'"

Maureen put the note back in its envelope and placed it in the drawer. "I had been beating myself up over my mistakes. You were right. But reading that note made me see that good came out of those mistakes. You came out of it. And I would never, ever trade my relationship with you for anything."

Natalia wiped tears of joy from her eyes. "I feel exactly the same way."

"Good." Maureen wiped her eyes. "Because I intend to be around for you a lot more. I want this to be your best year ever. I want you going off to college knowing you have an ex-stepmother in Tampa who loves you very much."

Natalia winced. "We really need to come up with something better than 'ex-stepmother.' That sounds even worse than stepmother."

Maureen's laugh was loud. Natalia loved the sound of it. "Very true. How about we just stick to Maureen?"

"Maureen it is." Natalia returned her embrace. "Welcome back."

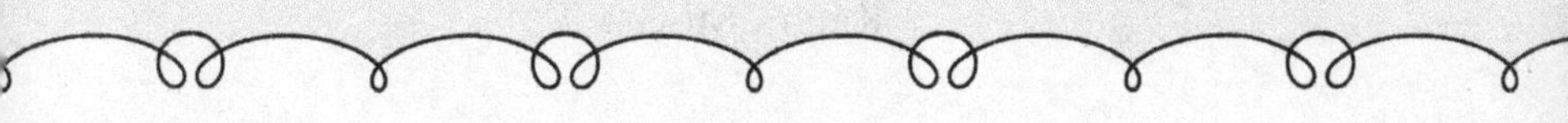

Chapter 47

"I can't believe you're getting on a plane again." Maureen pulled Natalia's suitcase out of her trunk.

Natalia's father called the day after she returned from Costa Rica. He had a business meeting in New York and wanted Natalia to fly up and meet him there. "I still wonder what he wants."

"Oscar's your father." Maureen slammed the trunk closed. "He wants to spend time with you."

"Are you sure you're okay?" Natalia knew the mention of him was difficult for Maureen.

"I will be." Maureen nodded. "I have my first appointment with a counselor today. I know I have a lot to work through, and I can't work through it all alone. Pastor Brian recommended her."

"I'm so proud of you." Natalia hugged Maureen.

"Hey, that's supposed to be my line."

Natalia spent the flight praying about how to broach the subject of teaching with her father. Time away from the girls hadn't lessened her desire to teach. In fact, it had just grown. She missed them so much that she tried to call Brian and see if they could offer a special class for the children of the students in their Thursday-night class. Brian hadn't returned her call yet. But he would. Natalia wondered at his avoidance of her lately, but assumed it was just the emotions of the mission trip. She felt it too.

Lord, how do I tell my papa I don't just want to teach, but I want to consider teaching overseas? That idea had settled into her mind and wouldn't stop replaying. She couldn't imagine anything more fulfilling than living in Costa Rica and teaching missionary kids. *I'd have to study Bible and education in college, but that would be exciting.* In researching online she learned that she could even complete her student teaching overseas.

Papa would understand. He was passionate, so he would appreciate the passion she had for this. Mamá would be harder to convince, but surely she would come around too. *They both love what they do. I'm sure they want the same for me.*

Peace washed over her as she exited the plane. God was going to work all of this out.

Papa began talking nonstop from the moment he greeted Natalia. She understood some of the business jargon, but most of it seemed like a foreign language—one she had no desire to learn. The pair took a car Papa had rented to a nice restaurant near the theater district.

"Dinner and a show for my best girl." Papa smiled as he pulled up to the valet parking attendant.

"What about Victoria?" The latest e-mails had contained news of their upcoming wedding in Segovia.

He waved his hand. "She was only interested in my money."

"You broke up with her?"

"I told her I was going bankrupt, and she broke up with me."

"You're going bankrupt?" Natalia thought her father's business had been doing well.

"No." He followed the waiter to a small booth in the corner of the restaurant. "But I told her that to see how she'd react."

"Maureen would never do that."

Papa pulled the chair out for Natalia. "No. Maureen was never very materialistic."

"Do you think you'd ever . . . ?"

"No." He opened his menu. "Women are plentiful, Natalia. I'll find another."

Natalia wanted to walk out of the restaurant. How dare her father treat marriage so callously. "Don't you ever wish you had someone to grow old with? Someone who knows you well and loves you anyway?"

He laid down the menu. "I've told you before—I am not made to be with just one woman."

Natalia's rage left, washed away with a wave of compassion. Her father's flings weren't something genetic, something he couldn't control. They were a reflection of a deeper need. He couldn't love the way he was meant to love because he didn't know the author of love.

"Papa . . ."

"Enough of this." The waiter came and took their orders. When he left, Papa continued, "I want to discuss your future."

She took a deep breath. Now was the time to tell her father the desire of her heart.

"You will work for me." Papa smiled and pulled out a manila folder. "I have spoken to your mother, and she believes, as do I, that you would make a superb partner: Lopez and Lopez. It will take time. You will need to study international affairs and go on to earn a master's in business administration. Preferably at Harvard. I have it all outlined here."

Natalia pulled out the papers. Her life planned out over the next five—no ten—years. Where she would go to college, what she would study, where she would intern. All ending with a few years working up the ladder to finally, by age twenty-eight, becoming a full partner. The number of zeros in her projected salary took her breath away.

"Papa, I—"

"No, don't say anything right now." His smile was broad. "I know it is overwhelming. But I believe you can do it. You are smart, hardworking, and you are a Lopez. When it comes time for me to retire, I will be content knowing the business will stay in the family."

She couldn't even eat the filet mignon the waiter laid in front of her. Papa talked more about the business, about his newest client, about how trends were changing in the international market, and how his company was on the cutting edge of those changes.

Natalia couldn't even enjoy the musical they went to see. *I can't turn him down, God. I can't. Papa is handing me the company he built. He is trusting me with it.*

As soon as the pair made their way to the hotel, Natalia

ran to her room, telling her father she was tired and needed to rest.

Rest, however, would not come. She picked up her cell phone.

"Oh, Brian." Natalia had hoped to catch Mrs. Younger, but a just-woken Brian answered the phone. She glanced at the electric clock on the nightstand. "It's after one o'clock. I'm so sorry. I had no idea. I'll call back later."

"No, it's fine." His tone changed. She could hear his concern, imagine him running a hand through his wavy hair. "Is everything okay?"

Natalia let out a deep breath. She wanted to hang up and deal with this by herself. What was she thinking, calling the Youngers in the middle of the night?

"Natalia." Brian's voice was teasing now. How she had missed that sound. "Don't make me come over there."

"I'm in New York City," Natalia teased back.

"What?" His voice changed from mockery to shock. "When?"

"I left this morning." Natalia placed a fluffy pillow on her lap. "Papa is in town and wanted to see me."

"That was nice."

"Not really." She squeezed the pillow. "He wanted to tell me that he and my mother have decided I will take over the family business."

"Wow."

Natalia waited. 'Wow'? That's it? I call for words of wisdom, and I get 'wow'?"

"Hang on. Let me go downstairs and get some Mountain Dew." Natalia could hear Brian's door open and his footsteps along the wooden floor. He came back on the line. "That should help in the wisdom department."

"You'll never get back to sleep."

"Natalia, this is Brian." His laugh was deep and comforting. "I can sleep anywhere, anytime."

"Ah yes. Well then, drink your Mountain Dew."

Brian did just that, narrating Natalia through the routine of opening the cabinet, pulling out a glass, getting ice, and pouring his drink. "Hear it fizzing? It's a beautiful sound."

"And I'm sure your family will appreciate the residue on the phone tomorrow morning."

"You mean this morning."

"Yes, sorry." She imagined Brian sitting at his kitchen table, drinking his soda and smiling into the phone.

"I'm ready now. Dr. Brian at your service. So your dad wants you to take over his business?"

In bantering with Brian, Natalia had almost forgotten the reason she called. "He has a whole plan mapped out and everything. He and Mamá even talked about it—and they don't talk about anything."

"But you don't want to take over his business?"

"I don't know." Natalia lay on her stomach and turned on the speaker on her phone. "I never considered that Papa would ask me this. It is an honor. And the money . . . as a Christian businesswoman, I could help so many ministries. Maybe that's what God wants. Maybe the desire I've been feeling to teach and work overseas is a desire to help, not actually go."

"You want to teach overseas?" Brian coughed up some Mountain Dew.

"Yes. I guess we haven't really talked since we got back from Costa Rica." The memory of Brian standing on the bridge came back, and Natalia remembered why.

Brian must have been thinking the same thing because their easy conversation suddenly stalled. "Okay, back up some and fill me in."

Natalia explained how her time in Costa Rica had shown her how much she loved teaching. "But not just that, teaching those kids. I understand being in a new country, adjusting. I'd love to be able to help children who are in that situation. To be a small part in helping missionaries go where they're called. How exciting would that be?"

Brian was silent, and Natalia checked her phone, concerned that the connection had been lost. "Brian?"

"Yeah, I'm here. Sorry. So teaching in Costa Rica or running your father's company in Spain."

"But it's more than that." Natalia flipped over onto her back. "My parents want me to do this, to take over Papa's company. And there's nothing wrong with that. It isn't a sin to be in business. It would be a whole mission field of its own. I could do good in either career."

"That's true. But this isn't about choosing the job that is the 'greatest good.' You need to ask God what he wants you to do. Being a missionary teacher isn't any better than being a Christian businesswoman. But doing what God wants you to do is better than doing what your parents want you to do."

"But what if what my parents want is what God wants?" Natalia thought of Spencer—his dad wanted him to be a lawyer, and Spencer was happy to go into that profession.

"Only God can tell you that. I'm just a lowly pastor's kid hopped up on Mountain Dew."

"Brian, you are much more than that," Natalia said softly, then she sat up in bed. "I should let you go. Papa is taking me with him on his meetings tomorrow, so I can get a feel for the business. It would probably look bad if I fell asleep during those meetings."

"It might make him rethink his offer." Brian laughed.

Natalia ended the call and fell back into bed, thoughts about her decision crowded out by thoughts of Brian.

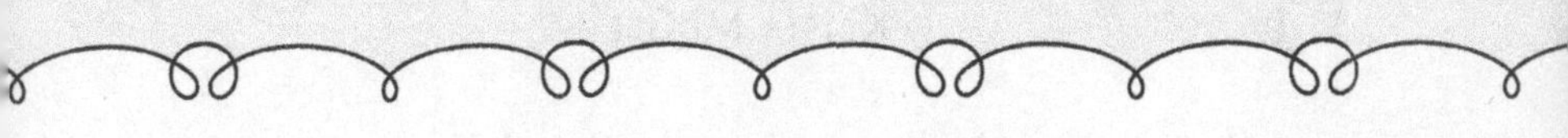

Chapter 48

"You sure you're up for this?" Brian was still shocked to have gotten a phone call from Spencer—much less a phone call telling him Spencer wanted to help renovate the ESL classroom.

"I asked my dad, and he said it was fine." Spencer lifted an old desk and carried it out of the classroom. "He's having new tables and chairs delivered in a couple of hours, so we need to get these out of here. I brought some paint too. These walls are looking rough."

Brian lifted a desk and followed Spencer. "I owe you an apology, man. I know I've been rude to you."

Spencer held the door for Brian. "If awards for rudeness are being handed out, I win. Hands down."

Brian couldn't argue with that. "So a new start, huh?"

"That would be awesome." Spencer bit his lip. "I need another favor from you, though."

"What's that?" Brian hoped it wasn't help with Natalia. He could handle being friends with Spencer. But a matchmaker? No way.

"I want to show my friends I'm different. But it's going to be hard." Spencer put a desk down and wiped his forehead. "I need someone to hold me accountable to the decision I made on the trip. Will you do that for me?"

Brian looked down at the former bully. *God, you really are amazing.* "You're giving me permission to call you out?"

"Yes, I am." Spencer grinned.

"And you won't come back with a smart-aleck remark? Or make fun of me when I walk away?"

Spencer lowered his head. "I've done that, haven't I?"

"A few times." Brian raised an eyebrow.

"I really do want to change. Will you help me?"

Brian slapped Spencer's back. "You bet I will."

The boys spent the morning cleaning and painting. And talking. Brian was impressed with the questions Spencer was asking, and he did his best to answer them.

"Do you think we can have a men's Bible study, like the girls have theirs?"

"At school?"

"We can meet on a different day than the girls."

"I think that's a great idea," Brian said. "You could even invite your friends."

"You think they'd come?"

"I think they'd lick the floor if you asked them to."

Spencer's phone rang, and he walked outside to greet the men bringing the new furniture. They were careful to place everything in the center of the room to avoid the wet paint.

"You guys need a couch in here so you can sit and talk

after class." Spencer looked at the back wall. "I'll work on that."

Brian sat in one of the new chairs. "The gang will be so excited when they walk in here on Thursday. They may even bring some more friends just to show off."

"Do you think I could come?" Spencer sounded almost apologetic.

"Of course. Anytime." Brian hoped he sounded sincere. The reality was that he hated the thought of Spencer intruding on the one thing that was just his and Natalia's. *But if this is what you want for her, God, I need to get out of the way and let it happen.*

"Natalia works with you too, right?"

Brian tried not to cringe. "She translates. But I think she'd like to start a children's class, so the ministry is expanding. We'll definitely need extra help."

"So you and Natalia . . . ?"

Brian heard the unspoken question. Spencer was asking permission to pursue Natalia. And given this new change in Spencer's life, Brian guessed Spencer would back off if Brian asked him to.

She's the girl of my dreams. You can't have her. That's what he wanted to say. But she wasn't his to claim. And if her actions were any indication, her affections were leaning toward Spencer anyway. "We're just friends."

"You sure?"

Brian nodded, not trusting himself to say anything.

Spencer's phone rang again. His father needed him. Renovations on their new bayside mansion were almost finished. "We might be able to have homecoming there after all."

"That's great." Brian thought of his work on that mansion, tearing everything down so it could be made into something magnificent for other people to enjoy.

Kind of like my relationship with Natalia.

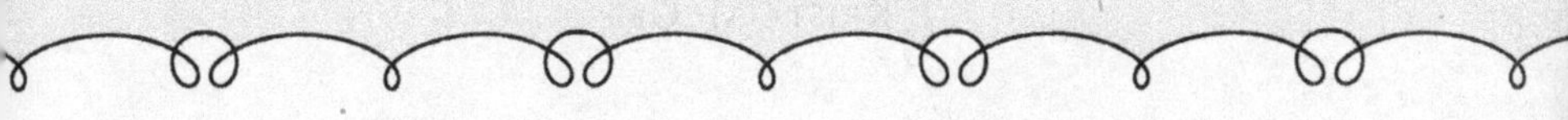

Chapter 49

Natalia laid her head back in the rental car and closed her eyes.

Business meetings were not fun.

She and her father had spent the morning in a conference room with people from several companies and at least three countries. English was the trade language, but when people became very worked up, their native tongues were let loose. Natalia could understand Portuguese fairly well, but she had no clue what the man from Japan was saying. Her father, however, responded to everyone in English, whatever language they spoke in.

"How many languages do you know, Papa?" Natalia forced her eyes open.

"I'm not sure." He shrugged. "I speak three—English, Spanish, and German. But I understand several. The basics, anyway."

"When did you learn them?"

"Along the way." Papa said this as if learning several

languages was a normal part of life. "You know I've spent a lot of time in different countries. I always made a point to immerse myself in their languages and cultures. It helps in business."

That part of business life did sound exciting. "So you just sat and talked with people?"

"And went to their theaters and concerts, their nightclubs and bars. You learn a lot by listening."

Why had her father never applied that to his role as father? She would have loved to have him try to learn "Natalia" as she was growing up.

Papa pulled into a parking space in the airport's parking garage. "So what do you think?"

"I think that's amazing. You are a wonderful businessman."

He turned to face her. "What do you think about the business? Ready to begin preparations to take over?"

Natalia had been dreading this conversation. She prayed all night that God would show her what she was supposed to do. Sitting through the meetings that day confirmed that this life was not one she was designed for. "Papa . . ."

His phone rang and he held a finger up to Natalia. For ten minutes, he spoke in German. Natalia didn't understand most of what was being said. That language did have some similarities to English, so she caught some of the exchange.

I don't want to spend my life in conference rooms and airplanes and traveling from one country to another. I want roots. I want a family.

Where did that thought come from? A family? She couldn't have that. Looking at her father, Natalia wondered.

Maybe she could. Was she living in fear instead of in truth? Was God not powerful enough to allow her to succeed where her parents had failed? Marriage and family were established by God. Why should she be afraid of it?

Natalia blinked as the reality of that truth began to sink into her soul, thawing what she had kept frozen for so long. She thought of the Youngers, of Jack and Carol. Marriages could last. They could be healthy. *God gives good gifts.*

"My man in Berlin." Papa ended his call. "Always a crisis with him. Patience and confidence—that's what helps men like Gustav. That's something you don't learn in college."

"Papa." Natalia took a deep breath. "I'm not sure I am the best choice to take over the business. Have you considered Ari? She is very smart."

Papa wrinkled his brow. "Don't underestimate yourself, Natalia."

"It's not that." She closed her eyes. "I just don't think business is for me. I don't think I'd enjoy it."

"Of course you'll enjoy it. Travel, money, power. What is not to enjoy?"

Natalia wondered if he was treating her like his German client. "But what if I want a family?"

"Then have a family." Papa unbuckled. "And give them everything they want. Just like I did."

Natalia wanted to tell him what she wanted most from him was something he never had—time. "I have found, Papa, that I really enjoy teaching."

"There is a great deal of teaching in our business. We explain the market to our clients . . . we train those coming up."

"But I want to teach children." Natalia spoke quickly, telling her father about Costa Rica, her girls, and her desire to return there after college.

"Natalia." He lowered his head. "You have returned from an exciting trip. I understand. The first time I visited this city, I was sure I wanted to live here, be a hippie in Greenwich Village. It all seemed very romantic. But then reality set in. As it will for you."

Papa was treating her like a child. Anger would have been better than condescension. He wasn't even taking her seriously.

"I believe this is what God has designed me to do. To help children who are moving to another country. It is much like what you have done—learning other cultures to make better relationships. I'll be helping children do that."

"And how much do teachers in Costa Rica make?"

"I don't care. It isn't about money, Papa. It's about a calling."

"That is easy to say when you have money."

Natalia sighed.

"Your flight leaves soon. We need to go inside." He opened the car door.

"Papa, I don't want to be a businesswoman." They stepped into the elevator.

He took Natalia's hand. "I want you to be happy. Being a teacher in a third-world country will not make you happy. Trust me."

"But what if it will? Will you allow me to try?"

"Try?" Papa's voice grew louder. "To try means studying

education instead of business. When you discover I am right, you will be years behind our ten-year plan."

"*Your* ten-year plan."

"What if you try my plan, and if you really don't like it, I will consider letting you go back to school to be a teacher?"

Natalia groaned. "I know after two days following you that I don't like this."

"That is just because you don't understand what is going on."

"I understand that you spent six years in school here in America so you could spend twenty years traveling the world building a company that requires all your time and energy. And I know that is not what I want."

Papa stepped off the elevator. "What you want, instead, is to be a teacher? To spend almost as many years in school as I did to make very little pay and have no control over what you do and where you go?"

"Yes, Papa. That is what I want more than anything."

"More than anything?"

"Yes."

Papa sighed deeply as he pulled Natalia's luggage to the security checkpoint. "I am a young man. I suppose I have time for you to sow these wild oats, come to your senses, and still train you to take over the business."

Natalia hugged her father. This was as close to a concession as she could hope for. Her own small miracle from God. "Thank you, Papa."

"You will see I'm right. Hopefully sooner rather than later."

I'm praying the same thing for you, Papa.

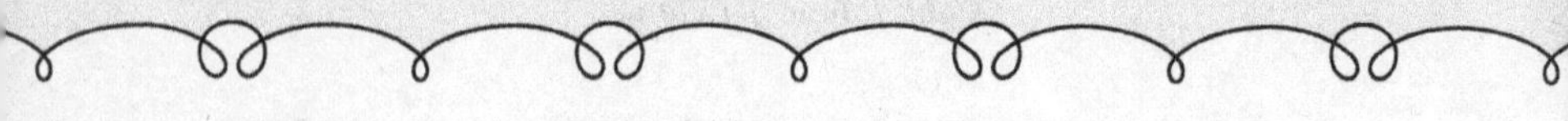

Chapter 50

"This was best class yet." Victor kissed Natalia's cheek. "Latin America is easy to love, yes?"

Natalia, Spencer, and Brian had shown the group their pictures from the trip to Costa Rica. Although the topic for the evening had been travel vocabulary, it ended being more about a group of friends sharing in a story of God's work.

"It certainly is, Victor."

"And I tell my friends about children's class." Victor opened the door to leave. "We will fill this room."

"I hope so." Natalia announced her plans to teach children while Brian and Spencer taught the adults. "Thanks for joining us, Spencer. I would not have been able to offer this children's class if it weren't for you."

"I wish I had come here earlier." Spencer grabbed an empty container and threw it in the trash. "This is great. We need a better projector in here, though. That one must be a hundred years old."

Brian laughed. "You sure are spending a lot of your dad's money in this room, man."

"I can't think of a better use for it." Spencer smiled. "Can I give you a ride home, Natalia?"

"Thanks, Spencer, but I need to talk with Brian about something."

"Okay." He looked from Natalia to Brian. "I'll see you at school tomorrow."

Brian watched Spencer leave. "Everything okay?"

Natalia sat on the new couch Spencer had purchased for the classroom. "Better than okay."

Pastor Mike poked his head into the room. "Hey, guys, I've got to run. The wife is asking for a tuna-salad sub."

Pastor Mike's wife was five months pregnant. He had joked about her cravings at church the night before. "Better than the anchovy salad, right?"

"Definitely." Pastor Mike laughed. "This kid is going to be a seafood lover, that's for sure. You guys done in here?"

"We are," Brian answered. "We're heading out in a few minutes."

"Excellent." Pastor Mike checked his phone. "She says to hurry. The janitor is here, so no need to lock up or turn off the lights. See you guys later."

Brian sat next to Natalia on the couch. He stretched out his long legs. "So what's up?"

Natalia's stomach clenched. She had spoken to Maureen the night before, admitted her feelings for Brian. Maureen, surprisingly, had encouraged Natalia to tell Brian how she felt.

"He's waiting for you," Maureen said. "Even I can see that. You need to let him know you're interested."

"Isn't that a bit forward?"

"Not at all," Maureen assured Natalia. "Men don't read minds well. You have to let him know what you're thinking and then he can decide what to do about it."

"And you really think it's all right?"

"I do, Natalia." Maureen's smile had been genuine. "You both are mature and have your focus where it needs to be—on Jesus first. And I can't think of a better young man for you than little Brian Younger."

But faced with "little Brian," Natalia's courage faded. So many "what ifs" floated through her mind.

"Natalia?" Brian broke into her thoughts. "I think I know what you want to talk about. I want you to know that I'm fine with it."

Brian spoke so matter-of-factly. And he still sat all the way on the other side of the couch. This was not at all how she had imagined this exchange.

"Really?"

"I knew you weren't made to never date." Brian shrugged. "That was just a coping mechanism because of all you've been through with your parents."

Natalia swallowed hard. Brian sounded like he was discussing a business transaction. Did he not realize how vulnerable she was making herself? Was he that unromantic? Natalia didn't expect him to fall at her feet and thank her, but this . . .

"What's wrong?" Brian's eyes softened.

"I didn't expect it to be like this." Natalia wanted to run out. This was terrible. What was she thinking?

"Natalia, we're friends. Nothing will change that. I

know it'll be different. It has to be. But we'll still be working here together. I'll still bug you for help in math."

Her heart sank. She couldn't bring herself to look into Brian's eyes. Was he saying he knew she was interested, but he wasn't? He just wanted to be friends?

"Spencer is not the same guy he used to be. I'm seeing that firsthand."

Natalia finally looked at Brian. "Spencer?"

"Yes, Spencer." Brian's eyes widened. "We are talking about Spencer, aren't we?"

"No." The pieces were falling into place. "I have been rethinking my commitment not to date. But not because of Spencer."

Brian turned to Natalia, his back against the arm of the couch. "You're not interested in Spencer?"

She tried not to laugh—the idea was so preposterous. "He's a friend. We have a lot in common. But, no, I've never been interested in him."

"But Costa Rica . . . ?"

Natalia stood and walked the length of the room. "Spencer was working through all that God was doing in his life. I was just helping him."

"You were helping him?" Brian was beside Natalia, his hand on her shoulder.

"What did you think?" Natalia's heart beat faster. She could feel the warmth of Brian's touch all the way to her toes.

"I thought that Spencer Adams had everything now—money, looks, Jesus. He's the perfect catch." Brian folded his arms and sat on the edge of one of the new tables.

"I'm sure there are some girls who think that." Lexi's face popped into her mind. "But I'm not one of them."

"Really?" The hope in Brian's voice gave Natalia goosebumps. "Why?"

"Because." Natalia heard her pulse in her ears, felt it racing through her body. She sat next to Brian and laid her head on his shoulder. "Spencer's not you."

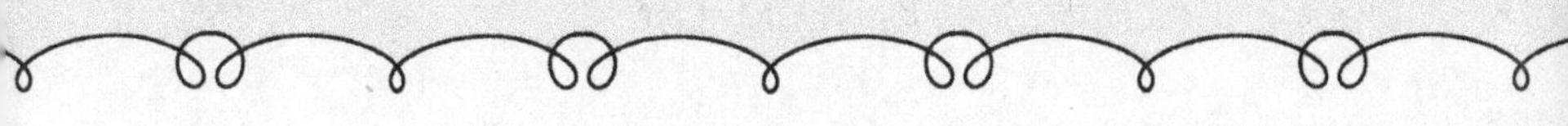

Chapter 51

"Woo-hoo!" Brian raced into his house. He pulled his mother up from the couch and swung her around in a huge hug.

"Brian." Mom pulled herself out of Brian's grip. "What is going on?"

"Natalia Lopez is what's going on." Brian put his hands on his mother's shoulders. "With *me*."

"Really?" She hugged Brian, gentler this time. "Oh, sweetie. I've been praying for that."

"You have?"

"Yes. Your father and I both felt like this could be the girl for you."

"She sure is." Brian still couldn't believe the events of the last hour. *"Spencer's not you,"* she had said.

For days Brian had been preparing himself for the inevitable. Natalia was interested in Spencer. Of course she was. Why wouldn't she be? Brian still couldn't believe that all this time, Natalia had been fighting an attraction to *him*. As they talked on the way home, she confessed just that—that from the first time she saw Brian she liked him.

"It was that hair," Natalia had said. "I came down the stairs the day you came to help assemble our things, and there you were. The tallest, whitest boy I'd ever seen, with the reddest hair and bluest eyes I'd ever seen."

"So I'm just a novelty?" Brian joked. "If I'd looked like Spencer Adams, you might not have been interested?"

Natalia held his hand, and Brian thought he understood how people felt when they were having an out-of-body experience. He couldn't think about anything but Natalia's hand in his.

She scooted closer on the truck's bench seat, and Brian thought his heart would explode. "I think you're the best-looking boy I've ever known."

Brian thanked God for the red light. "You need to sit over there."

Natalia's green eyes widened. "What?"

"I don't trust myself right now." Brian closed his eyes, fighting off desires he had never experienced in all his eighteen years.

"I guess you're right." Natalia moved back to her side of the truck, and Brian's heart returned to a seminormal state. "You really are a gentleman."

She wouldn't think that if she could see inside his head right then. "I am trying. But you sure don't make it easy." Brian had to tear his gaze away when the light turned green.

Natalia smiled. "Addy was very right."

"About what?"

She sighed. "God gives good gifts to his children."

"Don't rush," Mom warned, snapping Brian from his memories. "You need time."

"I know, I know." Brian sat on the couch. "Believe me, I know. But could we postpone that talk just a little? I just want to enjoy this for now."

"Of course."

"Oh no." Brian sat up, the joy of the moment suddenly shattered. "Spencer."

"Spencer?"

"He asked me about Natalia the other day. I gave him the green light to go out with her."

"What do you mean, you gave him the green light? She's not a commodity to be traded."

"I know, Mom." Brian rubbed his temples. "But he knew I was interested, and he asked if I would be upset if he went out with her. I assumed she returned his interest, so I said sure. What else was I going to say?"

"You need to talk to Spencer." Mom picked up the phone from its charger. "Now. This news will be all over school tomorrow. You need to be the one to tell him."

Thirty minutes later Brian stood in Spencer's driveway. This was not something he wanted to discuss over the phone.

"You and Natalia?" Spencer asked after Brian gave him a brief account of his conversation with Natalia—doing his best to make it sound as unromantic as possible.

"Are you mad?"

Spencer looked out over the pond beside his house. "A little. But not at you."

"Really?" Spencer's jaw twitched. Brian understood. He

had felt the same way when Spencer spoke with him a few days before. Natalia was one in a million.

"What am I supposed to say, 'You can't have her, I want her'?"

Brian stuffed his hands in his pockets. "You could."

"I want to." Spencer smiled. "But I kind of guessed. She talks about you a lot. You guys work together. You have the same interests. It makes sense."

She talks about me a lot. Brian still felt like he was in shock, that he would wake up very angry from the best dream ever. "I was sure she was into you. I still don't know what she sees in me."

"Look, man. You're better than you think you are."

"So we're good?"

"We're good." Spencer nodded once. "But don't ask me on any double dates with you guys for a while, okay?"

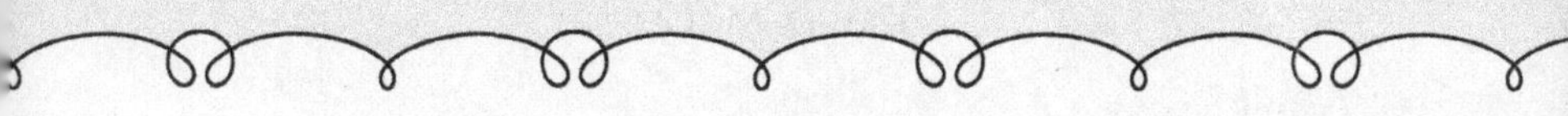

Chapter 52

"Did I tell you how good you look?" Brian laced his fingers through Natalia's as they walked the long driveway to Spencer's new home, decorated with lights and balloons for the homecoming celebration.

"I can't remember." Natalia squeezed Brian's hand. "Tell me again."

"You look good," Brian whispered in her ear, sending shivers down Natalia's spine. "And I love that you're wearing heels. Now you're only a foot shorter than me."

"Hey." Natalia laughed, standing straighter. "I am ten inches shorter now, thank you very much."

"Oh, excuse me." Brian gazed down in Natalia's eyes. "You ready for this?"

Although everyone at school knew Brian and Natalia were an "item," in the month they'd been together they had made a point to continue the way things were. They didn't want to rush into anything or to neglect their friendships for their budding relationship. Because of the sparks that flew every time they touched, they had committed not to be alone together, and they each had a friend keeping them accountable to that promise. This relationship was far too special to mess it up by letting their passions overrule their better judgment.

Tonight, though, they were coming to the homecoming party as a couple. Their first "official" date in front of the whole school. All the girls in the Bible study had been talking about it, helping Natalia pick out a dress and hairstyle. Her school in Madrid hadn't had homecomings, so this was new. The football game a few hours before had been fun and loud. Afterward she went to Lexi's house to change. Brian picked the two of them up in a borrowed convertible.

But now they were here. Lexi had run ahead, wanting to give the couple a little time alone before facing the crowd. Natalia enjoyed the peace and quiet, the feel of Brian's hand in hers.

Then Brian rang the doorbell. The spell was broken.

"Welcome." Spencer answered the door.

Natalia had dreaded this encounter more than any. Spencer had mostly avoided her in the last month. She understood why, but Natalia still felt bad. She didn't mean to hurt him. She was impressed, though, that he maintained his commitment to help on Thursday nights. With Natalia taking the children—a group that had already grown to almost twenty—in another room, she and Spencer didn't have much contact those evenings. Natalia was relieved that Spencer was confiding in Brian more and growing in his faith. The change that began in Costa Rica was real. Natalia was happy for him.

"Come on in." Spencer hugged Brian. "Enjoy the fruits of your labor."

Natalia looked at Brian. "What?"'

"I tore this place apart this summer."

"Oh, that's right. I had forgotten."

"Yep." Brian looked around. Natalia followed his gaze. The old mansion was beautifully restored, resembling pictures out of an interior design magazine. "The change is amazing."

"Kind of like me." Spencer smiled, this time meeting Natalia's gaze. "The old has gone, the new has come."

Brian slapped Spencer's back and walked into the large sitting room. Several couples from school were gathered around tables filled with delicious-smelling food.

The doorbell rang, and exclamations resounded from her classmates. She turned to see Kara McKormick and Chad Beacon enter. Their new show was boasting some of the highest ratings of any teen show ever. But, Addy had told Natalia, they wanted to come tonight because they wouldn't get a homecoming. Their school was on set, just the two of them. Kara had come to Tampa the week before to join some of the TCS girls looking for dresses at Lexi's mom's shop. Natalia enjoyed getting to know the extroverted star better. Natalia waited until the crowd dispersed before joining the celebrity couple.

"Hi, Kara." Natalia hugged her new friend. "Chad, I'd like to introduce you to Brian Younger."

The boys began talking about the show, school, and the

Bible. Natalia listened for a while and then turned to Kara. "Is Addy with you?"

"No. She and Jonathon will be here later." Kara smiled. "They have to wait for Secret Service, you know."

Natalia looked again at Brian, so handsome in his double-breasted suit and tie his mother had made to match her tangerine-colored dress. "I'm glad I don't have a boyfriend who is famous."

"Yes." Kara winked at Natalia. "Tall pastors' sons are more your style, right?"

"Definitely."

Lexi stepped in between Natalia and Kara. "Kara." She hugged the new celebrity. "I love the show. It is amazing. I don't know how you don't crack up all the time, though. The skits are so funny."

"We do crack up all the time." Kara took a drink from the table. "Whenever the camera cuts away from one of us, it's because we're laughing and we don't want the viewers to see. You need to come to one of the live shows again. You'll see it all then."

"You got it, girl." Lexi gave Kara a high five.

Natalia stood to the side and enjoyed the girls' banter.

"So who's your date?" Kara asked. "And I love the dress."

Natalia agreed. Lexi had continued with the "Gramps and Gran" diet plan and looked fabulous in her electric blue cocktail dress that enhanced her curves.

"Thank you." Lexi twirled around to show off her dress. "And I'm here with Jesus tonight. He's a great date. Doesn't care what I look like and loves me unconditionally."

Natalia glanced around the room and saw the many

girls who, desperate for a date or a boyfriend, had forgotten that truth. "You are the best, Lexi."

"I know." Lexi put a hand on her hip. "Me and Jesus need some more of those little meatballs, though. Catch you later."

"They're playing our song." Brian returned to Natalia and pointed to the dance floor set up under a white canopy in the backyard.

"We have a song?"

"We do now." Brian pulled Natalia outside. The air was perfect, about seventy-five degrees with a slight breeze coming off the Gulf. Heaven. Until . . .

"Ours is a Justin Bieber song?" Natalia grimaced as they walked past the impossibly loud speaker. "Really?"

"Just go with it." Brian wrapped his arms around her waist and pulled her close.

Natalia laid her head on Brian's chest, listening to his heart beat and moving in time to the music. She thought back to the day she arrived in Tampa, confused, unsure, wanting to get back on a plane to Madrid. She thought of Maureen's depression and her struggles with school and the culture, even the language.

Then she thought of the ESL group, the girls in her Bible study, her trip to Costa Rica. And Brian. Who would have known that one decision to get on a plane with her stepmother would have led to this? God had given her a purpose, a future, and a hope. He had replaced her fears with truth and given her far more than she ever thought she deserved.

"What are you thinking?" Brian pulled Natalia away and looked into her eyes.

"I am thinking that God is very good. Look at all he's done in just the last few months."

"It is amazing." Brian stepped closer to Natalia. "But this is only the beginning."

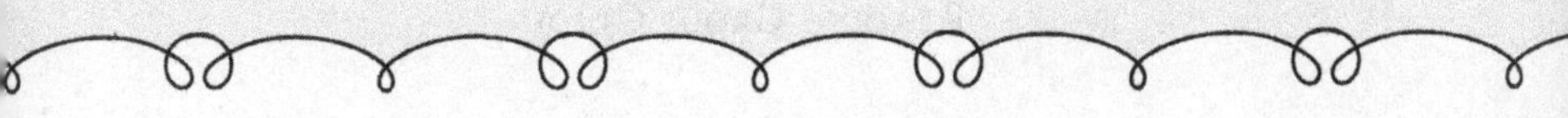

Reading Group Guide

1. Natalia's story is loosely based on Ruth. What parts of the biblical story did you see in *Right Where I Belong*?
2. Natalia moves from Spain to Florida. What difficulties does she face in making that move? If you had to make a major move, what would you miss the most?
3. As a pastor's son, Brian has faced greater scrutiny than some of his friends. Do you know any pastors' kids? Do they feel that way too?
4. Some of the girls at Natalia's school meet weekly to study the Bible together. How does that help them? Are you part of a small group like that?
5. Divorce has affected many characters in this book. Discuss which characters' struggles you most identified with and why.
6. Maureen is struggling with depression through much of the story. Have you ever known someone who is depressed? If so, how did you respond to that person?
7. Natalia and Brian help with the ESL ministry at their church. Are you involved in any ministries? What are they? If not, is there one you are interested in being part of?
8. When the group goes to Costa Rica, they spend part of their time working with missionary kids. Have

you ever known any missionary kids? What do you think would be difficult about going with your parents to serve God in another country? What would be exciting about it?

9. Spencer is an interesting character. What brings about change in him? Do you think he'll stick to the commitment he made in Costa Rica? Why or why not?
10. Natalia learns that God gives good gifts to his children. But it takes awhile for this lesson to really sink in. Why is this something some people have a hard time believing?

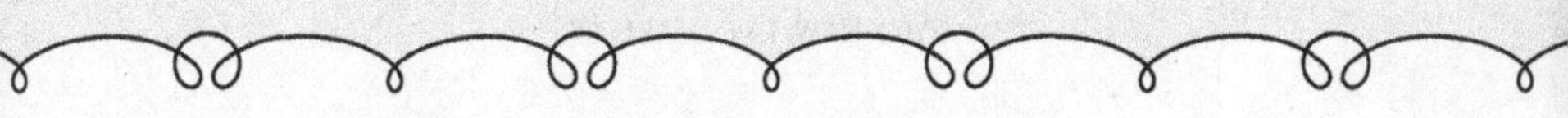

Acknowledgments

I always leave little pieces of myself in my novels. Writers have to do that. We can only write what we know. But in this book, I left huge chunks of me. I've been Natalia and I've been Maureen. I've even had my "Spencer" moments. Our family attended that language school in Costa Rica. A few years later we took a group down there to run a VBS for the missionary kids, just like a group had done for us when we were there. I've walked the cobbled streets of Madrid, and I still remember getting on the Metro that last time and crying, praying that God would give me friends as I left that beautiful city and prepared to move back to Tampa.

And God answered that prayer for me just like he answered Natalia's prayer. I teach at a school very much like Tampa Christian, where my students give me daily inspiration. They make me laugh and cry and, more than anything, they make me proud. I work with people who love Jesus and encourage others to do the same. I attend a church where God's Word isn't just taught, it is modeled. I am part of a Bible study with other women who encourage and challenge me to live a life that is pleasing to my Savior. I can only write what I know. I want to write truth and encouragement. These students, coworkers, and friends breathe truth and encouragement into my life so that, hopefully, I can pass that on to you, my readers.

I am incredibly blessed to be working with the Thomas Nelson Fiction Team. Amanda Bostic and Becky Monds are fantastic. They give me ideas, help, and hope when I am floundering. Julee Schwarzburg comes in and cleans up all my messes. You'd think an English teacher wouldn't leave modifiers dangling or use the word *look* 583 times. And thanks to Julee, you don't have to know. Except that now you do.

My husband, Dave, and my kids, Emma, Ellie, and Thomas, are my greatest ministry and, behind Jesus, my highest priority. I am a blessed wife and a blessed mama.

But the reason that I write, that I teach, that I get up each day is to bring glory to Jesus Christ. My prayer is that those who read my books will see that though the characters are fictional, the God they serve is not. He is real and active in our lives. He loves us more than we can fathom, and his plans for our lives are far better than any plans we can dream up on our own.